LAST RESORT

BY

SCOTT PRATT

&

J.D. PRATT

ACKNOWLEDGEMENTS

Thank you to Dan Pratt and Andrew Wolfendon for helping me bring this manuscript to life. Also, thank you to Captain Andrew Ford for helping us get an authentic feel for a day in the life of an inmate in Washington County.

To Mom and Dad – Save me a seat by the lake and have a Bud Light waiting on me if it isn't too much trouble. In a bottle. I'll find you when the time is right.

I loved you both before I was born and I'll love you both after I'm long gone.

—Dylan Pratt

This book, along with every book I've written and every book I'll write, is dedicated to my darling Kristy, to her unconquerable spirit and to her inspirational courage. I loved her before I was born and I'll love her after I'm long gone.
—Scott Pratt

I have long feared that my sins would return to visit me, and the cost is more than I can bear.
—Benjamin Martin (character), *The Patriot*

PROLOGUE

The Summer Before

"Steeee..." called the umpire, lifting his fist to half-mast. Eleven-year-old Abby Pruitt stepped out of the batter's box and shot a look back at him, not because she disagreed with the call—it was low and outside, sure—but because the ump seemed bored. He couldn't even bother saying the whole word: steee-rike.

Doesn't he know this is the city championship! So why does he sound like he's about to take a nap? Abby didn't usually have a problem with the old guy. He had umped tons of her games and had a decent eye. He walked with a limp and didn't say much, but there was a game earlier in the season where he had yelled, "Go Abby!" after she got a hit.

Abby had shot up three inches in the last six months—all of it in her legs—and her uniform didn't hang on her the same way it used to. She no longer felt like "one of the boys." And she was just fine with that.

Anything that gave her an edge.

She stepped out of the batter's box and stretched the bat high over her head, playing the moment for all its drama. It was the bottom of the sixth—the final inning in Little League—and Abby's team, the Detrick Funeral Home Tigers, was down to its last out and behind by one.

The small bleacher-style stands at the Church Street ballpark in Elizabethton, Tennessee were filled on this cool Saturday morning. Full or empty, the ballpark was Abby's favorite place to be. It was the only place where things made sense to her. The only place where she never got that twisty feeling in her chest—that thing her mom called "The Anxiety."

Abby stepped back into the box and dug in for the next pitch. The crowd quieted.

"Forget about the strike zone," she heard Coach Jack say in her mind. "If it's a pitch you know you can hit, take a swing. I trust you."

I trust you. No one had ever said that to her before. Not once. This was Abby's second year playing baseball, and she had already learned so much from Coach Jack Dillard. Abby was one of only three girls in the local league. At first Coach didn't seem to know how to handle her and bent over backwards to pretend he didn't notice she was a girl. But once he saw the way she played, he started taking a special interest. Until last year, Abby had never felt like she was good at anything or belonged anywhere. She and her mom, Verna, had moved around a lot, living in Hampton, Erwin, and Mountain City before ending up in a rental trailer here in Elizabethton. Abby loved her mom, who worked as a clerk at Food City, but it always seemed to Abby that if Verna didn't have a kid, she might be happier.

But here, in *this* place, with *this* coach, Abby felt a sense of belonging.

The ball whipped past her, smacking the catcher's glove. "Steeee…" said the umpire, slightly louder this time. Abby was down in the count, one and two. She looked up at the opposing pitcher in his blue and white Dodgers' uniform. He was huge and looked like he was already shaving. No way this kid was 12.

Time to notch it up. She gave the pitcher a crooked smile, wriggled her torso, and hunkered down for the next pitch. Abby was pretty, and she knew it. She wasn't above using her "charms" to try to distract an opposing pitcher—or an opposing batter if she was on the mound. It was as if she had suddenly developed some new brand of voodoo. All she had to do was flash her eyes and toss her head a certain way and boys—*guys* too— would smile and do things for her. She thought maybe that was even why her daddy had started coming around a bit more often.

The pitcher set himself and stared at her. Someone yelled at him from the stands, "Come on, Jordan, you got this. She's just a girl."

Just a girl. The magic words. The words that brought out the killer inside. Coach Jack had told her she had the purest swing he'd ever seen— and he'd been a bigshot player in high school and college, had even made the Minors. She might not be able to drive the ball into the parking lot like some of the boys, but she could slow the pitch down with her eyes and she could *connect*. Same thing with her pitching. She'd probably never numb a catcher's glove-hand, but she made up for it with control and deception. At age 11, she already had a bankable curveball and a filthy sinker. And she was *always* around the zone.

Control. That's what Abby had in spades. Control.

As she tapped her bat on the plate and adjusted her hips, she heard a voice yell, "See the ball, Hawk!" It was Coach Jack. He called her Hawkeye, Hawk for short. "Slow it down. Breathe."

Abby squinted her eyes against the sun and waited to see what kind of pitch was coming. She watched the ball come straight down the pipe to her favorite spot, a little high and outside, and she slapped it over the first baseman's head. She tossed the bat and flew past Coach Jack, who was waving her on from the first base coach's box. "Take second!" he yelled, and Abby slid in even though she'd beaten the throw by a week.

The crowd cheered, and Abby looked over at Coach. His face lit up with a smile. As she dusted her pants off, she glanced back at the right-fielder who'd made the throw to second. That's when she saw him. Greg. Her dad. Sitting on the tailgate of an old blue truck with a guy who had the biggest beard she'd ever seen. They had cans of beer in their hands and a red-and-white plastic cooler between them. "Hells yeah!" Greg yelled. "That's my kid!"

Abby felt blood rush to her face, and her mind began to race. *How long has* he *been here?* A jumble of feelings assailed her. Yes, she was glad her dad had showed up for a change. But a bigger part of her was cringing inside. You never knew how he was going to act. Why did he have to be here now? During the most important game of her life. In front of the person she most wanted to impress. Coach Jack. *Oh well, game should be over in a minute.*

"She took you to school, lard ass!" Greg shouted at the pitcher. Abby's face flushed as the kid on the mound turned to see who was yelling. Greg's bearded buddy roared with laughter. "That all you got, fattie?" Abby wished she had a hole to crawl into.

The next kid up to bat was Jeff, a decent hitter. As he strode out toward the plate, half the parents and guests stood and cheered for him. *If Jeff gets a hit and I score, we tie it,* Abby told herself. *We can win this. We really can.*

"Come on, throw some more of that garbage so my kid can score!" Greg Pruitt shouted. The pitcher looked pleadingly at his coach. "Just ignore him," the Dodgers' coach yelled. "Some grownups don't know how to act." Abby thought she saw the glint of a tear in the pitcher's eye as he glanced back to see how far off second base she was.

The first pitch to Jeff was way over the catcher's head. Abby took off for third. She held up there as the catcher rushed back to the plate, ball in hand.

The Dodgers' coach marched out to the mound to talk to his pitcher. "Yeah, give the little baby his bottle!" yelled Greg. Abby glanced at Coach Jack and saw rage flash in his eyes. *Does Coach know that loudmouth jerk is my father? God, I hope not.*

The Dodgers' coach patted his pitcher on the head and returned to the dugout.

"You got this, Jordan," a parent shouted.

"He don't got shit," yelled Greg. "He's a fat little momma's boy."

The pitcher no longer looked like a grownup to Abby. He looked like a fragile kid. She knew the feeling. Greg's words had the power to shrink people.

The instant the ball left the pitcher's hand, Abby knew she was going to tie the game. She started moving before she even heard the ping of the aluminum bat. The ball hit the dirt and skipped toward the shortstop, who fielded it cleanly and drew his arm back.

The throw to home would be close, for sure.

It wasn't. The ball sailed high, and the catcher had to step back and reach for it. Abby slid into home on one leg and was safe by a Tennessee mile.

"Yer out!" the umpire called.

Abby's world imploded.

Out? What just happened here? She *knew* she was safe, but the ump had said out. Which meant the game was over. Her Tigers had lost. *How?*

Parents jumped up, shouting and booing. Abby took a step back as Coach Jack strode toward the umpire to have a chat. And then suddenly, Greg Pruitt was right in the middle of things. Shouting and cursing at the old ump. Spit flying out of his mouth, eyes flashing like a crazy dog's. Coach Jack held his arm out like a traffic cop's, trying to calm Greg down. Abby rushed in to tell her dad to stop, but Coach blocked her and told her to go wait in the dugout.

That was when Greg made a move on the ump. Shoved him. Hard. In the chest. The old guy hit the ground with a loud "oooof" and a puff of dust. A collective gasp went up as parents rushed in to make sure the ump was okay.

Abby froze as Coach Jack stepped up to Greg and the two men stood face to face. Coach Jack Dillard had never looked so big before, and her father had never looked so small. "Leave. Now," Coach said, his voice calm but tight, "or I will *remove* you. Your choice."

A hush came over the bystanders as the two men faced off. Greg pumped himself two inches taller and leaned into Jack's face. "Oh, you the big man now? Coach Wonderful? You gonna be my kid's new daddy now, that it?"

"I mean it, Pruitt. You have three seconds." Abby's heart pounded. "…Two."

For a moment, Abby was sure her father was going to take a swing. But he just smiled, poked his finger into Coach's chest, and said, "You're gonna regret this…" And then he turned and walked off with the bearded guy, adding over his shoulder, "*Counselor.*"

PART I

CHAPTER 1

Tuesday, April 12

It was my fiftieth birthday, and I was celebrating the occasion by steeping in the aromas of human waste and industrial floor cleaner in the visitors' room of the Washington County Detention Center. My name is Joe Dillard, and it was rare for me to interview clients in jail these days. After more than twenty years in criminal defense, I now spent most of my work hours, which were down to about ten a week, in a largely advisory role at our small firm in Jonesborough, Tennessee. My son, Jack, and his fiancée, Charlie—Charleston Story, an auburn-haired beauty who reminded me of my wife, Caroline—carried the bulk of the caseload nowadays, and our legal secretary, Beverly, ran the office.

On this fine spring morning, however, Jack and Charlie had an appointment to tour a wedding venue called Millstone Manor, down near Greeneville. Thus was I "volun-told" by Beverly that I would inherit the honor and privilege of interviewing a court-appointed defendant by the name of Clovis "Badger" Daley.

According to his records, Badger was a semi-regular guest at the "Washington County Hyatt," though never for anything too serious. Until now. The door buzzed open and a deputy with a sagging, regret-filled face marched Badger in like he was a truck dolly and parked him on the other side of the table from where I sat. Badger was short, densely packed, and muscular—like his animal namesake. His dark-brown mutton-chop sideburns and heavy eyebrows, in tandem with the widow's peak tattooed on his forehead, told me the nickname was one he courted proudly. Maybe it's just me, but I've always believed that the day a man gets his first facial tattoo is the day he pretty much kicks the corporate ladder into the woodchipper.

Badger had been arrested on a second-degree murder charge, and my son Jack had caught the case, courtesy of one Judge Cora Mae Talbot. The DA's office had minced no words about its intention to press for the maximum sentence, and, frankly, I'd have done the same, back when I was DA. All evidence pointed toward a cataclysmically guilty client.

As the deputy left the room, the orange-clad Badger folded his arms, sat back, and grinned widely, unveiling a corncob of yellow teeth. He smelled like spoiled laundry and sweat.

"Hot damn. You's my lawyer?"

"For the moment. Are you Clovis Daley?"

"Badger. Ain't nobody calls me Clovis 'cept my Mamaw, and she been dead six years now. Say, ain't you the *famous* Dillard, the one I seen on TV a few times? I thought I'd be gettin' your kiddo, not the man hisself!"

For a man staring down the barrel of a murder charge, he seemed downright perky.

"Jack couldn't be here today, so I agreed to do your initial interview, Mr. Da... Badger."

"Well, butter my butt and call me a biscuit." He slapped his thigh with glee. "Looks like I'm in good hands. Like them ol' Allstate commercials. Think you can git me off?"

My mouth replied, "My son Jack will give you the best defense possible, I'm sure," but my brain was already thinking, *No way on God's green Earth.*

From what Jack had told me, Badger was found by police, sitting on the tailgate of his truck with a literal smoking gun in his hand, five yards from the murdered man, waiting to be taken into custody.

"Badger, I'm a little fuzzy on the details. Why don't you tell me what happened? I'm on my son's legal team, so anything you say to me is protected by attorney-client privilege."

"I shot that peckerwood Eddie Braun stone-cold dead with a Rock Island M-two-aught-six. You're welcome."

I had to admit, his candor was refreshing. Most inmates shout their innocence from the rooftops even when they've been caught dead to rights. Badger not only admitted his guilt, he seemed proud of it.

According to the report I'd read, the police had received a call the previous Thursday from a woman in Limestone, a sleepy community southwest of Jonesborough that ran along the railroad track. Mrs. Arnita Matthews told the duty officer she "might have found a dead man" on her property. When police arrived and looked behind her storage shed, they were puzzled by her equivocation: a male body was found, face down and covered with flies, rotting away in a pool of dried-black blood. Matthews reported having smelled what she thought was a dead animal for a week before finally taking a peek behind the cinder-block structure.

The ground behind the woman's shed was peppered with the short, sharp stumps of invasive bamboo stalks that had been cut off near the ground, and it appeared the man had fallen, impaled himself on several of the stumps, and bled out. The body, identified by the contents of the wallet in his pocket, was that of Clayton Daley. Badger's brother.

"Did you tell the police you shot Mr. Braun?" I asked.

"Do I look like an id'jit?"

I refrained from answering the question.

"Naw," he said. "All I told the boys in blue was that I done nothin' wrong. And that ain't no word of a lie."

"Explain, Mr. Daley. Er, Badger."

"I done the *right* thing by killin' that egg-suckin' dawg."

I sighed. "Why don't we start at the beginning?"

Badger surveyed my face with a crunched brow, took a deep breath, leaned back, and let his gaze drift into the middle distance.

"'Bout a month ago, Clay went missin'. ...*Again.*"

"That would be your brother Clayton? He went missing often?"

"More 'n never. Clay had a problem with booze and hillbilly heroin." Local slang for Oxycontin. Oxy was a major player in the opioid addiction crisis that had been sweeping the Appalachians like wildfire for years.

"He'd been gone pert' near a month when that lady found him a few days ago. They had me come down to the morgue to make sure it was him. 'Bout broke poor Momma's heart."

"I'm sorry about your brother, Badger, but the police ruled his death an accident. What does that have to do with Mr. Braun?"

"Weren't no accident. Braun killed my brother sure as I killed Braun. He's killed *lots* of folks, I reckon, peddlin' that poison of his to anyone who could rub two nickels together. That stuff's what done my brother in. 'Bout time somebody did somethin'."

"Help me understand."

"Clay couldn't kick the oxy. A few months back, he lost his license on account of takin' that poison, and he started drivin' one of them scooters." Small gas-powered scooters were the transportation mode of choice for those who had lost their driving privileges in the great state of Tennessee.

"Last Fri-dee around lunchtime I'm down't the Marathon station on 321, on my way to work, when this kid pulls in next to me on Clay's scooter. I recognize the decals. I as't the kid where he got it, and he says from Braun. So that night, when I get offa work, I head out to Braun's place to have us a parlay, and he tells me Clay sold him the scooter a few weeks ago to buy some more pills. 'Dumbass just took the pills and wandered off through them trees over there,' he says to me." Badger lifted his eyes to mine, redness rising in his face. "So, you see, Mr. Joe, when my brother turned up in that morgue a couple days later, I knew exactly who done it to him."

The report said the police received a call Sunday evening at 7:16 p.m. from the same woman who had found the Clayton Daley kabob behind her storage shed and who happened to live next door to Eddie Braun's single-wide. She told them she'd heard gunshots from the direction of the Braun residence. Twenty minutes later, a deputy arrived at the trailer to find Edmund Braun sitting in a lawn chair on his front porch, three bullet holes in his chest and belly, and Badger Daley sitting on the tailgate of his truck, a gun in his lap and an open bag of Brim's barbecue pork rinds in his hands.

I'd read the report, but I wanted to hear it from Daley. "So, what happened next, Badger?"

"I went back to see Braun and canceled his birth certificate."

"You shot him."

"No sense lyin' to a famous lawyer."

Badger was quiet for a minute as I took some notes. When I looked up, he was staring at me with tears in his eyes.

"I know Clay weren't no saint, Mr. Joe. He made his choices. But Braun just kept feeding him that poison, and Clay just couldn't kick it. *Couldn't.* You ever had someone do a thing like that to a person you love, Mr. Joe?"

I thought of my sister Sarah. When I was a boy, I walked in on my uncle Raymond sexually assaulting her. It was an incident that set off endless ripple effects in my life, not to mention Sarah's. None of them good. I was too young to do anything about it at the time, but I think if I'd had access to a gun, I'd have killed my uncle Raymond on the spot.

When I reached adulthood, I wasn't so powerless anymore, and I must confess there have been many times over the years that my anger has driven me to step outside the lines to protect someone I love. Even if they didn't strictly need protecting. It was only by sheer good fortune that I hadn't found myself on the other side of this table.

"Yeah, Badger. I've been there."

"Then you know, Mr. Dillard. Family's all they' is."

CHAPTER 2

After my meeting with Badger, I ambled out to the parking lot in the sweet-smelling Jonesborough air. The mountains of East Tennessee can be a bit oppressive, climate-wise, in the throes of summer, but most days in fall and spring made you forget all that. Today was sunny, just north of seventy degrees, you could practically hear the trees and flowers kicking up their heels in celebration. Part of me wanted to join them, but a rock of heaviness sat in my chest.

As I drove home in my truck, I felt the weight of the conversation I needed to have with Caroline and the kids pressing down on me. I had planned to talk to them on the drive back from the university hospital last Friday but couldn't muster the courage. How does one utter such terrible syllables?

So instead, I'd spent the weekend enjoying my family. Milking every drop of life out of every precious interaction. Trying to feel gratitude for what we still had.

Gratitude for my blessings was not my customary response to awful news. Historically, when life dealt me a blow I perceived as unfair, I went straight for anger. These last few days had felt different, though. And now, as I drove out along the Boones Creek Highway, heading toward Johnson City, I felt an almost *sweet* sadness. I noticed I was driving below the speed limit. How many times in my life had that ever happened?

As a younger man, I sped through everything, always in a big damn hurry to get to… who knows what. I crammed in a lot of living, but I also missed a lot. I wondered if today's slower pace stemmed from my talk with Dr. Seals or from turning fifty. Or both.

I crossed Kingsport Highway and drove out along Pickens Bridge Road, toward Boone Lake, where I had raised my family and where I still lived.

Fifty years. Damn. They'd been pretty good ones, though, hadn't they? Sure, there had been some tough times, some *really* tough ones, but, still, I'd been ridiculously fortunate. I thought of every precious day I'd spent with my wife, Caroline. I was still as crazy in love with her as I'd been in high school. Who gets to say that at fifty? I thought of how proud I was of our son Jack and the man he had become. Of our daughter Lilly and how much like her mother she was. I thought of everything I'd done to try to make a difference in this world, and, for perhaps the first time in my life, the old cliché rang true: I wouldn't change a thing.

Scratch that, I thought, pulling my truck into the garage. There was one *very large thing* I would change in a nanosecond. Caroline's cancer. I hated it to my core.

I felt the old anger rising again as I walked toward the house. I took a deep breath before entering, stopping on the porch to rub Rio's head. When my old German Shepherd was younger, he'd be so happy to see me he'd pee all over my shoe. These days, he just lay on his doggy bed and thumped his tail a few times. Guess I wasn't the only one who'd slowed down.

"Do anything exciting this morning, ol' boy?"

One tail-thump. No pee.

"Yeah… me either."

I stepped in the door and made my way to the kitchen, dropping my keys and briefcase on the table and draping my jacket over a chair.

"Just me," I announced.

My daughter, Lilly, poked her head out of the main bedroom.

"Back already?" she said, padding up to give me a hug and kiss.

"Amazing how fast things go when clients actually tell the truth." I nodded toward the bedroom. "How is she?"

"Same."

Last Friday, Caroline, Jack and I had taken yet another trip to Vanderbilt University Medical Center in Nashville to meet with Caroline's doctors. Lilly flew in from Boston, where her husband was doing his

SCOTT PRATT

residency, and met us at Vandy. She rode back to East Tennessee with us and was scheduled to return to Boston in the morning.

That meant no more deferrals. Today was the day "the talk" needed to happen.

When Caroline had first been diagnosed with breast cancer almost nine years ago, there was never any question: we would beat it. And we had. Many times. Caroline was the strongest, most determined person I knew. But cancer doesn't care. Cancer is like the monster from that movie *The Thing*. No matter how many times we knocked it down, it always came back. In some new form. Over the years, we had ridden the roller coaster of hope and heartache till we were flat worn out: A period of relative health, then more cancer. More treatments. More hope. Then a period of stasis or remission. Then more cancer. More tears. More pain.

At this point, she was sleeping at least sixteen hours a day. Which was a mercy, really. The pain she endured when lucid was so intense, Oxycontin was like baby aspirin. And when the oxy didn't cut it, it was on to the morphine.

There was no "next level" of pain medication.

"Is she asleep?"

Lilly nodded. "You going in to the office today?"

I shook my head no.

My self-imposed retirement was partly due to sheer weariness—hell, I'd been weary ten years earlier when I made my first attempt to get out of the legal profession. Lying clients, manipulative law enforcement officers, petty politics, and arrogant judges had taken a toll on my passion for the law. But it wasn't weariness that kept me home these days. It was Caroline. She needed a lot of hands-on care and couldn't be left alone for long. The real reason I spent so much time at home, though, was a selfish one: I didn't want to miss a minute with her.

When we took the trip to Nashville last week, I'd known things weren't good, but we'd been down that road before. And we'd always toughed it out, somehow. From time to time, some well-meaning doctor would mention "end-of-life care." That conversation never went well. We weren't going to give up. Ever. From the beginning, we had agreed that the moment we lost hope was the moment cancer won. Not an option for the Dillards.

This meeting at Vanderbilt had been different. The cancer, which had long ago metastasized to her bones, was adapting and becoming more aggressive. Over the past few months, the tumors had moved into the soft tissue. We were now monitoring several small spots on her liver, as well as a particularly sinister tumor that had drilled its way through her skull and was threatening to infiltrate the meningeal fluid around her brain. Once cancer cells start showing up in that fluid, it's game over.

After about thirty minutes of the usual examinations and questions, the lead oncologist, Dr. Janet Seals, asked me to step outside to sign some insurance papers.

There were no papers to sign.

"We're out of options, Joe." Janet had become more than a doctor to us over the years. She was a friend—kind and brilliant, unafraid to try something aggressive if she thought it would help. She read my eyes before I could even respond and said, "I know what you're thinking. You and Caroline have been abundantly clear that you will never throw in the towel, but Joe… there's nothing left that we can do."

"Quitting is not on the table."

"I knew you'd say that." She sighed. "And I *can* prescribe something if you want: a very old, very potent chemo drug that may extend her life by a few days…"

"We'll take it. We'll take whatever days we can get."

"…but they won't be good days, Joe. Not at all."

The rage flared up again. It is the curse of cancer medications that they are, for all intents and purposes, poison. Poison that's meant to kill cancer cells but invariably destroys a lot more than that. But I didn't even need to ask Caroline to know her answer—she'd want to try it. She'd want to keep fighting. Even if it meant her final days would be hell on earth.

"I'm sorry, Joe. Take her home. Be together. Tell me your decision when you're ready, but just know this: stopping isn't quitting." Her voice began to shake. "Quitting is when you don't try, and I have never, in all my years of oncology, seen anyone try as hard as Caroline Dillard. But sometimes, stopping treatment is… the right thing to do."

I'm not sure how long I stood there after Dr. Seals left, but eventually I went back into the room where Caroline and the kids were waiting. Caroline had nodded off but she half-opened her eyes and looked at me.

"Anything new?" she croaked.

"More of the same. It's going to take some time."

She raised her eyebrows. "You're pissed, I can tell. Why?"

"I was just hoping for... more progress."

The ride back to East Tennessee was painfully quiet. It was as if a ghost had moved into the car with us. On the way *to* Nashville that morning, Jack and I had talked about work and baseball—the Little League team he coached had made the finals last year, and he was excited about this year's prospects, especially a girl player named Abby Pruitt—while Caroline slept in the back seat.

On the long ride home, no one spoke.

We hadn't discussed the trip since.

CHAPTER 3

"This is our famous stone bridge," said the slight man in the seersucker suit and straw fedora. Ernesto was the events coordinator for Millstone Manor, a ten-acre indoor/outdoor wedding venue outside of Greeneville. Jack and Charlie followed him onto the gray stone bridge that arched over a babbling creek. "And everyone—I mean *everyone*—wants to do their formal shots here. You can see why."

Jack could indeed. The moss-covered bridge looked like it was plucked from a fairytale. Jack Dillard and Charlie Story looked out over the meandering stream and across a field of butterweed toward the stone manor, nestled against the tree line. They shot a knowing glance at each other. This was exactly the kind of venue they were looking for. Their plan was to host a simple but elegant wedding—outdoors, if possible—for a small group of family and friends. They didn't want to spend house-down-payment money on one day of pageantry; they were saving the money they earned at the law practice to build a future together. But still, they wanted their wedding day to be memorable. Millstone Manor offered a nice blend of elegance and affordability.

Jack wished he felt less distracted, though. He pressed his hand against the phone in his pocket for the tenth time, as if expecting it to vibrate any second.

Ernesto spun on his heels and led them back toward the manor, his uplifted palms saying *feast your eyes on these gardens and walkways.* Ernesto wore rose-rimmed sunglasses and a manscaped beard and looked like a three-quarter-sized version of a Hollywood actor. "From what you've told me," he said, "you'd probably be interested in our Intimate Gatherings package, for groups of fifty or less. That includes up to fifty chairs for the ceremony itself and another fifty for the reception. The beauty of the IG package is that we can switch from an outdoor to an indoor setting at a moment's notice, if the Tennessee weather gods decide not to cooperate. The Garden Chapel is a great sunny-day choice, but we can always..."

Jack tuned out. Part of him was thrilled to be making actual wedding plans with Charlie, the woman he loved, but part of him felt deeply unsettled. Ever since the trip to Nashville with his mother, a cloak of heaviness had sat on his shoulders. He felt like he was waiting for a shoe to drop. He placed his hand on his phone again.

"...And our award-winning chef has just released some to-die-for new menu options," Ernesto continued as he led the couple into his office at the rear of the manor. Jack tripped on the door jamb, snapping himself back to awareness. Ernesto sat at his desk and waved Jack and Charlie into the guest chairs. "Unfortunately..." Ernesto clicked a mouse and brought his computer to life. "We're booked *pretty* solid through December. We do have one opening at the end of June—the couple got into a fight over a pet tortoise and called the whole thing off—and then nothing till early October."

Jack and Charlie did a silent eye consultation. Ernesto took the cue. "Well, I'll leave you two lovebirds alone to talk. Can I bring you back some coffee? It's *good.*"

The couple nodded graciously, and Ernesto departed, leaving them alone.

"I love this place," Charlie said, eyes wide. "It's just what we were hoping for."

"It is," Jack concurred, but his enthusiasm level hit only a 7 out of 10.

"But...?"

"There's no but."

"Then why am I hearing one in your voice? Come on, Jack, what are you thinking about? Your mom, right?" Charlie herself had no family considerations. Her mother had abandoned her as a child, and her father had spent most of her life in prison. A few years back, he had been killed just before his release. Except for her horse, her dog, and Jack, Charlie was alone in the world. "You're worried about how she's going to—"

"This wedding is super important to her, Charlie. In fact, I think it's the one thing she's still looking forward to in her life."

"That's why we're here, making plans, instead of waiting. But if you don't think she'll like this place, we can…"

"No, no, it's not that."

"Then what?"

"It's more about… the timing."

"How so?"

"I don't know, Charlie. That trip to Nashville was…" He shook his head, looking down at the floor. "And you saw her on Sunday. She barely made it out of bed. The only time she came to life was when you showed her the venue brochures. And then she became *Mom* again. There was a light in her eyes and… I mean, it's almost as if…"

"You can say it, Jack: It's almost as if she's keeping herself alive *for* the wedding."

"People do that. They stick around for important events. Did you know that in China, the mortality rate among old folks goes down in the weeks before Chinese New Year? People stay alive for the holiday."

"And now you feel like we're holding your mom's fate in our hands?"

"Maybe we are," Jack said. "To some extent." He craned his head to look out the door for Ernesto, then lowered his voice. "I mean, I hope she's around for five more years. Ten. But what if her timetable is… shorter? In that case, the date we pick could be critical."

Charlie took Jack's hand and looked him in the eye. "Part of you thinks we should grab that June date, to be sure your mom…"

"Makes it," Jack whispered. His hand unconsciously groped for his phone again. No calls or messages. "On the other hand," he went on, "maybe if we go with the October date, we give her motivation to… stick around longer."

"That's possible. But it's also possible that if we wait *too* long…"

"Exactly."

Charlie took Jack's hand, cradled it in hers. "Jack, can I just say? You're overthinking this. And giving us too much power in the matter. Your mom will be here on this planet until exactly such time as she—and her Maker—decide. It's not on us. And besides, I don't think turning our wedding day into a death sentence for your mom is a super-great way to launch a marriage, do you?"

"No, but still. Choosing the date feels… significant." Jack's phone vibrated. The call he'd been half-expecting all day? He slipped his phone out of his pocket. A text. From his dad. Joe Dillard was not a texter—a text from him meant business. *"Can you come to the house before the b'day dinner?"* the message read. The whole Dillard clan was planning to go out to dinner together that evening—to celebrate Joe's fiftieth birthday and to get Caroline out of the house. *"I want to talk to you kids about something."* Oh, God. The last time Jack's dad had asked to talk to "you kids" was after his mother had received her initial cancer diagnosis.

Jack pulled in a shuddery breath. "Let's go with the June date."

CHAPTER 4

Caroline managed to look luminous as we strolled into Café Luna—despite her rail-thinness. She wore a sparkling violet top and a light-catching set of dangling earrings I'd bought her in the Caymans during a magical trip we took there years ago, along with her "good wig," which was combed to a sheen. But most of the sparkle emanated from her. It was hard to believe this was the same person I'd spent the last few days and weeks with; the person who barely got out of bed except to use the toilet. Maybe it was my birthday that was giving her the energy boost—if so, I would have a birthday every day—or maybe it was the prospect of dining at one of her favorite restaurants with her whole family around her.

I'd switched our reservation to Café Luna in Johnson City at the last minute, not only because Caroline loved it here but also because it had a private back room. I'd had "the talk" with the kids back at the house while Caroline was still asleep, and we'd discussed the terrible options before us. I had also given them their marching orders: tonight was for celebrating only.

So, we were all on the same page. But still, raw emotion was apt to rear its head. And if it did, I wanted us to have some privacy.

A young woman in a white shirt and black bowtie signaled to Caroline and me. "This way, Mr. and Mrs. Dillard."

Caroline's face lit up with a smile of recognition. I'd specifically requested Ashley as our server. She was a former dance student of Caroline's. For over two decades, Caroline had run a dance studio in Johnson City and had taught hundreds of local girls, many of them now women, how to chassé and pirouette. Her work had probably done more to uplift the collective spirit of East Tennessee than that of any ten therapists or priests.

Ashley led us to the table, set for seven, chatting with Caroline as we walked. We were the first to arrive, but the kids showed up a minute later. They'd come in a separate car: Jack and Charlie, my legal "protégés," and Lilly. Lilly was carrying a guitar case, which she quietly ditched in a corner of the room, and they all wore smiles that were a little too bright. Everyone told Caroline how incredible she looked as we made small talk and pretended to read our menus. The cuisine was not my personal favorite—tapas, which I think is Spanish for "not enough food." But tonight wasn't about the dining. It was about family.

Sarah, my sister, came in a few minutes later, carrying a wrapped present, her eight-year-old daughter Grace in tow. She handed me the gift, saying, "This is a giant scam, by the way, this whole fiftieth birthday thing. Because if you were really fifty, that would make *me* fifty-one. Which literally *can't* be true, can we all agree on that?" Everyone laughed.

Sarah and I had traveled a rocky road together over the years. There'd been the time she'd stolen Lilly's car and wrecked it, drunk, and I'd had her arrested; the time she'd driven drunk with Grace in the car and I'd forced her to enter rehab; the drugs; the bad choices in men... It was all fallout from the trauma she had suffered as a kid, of course, but that didn't make it easier to live with. For the last six years, though, she'd been doing amazingly well. Clean, sober, and running her own restaurant in Jonesborough. And somehow managing to look years younger than her kid brother.

At Sarah's bidding, Ashley brought champagne to the table, along with a split of the non-alcoholic stuff for Sarah. My sister hadn't been briefed on the latest news about Caroline, though, and so her energy level was at a higher pitch than the rest of ours.

Playing unofficial host, Sarah clinked a fork on her glass of faux champagne. "I'd like to propose a birthday toast," she said, hoisting her glass. "But first… I believe Lilly has a musical surprise in store for us."

Lilly, a dancer like her mother, had been teaching herself guitar lately, as she stayed home to care for our grandson, Joseph. Rumor had it—okay, Jack spilled the beans—she had written a song for my fiftieth birthday.

A humorous set of lyrics set to Dylan's *The Times They Are a-Changin'*. But right now, she looked like she would rather perform a tap dance in a minefield. "The talk" had shaken her to the roots.

"Maybe Lilly would rather save the song for later," I suggested.

Lilly beamed her gratitude at me, and Sarah took note of the somber undercurrent beneath our celebratory exteriors. An awkward silence descended. It was broken by a clinking sound to my right. Caroline, tapping *her* champagne glass.

"Actually, *I* have a toast," my wife announced, "and a bit of an announcement." Announcement? What was this? "But if I'm going to do this…" She raised her finger, catching Ashley the server's eye. "Could I get a Bud Light instead? No glass."

Everyone cheered as Ashley dashed off to fill the order. Bud Light was Caroline's go-to celebration drink. And she liked to drink it from the bottle, which never failed to delight me.

When Caroline had her Bud firmly in hand, she lifted it with her bone-thin fingers and said, "First, the toast. I'd like to wish a happy eight hundredth birthday to…" She paused and looked at me. "The kindest, strongest, handsomest, and just plain *good*-est man I've ever met."

"Aw, did you have to bring your boyfriend along?" I quipped. "It's my birthday."

My joke garnered more laughs than it merited, and then Caroline continued. "Seriously, Joe. In addition to things I can't say at a, ahem, family gathering, you've been my friend, my partner, my knight, my caretaker—which I never wanted you to be—and my rock. If I say any more than that, I'll cry. And I don't want to do that. Not tonight. Tonight is an unexpected gift. I didn't know if I'd ever sit around a table like this again with my favorite people on Earth."

"There'll be many more occasions like this," said Sarah, lifting her glass. "Many more."

The rest of us raised our glasses and echoed, "Many more! Many more! Many more!"

Caroline waited politely for the chorus to peter out to silence. "I appreciate the sentiment," she said, then shifted to a somber gear, "but we all know it isn't true."

The quiet of the room deepened to a well-like silence. Jack opened his mouth to protest, but Caroline shushed him with her hand. "I don't mean to be maudlin or self-pitying, just honest. And honesty is something I think we all need right now…" Glances shot around the table in anticipation of her next words. "Sarah, you might not want Grace here for this part."

Sarah wrapped her arm around her daughter, signaling Grace was fine to stay.

"I'm dying," Caroline said. A heartbeat passed. Then another. "I haven't spoken those words aloud before—refused to even consider them—but I'm saying them now. I'm dying."

The temperature dropped in my gut. If this was what honesty felt like, give me deceit.

"Stop it, Mom," said Jack, an edge of real anger in his voice. "I don't want to hear that kind of talk from you. None of us do."

"I'm sorry, Jack," Caroline replied. "I'm not thrilled to be saying it either. But it's true. I'm dying, and it's time we all accept it."

"Come on, babe," I said, attempting lightness. "We can talk about this later. Let's just enjoy our drinks and order some extremely tiny plates of food."

"Stop it, Joe. We need to do this first." She looked around the table, fierceness beaming from her eyes. "Do you really think I don't know what went down at Vandy last Friday?" she said to us all. "Joe, it was written all over your face. Do you seriously think I didn't call Janet Seals the moment I got home?"

That was exactly what I thought. Fool that I am.

"I know what my options are. Or rather, my lack of options. And I've made a decision. I'm not taking that last-resort chemo drug. Or any other horrific Hail Marys they may try to throw my way."

"What are you saying?" Jack snapped at her, almost shouting. "You're waving the white flag? Giving up? That's not my mother talking." Jack pushed his chair away from the table and stood up as if to leave. "I don't want to listen to this anymore. When you're ready to—"

"Jack! Sit!" Caroline thundered. Where was this resurgence of power coming from? Jack obeyed his mother, sheepishly. "Listen to me, all of you." She paused. "Life ends. At some point, life ends. Death—it's time we used the 'd' word—is not a defeat, it's a fact. I hate to break it to you, but none of us are getting out of this thing alive. My time is up. Sooner than we hoped, but it *is* up. Soon. And I have only one question for you. Do you want to help me? Or not?"

"You know we do, Mom," Lilly said. "Don't even ask that. But how can we help you if you're not even going to help your—"

"Lilly! You're not hearing me. Do you *really* want to help me? If so, I need you to be *with* me on this, not against me. I need you to accept my choice. I need you to accept reality. That means no more fighting this thing. No more shaking our fists at God. I'm dying, and I'm scared, and I need my family with me. On this final leg. What I don't need is you punching walls or covering your ears in denial because *you're* too scared to talk about it."

She looked around the table, locking eyes with each of us. Charlie met her gaze more fully than the rest of us and reached out to take her hand. Jack and Lilly nodded, looking down at the table. I squeezed my wife from the side and kissed her head.

"All right, then," she said. "This morning I called Nolichucky Hospice Care. I want to start hospice services tomorrow."

The air left the room at the word *hospice*. Hospice meant the end of all curative treatment and the start of purely palliative care. Make the patient comfortable and help them with their transition. Hospice was one-way only. And we all knew it.

But none of us protested.

"Accepting death doesn't mean we can't appreciate life," Caroline said. "In fact, it means we can appreciate it ten times more. Tonight, we're celebrating. Celebrating Joe's birthday. Celebrating my amazing, wonderful family. And I, for one, intend to enjoy the hell out of it." She seized the menu with wide eyes and a ravenous growl. "Let's order! I'm starving."

That was when it hit me: the burst of vigor she was exhibiting tonight was not because of my birthday or even because of the gathering of the clan. It was the energy one acquires when one has made an unshakable life decision.

CHAPTER 5

Five Days Later

The 911 call came in at 6:05 a.m.

DISPATCHER: 911, what is your emergency, please?

CALLER: It's my girl! My little girl! I can't find her anywhere. She plumb disappeared.

DISPATCHER: What is the address where the emergency is occurring, ma'am?

CALLER: I don't know where the emergency is occurring! I don't know where she is! Someone took her. I'm calling from the Baptist church out on Willow Springs. But that ain't where we live, me and my girl. We's over on Possum Hollow. They shut my phone off, so I had to come down here.

DISPATCHER: Your name, please?

CALLER: Verna. Verna Roy. R-o-y.

DISPATCHER: Are you able to stay where you are until an officer arrives? Can you do that, ma'am?

CALLER: Yes! The Holston Mountain Baptist Church.

DISPATCHER: We have the address. Can you tell me exactly what happened?

CALLER: I slept hard last night. Took a extra one of my pills, 'cause my thoughts was racin'. Mighta had a drink or two, I don't remember. But when my alarm went off for work, she was gone! No note, nothin', no cereal bowl in the sink. She never leaves this early. And she *never* leaves without writin' a note. Ever since we had that trouble last summer with that pervo prowlin' around these parts, she knows better. She's in trouble, I know it. You gotta find her!

DISPATCHER: Have you checked the places she usually frequents? Called her friends?

CALLER: My car ain't workin', and I told you, my phone's shut off. That's why she'd never leave without tellin' me. Somethin' bad happened. A mother knows. She can feel it in her belly, in her baby place. Besides, her bike's still at the house. Oh, I forgot to say that! Her bike's still at the house! She don't go nowhere without her bike. Somethin' bad happened!

DISPATCHER: What is your daughter's name?

CALLER: Abigail. Abigail Pruitt. We call her Abby. She kept her daddy's last name because he said he'd stop sendin' the checks if we changed it. Not that he sends 'em anyway.

DISPATCHER: The girl's father doesn't live with you? Is that correct?

CALLER: That's *damn* correct.

DISPATCHER: Can you tell me his name and address?

CALLER: His name's Gregory Pruitt. And his address is Somewhere in the Butt-Crack of Unicoi County. I'd tell you to check him out, but I know *he* didn't take her, because that would mean takin' some 'sponsibility for her. Which he ain't done since she was three.

DISPATCHER: Can you give me a physical description of the child?

CALLER: About five-two, tall for her age. Close to my height. Sandy hair, down to her shoulders. Pretty young thing. Prettier'n her mama. And don't she know it? Struttin' around, shakin' her hair and peekin' out from behind it, all coy-like. I keep tellin' her, you gotta watch that stuff. You don't know yet 'cause you're only eleven. That stuff's like gunpowder. If you ain't careful, it can get you into a world of hurt. Maybe it already done happened.

***

"And can you show us her bicycle, please, ma'am?"

Elizabethton Police Officer James T. Grandy was not having a grand morning. He'd slept the night on the old couch in the basement after arguing till twelve thirty with his wife, then polishing off a half pint of Fireball. The morning sun felt like a searchlight in his eyes, and his mouth tasted like burnt cotton as he followed Verna Roy from the house to the back shed. He and his partner, Officer Melissa Price, had met the distraught mother at the Baptist church where she made the 911 call. After questioning her there, they'd driven her home in the cruiser.

Home was a sixty-year-old house trailer on the side of a wooded hill about three-quarters of a mile from the church. The trailer's sun-faded, mustard-colored metal siding was dented all around, at shoulder height, as if someone had punched the place a thousand times. Its overgrown lot was strewn with abandoned objects: a bottomless rowboat, a car engine, two refrigerators, a stack of old bed springs.

Verna, clad in micro-shorts and a lacy gray baby-doll tank top that looked like underwear to Grandy, pointed into the doorless toolshed. A pink Huffy bicycle leaned against the rusty sheet-metal wall.

"This the only bike she owns?" Grandy asked.

"We look like the Kardashians to you?" Verna lit a cigarette with shaking hands. Grandy had trouble pegging her age. She could have been 40 or a hard-living 27. Good looks still in evidence but fading fast. Furtive-eyed and skittish.

"And does she ever walk anywhere from here?"

"There's nowhere *to* walk. Look around you."

"Just so you know, ma'am, the vast majority of children reported missing turn up in a familiar place."

"I'm telling you, there's no familiar place she can *get* to without her bike or gettin' a ride. She don't run in the woods like some kids. Coons and salamanders ain't her thing."

"You said she plays on a Little League team in town," Officer Price chimed in.

"Not at five a.m. in the morning she don't."

Grandy noted her eyeballs jittering from side to side. Chemically induced, he surmised. "How does she get to practices and games?"

"Sometimes by bike. Sometimes her coach picks her up. I think he got some kind of notion Abby needs rescuin' or takin' care of. She don't. I'm a good mom. They won't be makin' no Disney movies about me, that's for sure, but we do okay, Abby and me."

"What about the father? You said he lives over in Unicoi County. How often does your daughter see him?"

Verna raised her voice. "You gonna ask questions all day or are you gonna look for my daughter?"

"The only way we'll know where to look is by asking questions," said Price. "How often does she see the father?"

"Whenever 'the father' feels like showin' up. Which is usually about once in a blue frickin' moon. And then he's gone, fast as he came. Though lately…" Verna trailed off.

"Lately what, ma'am?" Price asked.

"Lately, I don't know… Seems he been comin' round more often. Maybe lingering a bit longer. Making noise about carin' about her."

"You're saying the father has taken a sudden interest in the girl?"

"I guess you could call it that." Verna folded her arms and looked at the ground. "I'm hopin' the reason's what I *think* it is, not… somethin' else."

"Ma'am?" asked Price, a note of wariness creeping into her voice.

"My daughter Abby, she's a heck of a ballplayer, officer. Last year her team went sixteen and two, made the finals, mostly on account a' her. And she's about to start a new season. I heard from someone I work with, over at the Food City, that her daddy was takin' bets on her games last year with all his no-'count drinkin' buddies. Makin' himself a lot more'n beer money, from what I heard. He denies it, a-course, but…"

"But what, ma'am?"

"…But I hope that's the reason it seems like he's been tryin' to—what's the word—'gratiate' himself with her these days."

"You *hope* the girl's father is taking bets on her Little League games?" said Grandy.

"Better *that* than…" Verna trailed off.

"Than what, ma'am?" Grandy prodded. He was not in the mood for Twenty Questions. "Than what?"

"You seen a picture of my daughter, officers?"

"We were hoping you'd provide one."

Verna Roy pulled a six-year-old smartphone out of her skin-tight back pocket. Its screen was cracked and cloudy, but the picture shone through clearly enough: a ten-year-old girl with twin bows in her hair, a huge grin on her face, and a missing canine tooth.

"That was Abby last summer," Verna said to the police. She swiped the screen a few times and brought up a new image: Abby, at age eleven, hair swept across her face, baby fat gone, a worldly glint in her eye. Pretty in a whole new way. "That's Abby last Tuesday, not even a year later."

Price turned her head to the radio on her shoulder. "This is unit seven. We're going to need to talk with the sheriff's department over in Unicoi. Make that a 10-18."

CHAPTER 6

"**W**hat time did you get in last night?" Charlie asked Jack as he rolled onto his back, wincing at the mid-morning light pouring through the bedroom window. Charlie looked like she'd been up and dressed for a while.

"I don't know. I didn't check the clock."

"I did. Two-thirty."

"Then why'd you ask?" He smiled to show he wasn't issuing a challenge.

Charlie sighed. "Let me take a blue-sky guess. You paid a visit to a certain family over in Bulls Gap—a family that maybe goes by the name of Colson."

Jack was silent for a moment. "How did you know?"

She tilted her head in a way that said *gimme a break*.

"I didn't go in the house this time," Jack said. "Didn't talk to anyone. Just dropped off a… package. A few games and toys. Couple other things. Nothing much."

The Colsons were the adoptive parents of Dustin and Leesey, the young children of Sheila Self, a troubled woman whose death Jack had inadvertently caused sixteen months earlier. Self tried to attack a client of the Dillard law firm outside the courthouse where he'd been cleared of wrongdoing in a high-profile, racially charged case. Charlie moved in to block the would-be assault and was stabbed in the arm. Jack then seized the woman and drove her to the ground in a body slam, unintentionally cracking her skull on the sidewalk. The injury was fatal.

In his mind, Jack was able to rationalize his actions. But his rational mind wasn't always at the helm. And it didn't help him sleep at night.

"Let me take another guess," said Charlie. "An hour or so after you dropped off your little CARE package, you found yourself sitting in your car with a bottle of Maker's Mark, parked on that dirt road overlooking the West Hill Cemetery."

The cemetery where Sheila Self happened to be interred.

"I didn't drive drunk, Charlie. I slept it off first. That's why I was so late getting home."

"Jack... I have no intention of playing the mother role in our relationship, if that's what you're expecting. I'm not going to be one of those wives who spends their life trying to change their husband's behavior. That's a fool's game. But at the same time, I gotta ask myself, is it wise to marry a man who has a drinking problem he doesn't want to address?"

"I don't have a drinking problem, Charlie." Jack sat up on the edge of the bed and planted his feet on the floor.

"That's what you said the last two times. A drinking problem doesn't have to be an everyday, falling-down thing. It can be a once-in-a-while thing that keeps on happening."

Jack didn't answer. Charlie crouched before him, hands on his knees, and stared him in the eye, giving him no quarter for retreat.

"I'm glad you feel some responsibility for those kids, Jack. I am. Frankly, if you didn't, you wouldn't be the man I love. But for the hundredth time, it's not your fault they're growing up without their mom. *You* didn't pull that knife outside that courtroom. *She* did. And some part of her knew, when she took that action, that she was saying goodbye to her kids. Forever. And that they'd be better off without her. And I hate to say it, but maybe they are."

"So, it was a *good* thing I did," Jack said, injecting a dose of irony into his voice. "Just want to get that straight. I'm a hero for killing a mother of two."

"Would you rather she had killed me?" Charlie snapped, jumping to her feet and turning toward the wall.

"Don't even say that."

"Well sometimes that's how it feels, Jack. When you wallow in regret this way. It's like you wish you could have a do-over. One where you didn't try to stop her."

"Of course I'm glad I stopped her. Jeez, Charlie." He stood and put his hands on her shoulders. She shrugged him off. "I just wish I had used more... control."

"Some things *can't be done* with control." She faced him again. "That's why the human body comes equipped with adrenal glands. To override the brain. To fire us up, make us do things that need doing before our minds can get in the way."

"It wasn't adrenaline that took me over that day, Charlie. It was..." Jack sat on the edge of the bed again. "...My father. That's what finally hit me yesterday, sitting in my car on that cemetery road. I'm becoming... hell no, I've already *become*... my father. And it terrifies me."

Charlie sat beside him and put her hand on his leg.

"I mean, I love my dad," Jack went on. "You know I do. I always thought if I could be half the man he is, I'd be twice the man I had any right to be. But I've also seen that anger of his. That rage. The way it moves into him like a demon and turns him into something he doesn't want to be. And he doesn't know how to control it. That's the scary part."

"Like I said, Jack. Sometimes control is... overrated."

"You don't know how it feels when the rage takes over."

"You have a lot to learn about me."

Charlie strode out of the bedroom, her auburn hair waving behind her, leaving Jack to ponder her final remark.

Jack and Charlie were renting this small farmhouse on Bugaboo Springs Road, about two miles outside of Jonesborough, while they searched for a post-wedding home. They had tried living on the fifteen-acre property on Buck Mountain that Charlie had inherited from her grandparents, but it hadn't worked out. The commute to the Jonesborough office had been too long, but there was a bigger issue. A few years earlier, Charlie had also inherited a five-hundred-acre property adjoining her family's farm. It turned out to be the hiding place for a huge cache of ill-gotten, Prohibition-era gold, which had brought a great deal of pain to Charlie's life. She dynamited the cave where the gold was stored and eventually donated the whole plot of land to the Appalachian Trail Conservancy. But still, living so near the "cursed" gold had proven too strong a distraction for Jack and Charlie, so they'd moved closer to work.

"What do you want for breakfast?" she called from the kitchen in a noticeably lightened tone. Jack felt a wave of gratitude toward her. He loved this woman. She never shied away from saying what needed to be said, but she also didn't hang on to negativity. She shook it off and moved on. No lingering resentments, no silent treatment. It was her special sauce, he thought.

"I'll make breakfast this morning," Jack yelled back. "It's the least I can do." He *had* texted her last night to let her know he wouldn't be home till late, but he still felt guilty about his disappearing act. "Just let me jump in the shower." Jack and Charlie both had ten o'clock appointments at the office. It was after nine already. They'd have to eat and run.

As Jack went to his dresser to dig out some fresh underwear, he heard the television pop on in the kitchen.

"Ja-ack," Charlie's voice called out before he could make it into the shower. He didn't like the tone of suppressed alarm he heard in it. "You'd better see this."

Jack stepped into the kitchen wearing only his briefs, as Charlie pushed rewind on the DVR/cable box. She stopped and hit play, cueing up a news segment at its start. The anchor of the Tri-Cities station, a middle-aged blonde who wore her hair like a country singer's, set her face in a "somber" cast and said, "Police are looking for help in the case of a missing local girl. Eleven-year-old Abigail Pruitt of Elizabethton"—a photo of the girl appeared over the anchor's shoulder—"was last seen by her mother at about nine thirty yesterday evening and is believed to have disappeared sometime during the night. Amy, we go live to you."

Jack's face went slack.

The video feed switched to a young on-the-scene reporter standing in front of the mustard-brown house trailer Jack knew well. "Thank you, Shirley. I'm here with Verna Roy, the mother of the missing girl. Ms. Roy, do you believe your daughter might have left home on her own or do you think she was taken by an abductor?"

Jack didn't hear Verna's reply. Nor did he register her plea to the camera—"If you took my baby, please bring her back to her mama." His brain had gone blank. Reporter Amy Campbell tossed the video feed back to the anchor desk.

"Police are also asking for help locating the girl's father," the anchor said. "He is believed to be residing at an unknown address in Unicoi County." A cell-phone photo of Greg Pruitt, with a beer in his hand and his arm around a bearded man whose face had been pixelated, appeared on the screen. Jack's hands tightened into fists, his nails digging into his palms. "His name is Gregory Pruitt, and he is wanted for questioning. No crime has been established, and Mr. Pruitt is *not* a suspect at this time, but if you have any information on his whereabouts, or those of Abigail Pruitt, you are encouraged to call one of these numbers."

The screen displayed numbers for the Elizabethton Police Department, the Tennessee Bureau of Investigation, and the Unicoi County Sheriff's Department. They all looked like hieroglyphs to Jack Dillard.

"Jack," Charlie said.

No response.

She snapped her fingers. "Jack," she repeated. "What are you thinking?"

"That maybe you're right. Maybe control is overrated."

He strode out of the kitchen toward the bedroom, where his day clothes awaited.

"Jack, what are you doing? Jack? Jack?"

CHAPTER 7

A bump in the road awakened Abby from the half-dream she'd drifted into. The green grass of the baseball field dissolved into the green glow from the light-stick illuminating the interior of the truck's cargo bed. Reality came crashing back in all its harshness.

Abby couldn't believe how stupid she'd been. Trusting a grownup! A *strange* grownup to boot. Two of them, actually. Abby prided herself on being smarter than that. She knew grownups always lied. She knew that when grownups told you to do something, it was only because it was good for *them*, not for you. But she had walked out the front door of her home with those two strangers, as if they were all heading to Dollywood for a prize vacation.

What an idiot. And now here she found herself, in the back of a dark freight truck, heading to who-knew-where. Someplace far away from home, that was all she knew. The truck had been on the road for hours. Mostly highway miles, it seemed.

The terror welled up in her again, and she felt more scared than she'd ever been in her life. For the hundredth time she talked herself down. "Being scared doesn't help," she said aloud to the empty space. "Being scared makes you stupid"; she'd learned that from the talk Officer Price gave at her school. She needed to stay sharp. In mind and body.

If they wanted to kill you, you'd already be dead. She found thin comfort in the thought but repeated it nonetheless. *If they wanted to kill you, you'd already be dead.*

The grownups had been clever, she had to hand it to them. They dressed and looked the parts they were playing, and they talked a good game. No wonder she'd fallen for their trick.

At about 12:25 a.m. a knock on the trailer door had awoken her. That wasn't anything new. Sometimes guys came to the house at night, and her mom let them in. Sometimes there'd be a few mumbled words and the guy would leave a minute or two later. Other times the guy didn't leave right away, and she'd hear the door to Mom's bedroom closing softly. She'd hear other sounds too, sometimes. Sounds her mom didn't think she heard. But Abby wasn't stupid.

Some nights she was pretty sure it was her dad coming around. Some nights… not.

Last night, though, Mom didn't answer the knock. And then it came again. Abby waited, but there was no movement from her mother. Another knock. Still nothing. No way Abby was opening the door. Not to a late-night guy. Nope. When the knock came a fourth time, she started to worry. Why wasn't her mother getting up?

Abby slipped out of bed in her sleep-sweats and went to check her mother's room, adjacent to hers off the narrow hall. The door was open, and by the moonlight streaming past the knotted-together curtains, Abby could see her mom wasn't in bed. Abby padded, barefoot, into the TV room. The TV was still going, the lamp still on. And there was her mom, lying on her back on the couch, open-mouthed and still. Her head and shoulder hung off the edge, almost touching the coffee table, and her wrist was pressing down on the edge of the Little Caesars pizza box from earlier. Abby's heart did a giddyup of panic, but then Verna hauled in a ragged breath. Whew, she was okay. Well, alive anyway. Abby shook her mom, but she didn't wake up. She was about to shake her a second time when a rap on the glass behind made her jump and turn. A man's face leaned into the window.

Abby had been spotted; there was nothing she could do about it. *Great job, Mom! Falling asleep with the shade up and the lights on!*

"Abby Pruitt?" said the man through the thin glass. "Can you open the door, please? We're from the Department of Children's Services." *What?* "We've had a report about this house, and we need to come in."

He held up an official-looking ID of some kind. Abby should have checked it. She should have asked him a pile of questions before opening the door. Like, *Why isn't a cop with you at this time of night?* But she didn't.

"My name is Mr. Sanders," said the man after stepping through the door Abby opened. He had thinning hair and wore a pair of round, wise-owl glasses, along with a shirt and tie and a light zip-up jacket. He seemed harmless enough. He waved his hand back toward the door, and a lady came in behind him. "And this is Ms. Oliverez; she's a social worker."

"Oliverez" was a Latina-looking woman—*one of them Hispanics*, Verna would have said—and she wore a dark suit-jacket over a striped sweater and a pair of new-looking jeans. A card with her picture on it was clipped to a long cloth cord hanging around her neck. "Oliverez" smiled at Abby in a kind way but didn't show any teeth.

"Someone called in a report of a minor being left in the care of an incapacitated adult," said Sanders. "That means a grownup in not-too-great shape."

"Who called it in?" Abby asked reflexively. "My father? Nobody knows us around here. Is that how you knew my name? Did my father call you?"

Sanders didn't answer. "An ambulance is on the way for your mom. But meanwhile, we need to take you somewhere safe for the night."

"I'm safe here," Abby protested. "Mom!" she shouted at the figure on the couch. She stepped toward her mother to rouse her, but Sanders blocked her path. "Mom!" Abby shouted around the man. "Mom!"

"Get some clothes together, Abby, you're coming with us for tonight."

"Clothes? Why? When am I coming back?"

"As soon as we can ensure your safety in this home. Which we'll all be working toward."

"I have practice tomorrow. Will I be back in time for practice?"

"We'll see," the man said. The woman still hadn't spoken. "But we can't make any promises right now. Get those clothes now, Abby."

"No! Just wake her up. She took too much medicine is all. She does that sometimes. She'll be okay."

The strangers were unresponsive to her pleas. Sanders pointed to her room.

Abby, in a daze, stuffed some clothes, a hairbrush, and a toothbrush into a plastic Food City bag and exited the house, bookended by the two adults. They marched her out to a blue car that *looked* like one a social worker might drive—not a pickup truck or some old beater—and Abby slid reluctantly into the backseat. She felt scared, but not for her *life*. In fact, she didn't start to suspect anything fishy about the grownups until about ten minutes into their drive, when "Oliverez" turned to say something to Sanders, who was at the wheel. That's when Abby noticed Oliverez had "meth mouth," that jumble of rotten teeth and bad gums that was the hallmark of a longtime tweaker. You didn't expect a social worker to have meth mouth. No wonder Oliverez hadn't opened her mouth in the house.

Abby knew for sure she was in trouble when the car stopped next to a rusted-out bus in a dirt lot behind an old warehouse. The grown-ups yanked her out of the backseat and Oliverez said, "You're going with these guys now," was all they said.

Abby felt her arms being grabbed by strong hands from behind, and she was marched away. Her heart dropped out of her chest. She wanted to scream and kick and thrash, but something told her that would only make things worse. *Control, Abby, control. Breathe.*

The new men made her do some strange things they didn't explain, while they took videos and photos with their phones. They also stuck a big needle in her and drew out some of her blood. Then they put her in the cargo truck.

Now here she sat like a piece of freight. Her captors had created a "chamber" for her back here, surrounded by walls of stacked boxes. They had provided her with a few small "comforts" as well: a pile of blankets; a plastic bucket for going to the bathroom; several bottles of water; a bag of snacks—Doritos, peanut-butter crackers, Little Debbies; a couple of glowsticks; even a thrift-store-looking Nintendo DS that was older than she was. There was an electric air cooler/circulator of some kind, too, with a fat hose that ran up to the ceiling and was duct-taped in place there. And they'd provided a walkie-talkie for emergencies, saying that if she received a call from them, she was to obey their instructions without question, or else her mom would die.

The terror arose yet again, threatening to close her throat.

"Put on your game face, Hawk," she heard in her mind. The voice of Coach Jack. The only adult she did trust—although maybe she had been wrong about him too. She was starting to think maybe all adults were liars and users. Maybe that was what happened to you when the hair grew in under your arms; you just became selfish and evil. In that case, maybe dying before she grew up all the way wasn't the worst thing in the world.

No! Coach wouldn't like that kind of talk. He wouldn't let her give up like that.

Coach would expect her to fight. And to win.

Right. That settled it. She wasn't going to let Coach down. Or herself.

She put on her game face. What moves could she make? What pitches did she have in her arsenal? Escaping from the truck didn't seem possible. Especially when it was flying down a freeway, like it seemed to be. What other ideas could she try?

To answer that question, she would need to understand why these men had taken her. What did they want with her? What were their plans?

They couldn't have taken her for money, she reasoned. Her mother could barely pay the rent on the shoebox they lived in and keep food on the table. "Look, we're hundredaires!" Verna would say on Thursdays when she cashed her paycheck.

People didn't kidnap hundredaires' kids for ransom.

Maybe this was "human trafficking." She'd heard about that, but she didn't really know what it was. She thought maybe it had something to do with forcing people to work for free in factories and stuff. But why pick her? Her mom said she wasn't a very good worker. In fact, there was nothing special about her at all.

But wait. That wasn't true, was it?

Her ball-playing. Coach Jack said "the sky's the limit" when it came to her ball-playing talent. She wasn't sure what that meant, but she knew it was good. A couple of times lately, when her mom was drinking, she said Abby's dad had made some money taking bets on her games. So maybe she *did* have value. As a ballplayer. Maybe her captors were taking her someplace to play baseball. For money. Someplace like Japan. Or the "Minican Republic."

But no. That would be too risky. Putting her out in front of crowds and cameras. Someone might recognize her.

An alarming thought struck. What if they wanted her for… the other thing? Her mama was always warning her about the way she moved her hips and flipped her hair. She said Abby was gonna get herself in trouble young. She said men only thought about one thing and that she was giving them ideas. She knew what her mother was talking about, too: the sex. Abby couldn't imagine why a man would want a girl for sex who wasn't even a woman yet, but she'd heard rumors about guys who did.

Oh no. What if that's it? What if they want me for doing the sex?

Abby lunged for the toilet-bucket to throw up. After dry-heaving a few times like Verna on a Saturday morning, she plunked herself down on the truck-bed floor.

She couldn't allow them to use her that way. No, no, no. Not even once. She *had* to get away before that happened to her.

She thought harder than she'd ever thought about anything and came up with an idea. It wasn't MacGyver-level stuff, and it probably wouldn't work, but it was the only idea she could think of. It was worth a try.

CHAPTER 8

'd managed to talk my son down after Charlie called me in a panic. Jack had promised me, by phone, not to hunt down this Greg Pruitt guy and strangle him, and I'd agreed to meet him at the office later on to strategize. I had never heard him so upset.

Thoughts of Jack—and the missing girl—assailed my mind, but there was nothing I could do about that situation right now. For now, I had an important appointment, one I could not and would not miss: my "date" with Caroline. My wife usually had a period of wakefulness in the mid-morning, after the visiting nurse left, when the pain tended to ebb a bit. That was when we liked to schedule our daily "dates." I would bring her some herbal tea and sit beside her on the bed, propped up against some pillows, and we'd just hang out together. Some days I'd read to her, other days we'd look at stupid dog videos or play Scrabble on her iPad. Mostly we'd just chat or hold hands in silence.

Silence. That was the big thing with Caroline lately. She seemed to embrace it in some new way. It often seemed like she was using the silence to tune into some frequency I couldn't hear. As for me, silence made me nervous. Always had. But I was getting better with it, in my own crude way.

Part of that was attributable to the "communication training" my family was receiving from the hospice agency. I admit, I had been skeptical at first, but our outreach worker, Lou Anne, turned out to be a wise individual. She was teaching us the importance of what she called "just being there." Families of hospice patients, she said, tend to want to "fix" things and *do* things for the patient, but it was important for caregivers to learn to just sit with them and be present. No fixing. No solving.

Sometimes just silently squeezing a person's hand was the best thing you could do. And that was enough. Lou Anne was also teaching us something called "responsive listening," where you didn't try to answer difficult questions like "Is God punishing me?" with dumb platitudes like "Of course not, Honey." Instead, you asked open-ended follow-up questions like, "Is that what you feel is happening to you?"

I stunk at responsive listening. But I was learning to get better at that too. I was learning a lot of things. Death is a great teacher, turns out.

"Are you going in?" Lilly asked me, nodding toward the bedroom, after the nurse said her goodbyes. My daughter had returned to Johnson City a few days after my birthday party and was staying at the house indefinitely, along with our grandson Joseph. That was one nice side benefit to all of this.

"Yeah. Maybe you and Joseph can visit her later, when I leave for the office."

"I'll see if she's up for it. I've been trying to get the little guy to coordinate his naps with Grandma's. Not having a huge amount of success."

I smiled at Lilly and kept the smile plastered to my face as I stepped into the bedroom to greet my wife. The emergent situation with Jack and the missing girl was gnawing at my gut, but Caroline didn't need to know about that. She sat up and twinkled her eyes as I entered, patting the mattress for me to join her. Caroline had changed since we started hospice. Somehow, she'd gotten more beautiful, despite the ravages of the disease. Maybe it had something to do with finding inner peace. Not that I'd know anything about that.

"So how is Joseph Jackson Dillard doing with week one of the Mortality Acceptance Plan?" she asked as I settled onto the comforter beside her, laying my phone on the nightstand.

Sometimes it stung me how glib she was about her condition. But I supposed it was better than the opposite.

"Bad," I answered, honestly. "But working on it."

We went through my daily round of questions about how she was feeling and how things had gone with the visiting nurse, blah blah, and then she took my hand and leaned back into the pillow, creating a pregnant moment.

"What is it?" I asked, sensing she had something on her mind.

"I want to tell you about something that's been happening to me, Joe, if you're ready to hear it. Something I've been keeping inside. It's kinda spooky, but also kinda awesome in a way, and it's been going on for the last few days. But I only want to tell you if you promise not to freak out or clam up."

I tamped down my irritation at her low expectations of me. "I promise."

"All right, then." She nestled up close to me, stifling a wince of pain. In a hushed voice she said, "I'm starting to get glimpses, Joe. Of... 'the other side.'" My hand began to clench, but I turned it into a gentle squeeze of her hand. "It's coming into focus, like a real place. It's like I'm starting to have one foot in each world. Sometimes I'm moving more toward *that* world, sometimes I'm moving more toward this one. Back and forth."

Caroline seemed almost excited about her new experience. I felt like I'd just been poured a concrete shirt.

"And do you know what that place looks like, Joe? You'll get a kick out of this." I doubted that. "Remember the bay, down on Grand Cayman, the one with the glowing plankton?"

Remember it? I'd never forget it. When Jack and Lilly were younger, we took a family vacation to the Caymans. One night, when the kids were doing a 'science sleepover' event, Caroline and I went off by ourselves. We rented a double-seated kayak at Bioluminescent Bay. That's the decidedly unromantic name they give the place, but our evening was far from unromantic. In this bay live trillions of tiny phytoplankton that light up briefly when agitated. So, when you put a boat paddle—or your hand—into the water, swirls of blue-green light erupt below the surface, creating these wispy, ghostly patterns. Caroline and I were in awe. We became like children and lost track of time. It was the closest I've ever come to seeing God. We drifted around that bay for hours, stirring up a light show that rivaled the heavens above. And talking. About everything. Soul to soul—saying things we'd never spoken aloud to anyone. When we got back to our room, we made love in a way that could only be described as a religious experience. That night still stands as my gold standard for the heights human intimacy can reach. So yeah, I guessed I could coax that memory out of the vault if need be.

"Well, sometimes when I close my eyes now," she said, "I'm *there*. On the bay. It's not a dream or a hallucination. It's real, somehow. I'm there, in a kayak. But you're on the shore and so are the kids. Some days I start drifting out to sea—and the night sky and the ocean start to meld together into one glowing field—and that's when I know I'm losing my grip on this world, transitioning to the next one. Other days, my boat stays closer to shore and that's when I feel more tethered to life. Those are the days the nurse tells me my vitals are stronger."

I was both touched and terrified by the scene my wife described. I pushed the terror aside and asked an "open-ended question," the only one I could think of: "Where is your boat today?"

"Close to shore. ...But drifting out."

Drifting out. No! I wanted to jump out of the bed. I couldn't lie there anymore. I needed to move. But I also needed to honor my promise not to freak out. The truth was finally hitting home, deep in my belly: my precious Caroline was going to *die*. We had run out of deferrals. Out of backup plans. Out of Hail Marys. The end was coming and right soon. This thing was real. Real as a pair of steel rails heading to an unchangeable destination.

And I literally couldn't take it lying down.

I rose with controlled slowness. I walked to the bedroom door and back again. Repeated the loop a second time.

"Joe...?"

"I'm sorry, Sweetie. I'm not freaking out. I just need to digest this."

That was when I saw my phone light up on the nightstand. Incoming call. From Charlie. About Jack, no doubt. He was probably losing it. Gearing up to do something stupid and impetuous. Like his father would. And Charlie didn't know how to handle him.

Jack's situation demanded an immediate response, but I couldn't pull myself away from what was happening here in my bedroom, with my dying wife—who certainly didn't need to know what was going on with our son.

Two emergent situations, side by side, both of them requiring a hundred percent of my attention. And me at forty-percent capacity. It was more than I could handle. I felt ready to split in two. My breath became choppy, and my jaws and shoulders tensed into rock. My hand formed a fist and, as it did, part of me stepped back, observing myself from an objective distance. I knew what I was about to do before my arm drew back. I was going to punch the wall. With everything I had. Caroline knew it too. Her eyes flashed wide.

"Joe! You promised!"

I arrested my fist. Took a breath. Another.

"I'm sorry, Sweetie," I said, appalled at my near eruption.

"What's going on, Joe? With you? This isn't just about me, I can tell. This is your I've-got-stuff-on-my-mind-but-I-don't-want-to-burden-Caroline-so-I'll-hold-it-in-till-I-explode routine. I know it well. So spit it out. I'm not dead yet. I'm still your wife. And I can still help you."

I sat on the bed and the floodgates opened. I told her all about the Pruitt girl's disappearance and my worries about Jack. In full detail. Needless to say, she echoed my concerns. And then some.

"This is going to kill him, Joe, if it doesn't end well. He's become almost like a father to that girl. I don't think he can take another loss right now. He's barely been holding himself together since what happened to that Self woman. And with everything that's been going on with me—especially since our talk at the restaurant..."

"He's had a lot on his plate, no question about it. And I don't like what I'm hearing about his drinking, either."

"Planning the wedding with Charlie and coaching that ball team are the two good things he's done for himself over the last year and a half. If that girl doesn't turn up... Or if she turns up hurt or... *worse*, God forbid, he's going to take a fall. A big one."

"I know."

"And the thing is, Joe, I don't know where bottom is for him. I never have."

"Me either. I'm afraid it might be pretty far down."

"And that poor girl. What about *her*? She's been blossoming like a spring bluebell ever since Jack took her under his wing. Charlie tells me about it all the time. What kind of hell is *she* going through right now?"

"I know. I know. Unfortunately, there's nothing we can do about it right now. Except give Jack our love and support."

My wife settled back on the pillow and gave me her patented Caroline laser stare.

"What?" I asked.

"That's not really true, is it?"

"That there's nothing we can do about it?"

She turned her laser up another notch.

"What?" I said again. "What are you saying?"

"You need to do it, Joe. You need to go find that girl."

"'Go find that girl'? Caroline, come on. Just because I got lucky that one time hardly makes me an expert on tracking missing children." A few years earlier, I'd helped find Lindsay Monroe, a dance student of Caroline's who had gone missing.

"When has 'lack of expertise' ever stopped you from doing what's right? From where I sit, all I know is this: When Joe Dillard decides a job needs doing, there's no one on Earth more capable of getting it done."

"Sweetie, I'm sure the police, the sheriffs' departments, and the TBI are on top of the situation and doing everything they can."

"Which might be enough. *Might* be. You, on the other hand, have some rather powerful resources of your own. You have a team that includes Jack and Charlie..." Charlie had one of the sharpest minds I'd ever known, and Jack had acquired some pretty good investigative skills when working for me through law school. But they both had their hands full at the firm. And Jack was too emotionally close to get involved. "Stony..." continued Caroline. Susan Stoneman was a PI who did some work for the firm. She was good, but was she better than the TBI? "Leon Bates..." Caroline went on. Leon was Sheriff of Washington County and a man I counted as a friend. He was known to slip me inside information and a helping hand from time to time, but his first duty was to his job. "And last but not least, you have Joseph J. Dillard, Attorney at Law."

"Right: Attorney at Law, not Licensed Private Investigator. I'm sure a dozen people more competent than me are already involved in the case."

"The same people you usually dismiss as hacks, drudges, and scoundrels. Are you sure your reluctance to get involved isn't about something else? Like, for instance, the fact that it will take you away from home when your wife's time on Earth is running short?"

I opened my mouth to answer, but nothing came out.

"Go find her, Joe. Now. She needs you. *Jack* needs you. Go find that girl."

CHAPTER 9

Trying to find a man who may not want to be found, in Unicoi County, in Upper East Tennessee, is like trying to find a specific penny at a Coinstar processing plant. Unicoi County is nestled entirely within the Blue Ridge Mountain Range. It is rural, mountainous, and home to only two towns: Erwin and Unicoi. The rest of the county—about ninety percent of it—is unincorporated territory. Half of Unicoi's population of eighteen thousand dwells in the two towns; the rest is spread throughout the verdant hills and forests fed by endless branches of the Nolichucky River. The fishing and hunting are good in Unicoi. Trail-hiking too. The word itself, Unicoi, comes from a Cherokee term meaning "fog-shrouded." And the shadowy valleys of Unicoi County are indeed graced by frequent fog. But fog-shrouding is more than a literal term here. Folks who live in and around the county know that things happen in Unicoi that elude the eyes of the rest of the world.

The TBI had gotten lucky, though. They'd found the place where Greg Pruitt was living fairly quickly: a tin-sided cabin about two hundred yards from the nearest dirt road.

Agent Anita White, Special Agent in Charge of the Johnson City TBI office, had placed herself in charge of the effort to find the missing girl's father. Normally, such a case would have fallen to a subordinate, but she had a feeling this one could blow up in her face. So she opted for hands on. She was coordinating with the Unicoi County Sheriff's Department and the town police in Erwin and Unicoi. There hadn't been much to go on at first; only the word of the girl's mother, who claimed Pruitt was living somewhere in Unicoi.

Pruitt, they'd learned, was a small-time offender with two assaults, a handful of drunk-and-disorderlies, and a petty larceny under his belt, but nothing recent. Everything in the public records showed him to still be living in an apartment in Washington County, near Oak Grove, but the property's landlord said the shared apartment had been vacated several months earlier. Agent White couldn't get a warrant to track Pruitt's use of bank or credit cards—if he even possessed any—because there was no evidence a crime had been committed.

But putting the photo out early had proven fruitful. After the news segment played, over two dozen calls came in to the various agencies. Employees at the Tractor Supply Co, the Dollar Tree, and the Food Lion—all located in the same quarter-mile stretch of Erwin—reported having seen Pruitt numerous times. A couple of residents out along Canah Hollow Road had called the sheriff's office and reported encounters with him, narrowing the search area. It seemed likely that Pruitt was residing somewhere down a dirt hunting road that wound from Canah Hollow Road through a mountain pass called the Canah Gap and up into the surrounding hills. Deputies from the sheriff's department talked to a guy who had sold Pruitt half a cord of wood in late February. He had delivered the load himself, using an oversized wheelbarrow, in multiple trips, to traverse the long path from the road to the secluded cabin.

And now it was time to move in. This wasn't a SWAT-like operation. At this point, they just wanted to talk to the guy. But still, a child might be in jeopardy, so Agent White had brought along a partner from the TBI and a pair of deputies from the sheriff's department. An extra cruiser was stationed nearby as backup.

As White's squad emerged from the wooded path, they saw no signs of human life at the hillside cabin. Bath towels had been tacked, from the inside, over the two visible windows. White approached and knocked on the tin-sheathed door. "Mr. Pruitt. TBI. We'd like to ask you a few questions. Can you open the door, please?"

No answer.

"Mr. Pruitt? Gregory Pruitt? If you're in there, open up, please."

One of the deputies pushed on the door, and it swung inward easily. White announced herself again and stepped inside. The place had a hastily abandoned look. The shelves on the kitchen's plywood walls stood empty, the floors were strewn with trampled debris, and the two mattresses on the floor in the back room were void of blankets. But a slice of bologna on the kitchen counter, still in its Oscar Meyer packaging, looked fresh enough. And White noticed the smell right away—the familiar, cat-urine-like stink of ammonia, cooked into the walls.

Not five minutes later, Deputy Henderson found a trio of Glad Lawn and Leaf bags tossed over the edge of a short cliff behind the cabin. They contained a telltale assortment of items: empty boxes of pseudoephedrine cold pills, discolored coffee filters, empty plastic soda bottles with extra holes punched in them, Red Devil lye, masks, rubber hoses, flasks.

"It appears we have a bad news/good news situation on our hands," said White.

The bad news: Greg Pruitt must have gotten wind of the fact that the police were looking for him—that was the risk you ran by going public—and had vanished, maybe with the girl. The good news: Pruitt's little backwoods meth kitchen now rendered him a criminal suspect.

The hunt for Gregory Pruitt had acquired teeth.

***

My meeting with Jack and Charlie had gone pretty much as expected. Jack was beside himself with worry and anger. He shared Verna Roy's opinion that Abby wouldn't have gone anywhere without her bicycle and that her disappearance in the night had been at the hands of an ill-intentioned adult. And he had little doubt as to who that adult was.

"You don't know this guy, Dad," Jack said to me. "I've had a couple of run-ins with him. He's got that 'perfect storm' combination of violent personality, fragile ego, and the emotional maturity of a nine-year-old. He sees everything as a slight to his manhood. There's a reason he never got joint custody of Abby. He's not even supposed to visit her unsupervised. But now that she's developing some ballplaying talent, he's got fantasies of her making him rich somehow. Suddenly he's Daddy Dearest again. If Verna tried to block him from seeing Abby, in any way, I wouldn't put it past him to take the kid out of state, maybe even hurt her—or worse—to get even. Abby's just an object to him. I don't know what he's capable of."

I listened patiently to Jack, then read him the riot act: he was not to get involved with the Greg Pruitt situation. Period. Jack countered by pointing out, in judiciously chosen terms, that I was not the boss of him. Technically I *was*, but I didn't bring it up. Instead, I made a bargain with him. If he and Charlie would sit tight and take care of business for the firm, I would use the firm's resources—i.e., me and Stony and our network of connections—to find out everything we could about Abby's disappearance. Charlie ultimately persuaded my son that this was the wisest course of action. He acceded. For now.

Which meant I had suddenly appointed myself to a position I had no desire to hold: Missing Persons Investigator. I could almost feel Caroline's nod of approval from twelve miles away.

My first task in my new role was to stop at the home office of an actual, licensed investigator. Stony. Over the past couple of years, Susan Stoneman had become a trusted and valued member of the Dillard law firm team. A former FBI agent, Stony tended to live up to her nickname, personality-wise, but she was a skilled PI, and she could sometimes be persuaded to color outside the lines if she believed in a cause.

"What's the word, Stony?" I said, joining her on the screened-in porch of her house where she had set up a workstation on a picnic table to enjoy the spring air.

"Well," she said, "I made some calls, like you asked." Given Stony's dearth of warmth and fuzziness, it was surprising how many friends she had developed within the local law enforcement agencies. "And it seems this Greg Pruitt charmer is still Person of Interest Number One. Word has it he's been making efforts of late to get back into the girl's life. And there's been some fighting with the mom. Now suddenly both the girl and the dad go missing on the same day. It would be pretty weird if it *wasn't* him who took her. Especially given the stats."

"*How* weird, though, exactly?"

"Like, 'not worth looking anywhere else for the perp' weird. There is one twist in this thing, though." She explained to me that the address where Pruitt was last seen turned out to be a hastily abandoned meth lab in the hill country outside Erwin.

"So it's possible," I said, "that Pruitt saw his picture on TV, knew that people would be looking for him, and blew town because he was running a Mr. Meth franchise in his kitchen. Not because he was kidnapping his daughter across state lines."

"Possible. But my recommendation is that we just sit tight for now and let the authorities do their job. Now that Pruitt is officially a criminal suspect, they'll turn up the heat. They'll get warrants to trace his cellphone, his debit cards; they'll do road-watches and roadblocks, the whole nine yards. Unless he's smarter than he's ever given anyone reason to believe he is, they'll nab him pretty soon. And the girl too, I'm willing to bet."

"Here's my dilemma, though. I promised Jack—and my wife—I'd do something."

"Want to do something, Joe? Go play Words With Friends. Chill. Anything else might be considered interfering with a police investigation."

I knocked on the picnic table as if to say "understood," then stood and headed for the screen door. Before exiting, I turned to her. "Stony? If it wasn't the father, what other reasons would someone have for taking an eleven-year-old kid?"

"You know the answer to that question, Joe, as well as I do. And none of the reasons are good."

"You once told me the FBI monitors the dark web for pedophiles, kiddie porn buyers, people like that."

"Yeah, sometimes these sickos like to brag or share tips and strategies."

"Do you know any feds who work in that area?"

"I know people who know people… maybe."

"Can you put out a feeler? See if anyone has picked up any—I don't know—chatter or whatnot coming out of Upper East Tennessee. Anything about a missing girl."

"If she was taken by an individual for personal sexual assault purposes, it's highly unlikely the assailant would be bragging about it. It's also highly unlikely she was grabbed by a sex-trafficking organization. That kind of outright kidnapping is much rarer than people think. Most sex trafficking happens through people the kid knows."

"Can you put out a feeler anyway? Just to humor me."

"Joe, there is a 'favor economy,' as you well know. You don't blow your asks on longshots."

"*I'm* asking *you*, Stony. And I understand that I'll owe you one."

She tossed her hands up as if to say, *I'll see what I can do.*

I smiled my thanks. As I headed toward the screen door, Stony said over her shoulder, "Don't do anything stupid, Joe."

CHAPTER 10

I was about to do something stupid.

Passing Sycamore Shoals Park on West Elk Avenue, I steered my truck out along 321 toward Elizabethton. My plan was to talk to the girl's mother. Why? I didn't know yet. But maybe by talking to her I'd learn something. I figured she'd probably had her fill of questioning by this point in her awful day, but maybe she would confide in me because of the Jack connection. Jack was an important figure in her daughter's life.

As I drove, I put in a call to Leon Bates, the sheriff of Washington County. Leon and I'd had our share of adventures together. We liked and trusted each other, and, after fifty years on this planet, I couldn't say that about many people.

"Hello, Brother Dillard," he answered his phone. "What brings you crawling out of the rocks on this sunshine-y afternoon?"

I told him the reason for my call. I figured Bates wouldn't be involved in the Pruitt case because Abby lived in Carter County and the father was over in Unicoi. But I also knew Leon kept his antennas up. Nothing happened in East Tennessee law enforcement that he didn't know about. He surprised me by saying there was a chance he might end up involved in the case, which could limit his ability to talk, but he agreed to meet me the following morning.

"Coffee at the usual place?"

"Be there or be square."

The "usual place" wasn't a diner, it was the parking lot behind the old Highland Church of Christ, a place we'd met many times to avoid local ears. But tomorrow's meeting was tomorrow's concern. For now, I had other priorities.

***

When I pulled up near the Roy/Pruitt address in the hills of outer Elizabethton and parked on Possum Hollow Road, I was surprised to see a dozen other cars arrayed along the wooded street and a small crowd gathered on the road sloping up to Verna Roy's mobile home. A stocky woman with a marine-style crew cut and green camouflage sweatshirt was addressing the group from the hillside in a bullhorn-like voice.

"Again, my name is TJ, and this is my partner, Sherry." She pointed to a waifish-looking woman with long, dyed-green hair, holding a clipboard. "We will be the official HOLDERS OF THE MAP." She enunciated the latter phrase as if teaching it to schoolchildren. "We have fourteen volunteers today. We will work in four teams. It is the role of team leaders to ensure each team has a ROLL OF ORANGE TAPE, which I will hand out, and at least one CELLPHONE CAMERA. Remember: if you come across a suspicious item, do not touch or disturb it. Report it to your team leader, then MARK THE LOCATION WITH ORANGE TAPE and PHOTOGRAPH THE ITEM IN PLACE..."

I'd timed my arrival uncannily well. A volunteer search party had apparently been organized to comb the woods behind Verna's house, and map-holder TJ was in charge and ready to roll.

"Please maintain ARM'S-LENGTH DISTANCE from your teammates and walk at a consistent pace," she went on. "Remain alert at all times and do not ignore TREES, DITCHES, AND RAVINES..." TJ spotted me as I neared the group. "Sir, are you here to join the ground search?"

Without thinking, I responded, "Yes," and then added, for reasons unknown, "My son is a friend of the missing girl."

"We thank you much," she said in a rote tone. "Please give your name to Sherry, and she will assign you to a team."

As TJ resumed her spiel, I cast my eyes about and spotted Verna Roy, standing up near the trailer, apart from the group. I recognized her from the video on the news channel's website. She was smoking a cigarette, shifting her weight from one foot to the other. It didn't look like she was planning to join the search.

"The search will commence in..." TJ looked at her phone. "Five minutes. Please use this time to gather needed items from your car—such as bottled water, walking sticks, and first aid items—and to apply insect repellent and sunblock…"

I took the opportunity to make a beeline for Verna. She didn't notice me till I spoke.

"You've probably figured out who I am," I said to her. Jack and I both stand around six-three and have faces poured from the same mold. But Verna Roy didn't look like she was doing much figuring-out today. Her pupils were the size of pinholes, and she was rubbing her arms as if she was freezing, though the day was sunny and mild. I introduced myself as Jack's father, and she seemed to look right through me, not *at* me.

"They ain't gonna find her out there in them trees," she said in an airy, sing-song voice. "I already told 'em that. They ain't gonna find her in them trees."

"What do you mean, ma'am?"

She smiled vacantly, her eyeballs dancing about. "She ain't no forest fairy. And I ain't no forest fairy mama. That's for sugar-dee-damn-well-sure."

Verna Roy was baked. I wasn't going to get anything useful from her. Not today.

"I'm here because I'm trying to find your daughter," I told her. "I was hoping maybe—"

Verna floated off toward the house, tuning me out.

"I'll leave my card in the door," I called after her. "Maybe we can talk when you're feeling… ready."

Verna Roy, over and out.

***

I was assigned to search team B, along with a retired schoolteacher, an unemployed lab technician, and a night-shift bakery worker. Kathy, the teacher, was our team leader. She had a computer-printed map of the area we were assigned to search, with key landmarks circled and labeled in black marker, such as "big rock" and "sharp drop-off."

Our search area looked to be roughly a half-mile square, and our job was to make repeated sweeps as a team, back and forth, like a lawnmower cutting grass. The trees, ground brush, and rutted terrain would make it tricky to ensure thorough coverage.

"I'm probably stating the obvious," Kathy announced as we embarked, "but we're not really looking for a living child, this close to home. So be prepared."

As we headed up the forested hill, eyes sweeping the ground, I had little expectation of our finding anything useful. It came as a surprise when, less than five minutes into the search, we heard a voice call out, fifty yards to our right, "Found something!"

Team D, it turned out, had found a cellphone lying in an open area just a stone's throw from the mobile home. It was a cheap model of the burner variety.

If I had known the trouble that phone would bring into my life, I would have made sure I was the one to find it. And I would have slipped that phone into my pocket. And I would have thrown it as far as I could into the Nolichucky River.

CHAPTER 11

I waited in the lot behind Highland Church at 7:15 a.m. I'd been the one to request the meeting, so I brought the coffee, two larges from the new Dunkin on Oakland.

"Morning, Beautiful," said cowboy-hatted Bates as he pulled his cruiser up to my truck, facing the opposite way so our windows aligned. Tall, rangy, and slow-talking, Leon reminded me of Dennis Weaver in that old *McCloud* show that was on TV when I was a kid. But many a man—and woman—had paid a steep price for underestimating Leon Bates' brains and steel.

"I've made a decision," I deadpanned. "I think we should start seeing other men."

"Fine, but I keep the dog." He accepted the coffee I handed him with a tip of his hat.

I hadn't spoken to Leon since Caroline had made her decision to enter hospice care, so he and I had some personal ground to cover before talking business. Bates took the news to heart. There was a shake in his voice and a glisten in his eye as he clasped my forearm and said, "You tell that fine, fine woman of yours that I will be by to see her just as soon as I can."

We moved awkwardly on to the matter at hand. "There's been a development," he informed me. "Gregory Pruitt was taken into custody last night." My eyes went wide. "Yep, they nabbed him at a checkpoint on 23 North in Kingsport, hiding in the trunk of his meth-buddy's car, trying to cross the Virginia line. Not a man of surplus I.Q., it turns out. But the bad news is: they didn't find the girl."

"Crap."

"You said that right. I spoke to Anita White this morning." Anita was a TBI agent we both knew and respected. I'd first met her on a case when she was a field agent out of Johnson City. She later became Assistant SAC—Special Agent in Charge—at the Knoxville office and had recently returned to the Johnson City office to serve as full SAC there. "She said her people went at him pretty hard, and they're convinced he didn't take the girl. Still, there's something about him she doesn't like. Besides, of course, the fact that he's almost certainly guilty of manufacturing crystal methamphetamine. Every time they asked him about the girl, seems he got kind of squirrely. Anita's troubled by that."

"Why? What is she thinking?"

Bates pulled the drink tab off his cup lid and peered into the dark liquid within. "Did you know, Brother Dillard, that over forty percent of the time, when a child is sold into sex trafficking, a family member is involved? Usually a parent."

"Parents selling their own kids for sex? Good God." My coffee suddenly tasted bitter in my mouth. "Just when I thought my opinion of the human race couldn't sink any lower. Is that what Anita thinks happened here? Pruitt *sold* her?"

"Too early to say." Bates sipped his brew thoughtfully. "At this point, it's just a hunch she can't seem to shake. Pruitt checks a lot of the boxes, though."

"Such as?"

"Narcissistic personality, for one. These narcissists, they lack empathy. They don't see other people as having intrinsic value. They're users. Even when it comes to their own family members. Pruitt's also got a hair-trigger temper and lashes out at people who cross him."

"People like the girl's mother?"

"Possibly. Plus, he's money-driven and already sells a black-market commodity. There's a high correlation between people who sell any type of illegal goods and those who sell kids. He had a lot of cash on him last night too—more than might be warranted by a small-scale meth operation. And here's another red flag: he's already *been* making money on his daughter."

"What do you mean? How so?"

Bates explained how the previous summer Greg Pruitt had turned Abby's Little League performances into a cottage industry for himself, taking bets among his cronies. "Parents who use their kids financially," he explained, "are *much* more likely than the average bear to be involved in child sex trafficking."

"I think I want to kill him."

"You may not get a chance. He's at the Washington County Detention Center pending arraignment on the drug charges."

"Really? What's he doing in *your* house?"

"It's on account of his last official address. But if word gets out that he might be wanted on child sex charges, well, we know what can happen to guys like that in the hoosegow."

"Right. They find themselves singing in the *soprano* section of the inmate chorus."

"If they're lucky." Bates toasted the heavens with his coffee cup. "There's something else that's troubling in this case, Brother Dillard. It's the girl herself. She's a pretty young thing, God bless her. An early bloomer. Anita tells me that because of her age and 'type,' she could fetch a high premium amongst a certain 'clientele' on the sex market."

I shook my head in dismay. "We better pray that's not what happened to her."

"Actually, we better pray that's what *did*."

I shot him a puzzled look.

"At least that way, she's probably still alive. Which means there's still a chance to find her before too much damage is done. But if something else happened; if some sick individual took her for his own 'uses'—and she's at the most common age when that kind of thing happens—time is not on our side. It's already been thirty-six hours, and you know what they say."

"If you don't find them within the first twenty-four hours…"

Bates nodded soberly. His cellphone rang on his console, and he looked at the caller ID with a knitted brow.

"Hang on, I've got to take this."

Bates rolled his window up and answered his phone. He listened, giving short answers, for a minute or two and then did something I'd never seen him do before. He dropped the gearshift into D and pulled ahead, parking about three car lengths away from me to finish his call. The meaning of the gesture was clear: our "brotherly" conversation was over. He was now the Sheriff of Washington County, conducting official police business. In private.

I watched him in my mirror as he spoke on the phone. While he talked, he seemed to be tapping the keys of a laptop or tablet on the car's console. When he was finished, he leaned back in his seat and sat eerily still for what felt like a very long time. And then he put the cruiser in reverse and backed slowly toward me.

He rolled his window down, his face ashen.

"Who just had a dance party on *your* grave?" I inquired.

Bates was not amused. "Evidently," he said, then paused, "a kid on the ball team has come forward to report some suspicious adult behavior he observed around the Pruitt girl." He looked down at the tablet device. "And then *these* came in on the tip site. If the time stamp on these photos is correct, they were taken after the girl disappeared."

Bates sighed and handed the tablet device to me as if it had the weight of cast iron.

The screen displayed three nighttime photographs of the Pruitt girl in the front seat of a car with a man. The two looked to be embroiled in an intimate, face-to-face conversation. The man wore a baseball cap and was making intense eye contact with Abby. In one of the photos, his hand rested on the girl's shoulder.

The man in the photographs was my son Jack.

CHAPTER 12

10:17 p.m., near Black Canyon City, Arizona

Tommy switched on the U.V. light on his NinjaGrip-360 bug grabber and readied for action. Using a stick in his other hand, he flipped aside a chunk of dead-cactus debris. Bark scorpions! Yes! Two of them. Nice, fat ones, each almost three inches long—glowing in the U.V. light, just like those glo-in-the-dark rubber critters his mom used to buy him. Before she ran off.

Tommy squeezed the trigger on the long, pole-like device and snagged one scorpion, then the other, and dropped them into a pail. Tommy was supposed to kill the scorpions, but he liked to keep them alive. He had a terrarium full of them in the toolshed behind the house. Nobody paid any attention to what Tommy did in the toolshed.

"Hey, Goof-tard!" a voice sang out in the Arizona night. Tommy looked up toward the silhouetted house on the hill and the huge saguaro cactus that stood sentinel beside it. The dark forms of two men headed down the hill toward where he was working—a patch of desert plants about twenty yards behind the house.

"There you are, Goof-tard," said the lead man, catching his breath. Shane was a staff person at the residence. He was about thirty years old, softly muscular, and kept his head shaved in a buzz cut.

"Mr. Paolo don't like it when you call me that," Tommy said, his eyes fixed on the ground.

"Well, Mr. Paolo's not here tonight, is he? Hey, Tommy, you know I'm only joking when I call you Goof-tard, right? But here's a tip: quit acting like one and I'll quit calling you one. Ha!"

Tommy kept looking down.

"Hey, that's a joke too. What's the matter, you on the rag tonight?"

Tommy shuffled his feet, waiting for Shane to say his piece and leave.

"So listen, Tommy. This is Rami." Shane gestured toward the man beside him, also around thirty, bearded and shaggy-haired, dark complected. "He's going to be working here."

"What happened to M-Marco?" Tommy asked.

"M-Marco m-messed up. Marco sampled the wares. Marco's probably being ch-chopped up into coyote ch-chow right about now. Ha!" Shane turned to his new colleague. "Rami, this is Tommy. He used to be one of our 'associates,' but he got a little old for our clientele. Right, T?" Tommy had recently turned 17. "He just sticks around 'cause the boss has a soft spot for him. Or maybe it's a hard spot. Ha! Tommy's kinda like our mascot, aren't you, T? He cleans up, does odd jobs around the place. Why don't you tell Rami what you're up to tonight?"

"C-catching scorpions, so they d-don't get in the house."

"Scorpions? Really?" said the new guy, pulling his head back with a grimace.

"Get used to it, pal," said Shane, gesturing out at the rugged desert wilderness and surrounding mountains. No other house lights could be seen in any direction. "What was it that guy in that movie said? 'Everything out here that isn't *you* wants to kill you.' Ha! We got rattlesnakes, poison centipedes, black widows, fire ants, Gila monsters, cholla cactus—they're the worst! And go ahead and tell him about the scorpions, T."

Tommy cleared his throat and launched into his memorized spiel. "The scorpion is not an insect b-but a member of the arachnid family, like the spider and tick. It has eight legs, a segmented b-body, and a vemenous tail."

"*Venom*ous, Goof-tard."

"Ven-om-ous," Tommy repeated, overpronouncing. "The bark scorpion, which we have here"—Tommy pointed to his bucket—"is the most ven-om-ous scorpion in North America. Its sting can cause severe pain, breathing problems, muscle stiffness, and even death."

Shane applauded. "Okay, Great White Hunter, put your weapon down. I want you to come with me while I show Rami the ropes." Tommy leaned his bug-grabber against a rock and followed the two men toward the house.

Shane spoke to the new guy as they walked. "So usually, we have anywhere from five to seven 'associates' on premise at any time. Mostly female, but some male too. They stay a few weeks, a few months, some longer, then they get moved out. Where to? We're not told. There's a new crop coming in a couple of days, that's all I know. Our main job is to supervise them in the house and transport them to the meeting locations with the clients. Usually that's in metro Phoenix, but it can be Tucson, Prescott, Jerome, wherever."

Shane opened the back door of the adobe-style house and ushered Rami inside. Tommy followed the men. "This is the kitchen. Obvo." The decor was contemporary Southwestern—desert tones, wood accents. "Tommy keeps it nice and clean, don't you, T?" Shane strode across the tile floor to a pair of refrigerators. The one on the right was padlocked. Shane opened the left one to reveal dozens of cans of Budweiser, Smirnoff Ice, Mike's Hard Lemonade, Four Loco, and Coors Light, as well as assorted soft drinks. "They can help themselves to any of this stuff. The other fridge has food and snacks. They have to ask staff to unlock that one. Mr. Paolo don't want 'em getting fat. They can have these whenever they want, too." Shane tapped a glass jar on a counter. "Weed gummies. They can have other 'goodies' too, but they gotta see Mr. Paolo for those. Knives and other sharps get locked up over there. Come on, let's meet the zoo exhibits."

Tommy followed Shane as he led the new guy through the living room, then down the hall. "No locks on the bedrooms," Shane explained to Rami. He knocked on the first door on the right, then pushed it open. Three of the four bunkbeds in the room were occupied by tweenaged girls, none of them over 14. One was lying back on a pillow, listening to AirPods, a can of Smirnoff Ice in her hand, the other two lay on their stomachs using tablet devices.

"Girls, this is Rami. He's our new staff member. Rami: Alexis, Nicole, and Brianna." The girls offered absent nods and waves. Shane pointed to the empty bed. "Madison is working tonight." He shut the girls' door. "They can't have phones, for obvious reasons, but they can use other devices. There's no Wi-Fi here, so..."

Shane went to the next door down, knocked and opened it, again without waiting for an answer. A boy of about 14 with combed-back hair and a sweatband around his head sat on the bed playing a shooter game on a big TV screen, cigarette clamped in his teeth. "Aaron, meet Rami—he's staff. Rami, Aaron." Aaron grinned around his cigarette in greeting.

Shane turned toward the door across the hall and knocked. "The little angel in this room is Luka. She's in a single room 'cause she don't play well with others." Shane knocked again; no response. He pushed the door open.

Tommy watched from the hallway as Shane entered the room and stood over the girl's bed. "Wake up, Sleeping Beauty, time to meet the new staff person. Come on, I know you hear me. Come on, Luka…" Shane's fingers snapped. "Eyes open! Up!" There was a pause, and Shane shouted, "SHIT!" in rage and panic. He tore out of the room holding up an object: a disposable box-cutter with a yellow plastic handle, sticky with blood. "How the hell did she get hold of *this*?" he raged at Tommy, as if Tommy should know. "Shit, shit, shit!"

The two doors across the hall flew open and stunned faces appeared in the doorframes. Shane shouted at them, *"How did she get hold of this?"* The young people ducked back inside.

Shane looked at Tommy and Rami, his face red, his teeth bared. "You two, wait here while I call Mr. Paolo. He ain't gonna like this!" Shane stormed toward the kitchen, swearing and snarling, fumbling for his phone.

Two minutes later, he stormed back. "Mr. Paolo ain't happy. Not one bit. Not one tiny bit. But come on, we got a job to do. Quick." Shane stomped into the bedroom, signaling for Rami and Tommy to follow him.

Tommy braced himself but still wasn't prepared for what he saw when he entered the room. The *amount* of blood soaking the bed was what caused a whoosh of air to fill his lungs. And 13-year-old Luka's face—God, it was almost as white as her pillowcase. The framing of jet-black hair around it made it look all the whiter. Shane took hold of the girl's left arm and pointed to Rami. "You: grab her other arm and shoulder." He looked at Tommy. "And you, Goof-tard, grab her feet!"

"M-Mr. Paolo said I don't gotta do jobs like this."

"Grab her feet, Goof-tard, or I'll tell him you're the one who gave her the razor knife."

Tommy grabbed the dead girl's feet. They felt cool and dry. Like leather slippers. Awful.

In his mind, Tommy recorded the details of the scene and put them on his List. He filed them away with all the other very-bad-things he had seen and the people who had done them. No one knew about Tommy's secret List, just like no one knew about the scorpions in the toolshed.

Shane barked at the new guy, who was still hanging back near the door. "What are *you* thinking: 'I didn't sign up for this'? News flash, *yeah*, you did. It's exactly what you signed up for. So snap to it if you don't want to end up where she's going."

Rami hustled to join Shane at the head-end of the body.

"Consider this part of your orientation," Shane said to the new guy. "You're about to learn what happens to associates who don't 'make it in the program.'"

CHAPTER 13

'd called a family meeting for 3:45 at the house. I figured if we met in the kitchen, behind closed doors, we'd be safe from Caroline's ears. Not that we really needed to worry about that anyway. As great as it had been to see her come alive at my birthday dinner, the cost had been dear. Since that night, she hadn't ventured out of the bedroom/bathroom area even once, and her stamina had halved.

I'd chosen 3:45 because I knew Lou Anne from the hospice service would be here at four. I wanted her advice on how to handle the Jack news.

I'd already talked to Jack privately, of course. He assured me of what I already surmised on my own—that the anonymously uploaded photos of him and the Pruitt girl in his car were not taken the night she disappeared, but at an earlier date. The time stamp, therefore, had been forged. Not a difficult thing to do, presumably. But who did it and why?

The photos looked damning, regardless of when they were taken, but Jack explained to me that he often had heart-to-heart talks in his car with Abby, in his ongoing efforts to counsel and encourage her. Jack's big problem, above and beyond the photos, was his lack of a decent alibi the night before last. Unless someone had witnessed him passed out, drunk, in his car on that cemetery road, no one could vouch for his whereabouts during the timeframe of the girl's disappearance. Even worse, Bates had called me this afternoon, hinting that something more damaging might be coming down the pike. More "evidence" against Jack. Leon also said he couldn't talk to me about the case anymore—which caused the hairs on my back to bristle.

Jack's predicament was vexing enough on its own, but there was an added consideration. How to handle it with Caroline. Hence, the family meeting.

***

"But what about the CARE package Jack dropped off at the Colsons' house?" Charlie said to me and the other family members gathered around the kitchen table. "The games and toys for the kids? Doesn't that help corroborate Jack's version of the story?"

"You're a lawyer, Charlie," I replied. "Think of how a prosecutor would spin that. Jack's last verifiable activity before the Pruitt girl's disappearance was lurking outside the home of two *other* children. Leaving gifts for them and then sneaking off unannounced."

"Jeez, Dad," said Jack. "Lurking? Sneaking off? Why don't you tell me how you *really* feel?"

"I'm telling you how they'll make it sound, son. You've been practicing law long enough to know: truth doesn't matter in a courtroom. It's whoever can spin the best story from the known facts. And a prosecutor would have a grand time spinning *those* facts."

"But Jack didn't do it," said Charlie. "The more they dig into this, the more they'll know he's not their guy."

"Maybe. And maybe this *will* blow over quickly, but…"

"But what?" asked Jack.

I explained to them that Leon Bates had hinted at the prospect of more evidence to come. "We have to prepare ourselves," I said, looking around the table, "for the possibility that this may get worse before it gets better. And the fact is, right now, they're not looking at Greg Pruitt, the father, anymore. They're looking at Jack."

Faces paled.

"Mom can't find out about this," said Lilly. "I mean, she *can't*. It will kill her, flat out."

"That's why I wanted us to talk. How do we present this to your mother? Or do we not tell her at all?"

A vote was taken, and the verdict was unanimous: we shouldn't tell Caroline.

Lou Anne, the outreach worker from Nolichucky Hospice, arrived at her appointed time, and I invited her to join us at the table. After explaining the Jack situation to her in broad terms, I asked her opinion on how to handle it with Caroline.

"Sometimes withholding information from a patient is justifiable," she said, "but generally it's a mistake for caretakers to set themselves up as 'truth filters.' The patient is an adult and has a right to know things. Secrecy also requires a certain amount of… subterfuge, dishonesty. Keeping the truth from a patient can become complicated. The greater the number of people who know about it, and the more public the information is, the harder it is to keep secret."

"That's true," said Lilly. "She's on *that* thing all day long now." Lilly pointed to Caroline's iPad, in its floral-patterned case, plugged into a white cord on the counter, a few feet from where we sat. "If the stuff about Jack becomes public, it'll pop up on one of her news feeds. Is that how we want her to find out about it? On the Internet?"

"Why is her iPad out here anyway?" I mused aloud. She didn't usually let it out of her sight for long.

"She asked me to put it on the kitchen charger while she napped," said Lilly.

We all looked at the device, then at each other, and I knew what we were all thinking: Did we *have* to give the iPad back to Caroline? "We could say I broke it somehow. Dropped it and stepped on it. Buy ourselves some time."

"Listen to yourselves," said Lou Anne. "This is what I mean about complications. You're talking about withholding Caroline's personal property from her to prevent her from learning inconvenient facts."

Lou Anne was right. This thing was going to get complicated. Fast. We might be able to keep the news about Jack from Caroline for a short while, but not for long. Not without paying a price, on many levels. Which meant only one thing: we had to stop the Jack story from *becoming* a story. We had to nip it in the bud. We had to find out the truth. Fast.

Not just for the girl. Not just for Jack. For Caroline too.

***

It was eight p.m., and I was en route to Lake Norman, North Carolina. I hated being away from home these days, and I especially hated taking trips. But this one was critical. I was on my way to see Erlene Barlowe.

Erlene was the proprietor of the Mouse's Tail, a strip joint outside of Johnson City, and a woman with whom I'd had multiple "dealings" over the years. My relationship with Erlene was many-sided, and we'd been on the outs once or twice, but I still considered her more friend than foe. I believed the feeling was mutual. I'd learned from Leon Bates—who also had a "many-sided" relationship with Erlene, to put it mildly—that Erlene had recently bought a lakeside home in North Carolina, where she was considering retiring. I didn't believe it would happen. Erlene was too involved with the running of the club, and with the lives of the girls who worked there, to ever retire. But evidently, she was giving the idea a trial run and was currently spending a few days at her Lake Norman house.

I could have tried speaking to her by phone, but I didn't trust her not to record the call—Erlene liked to collect dirt on everyone, friend *and* foe—and besides, I'd learned over the years that in-person conversations with Erlene tended to be more productive. The reason I was going to see her? Sex. Erlene knew everything about the sex life of East Tennessee. She knew who had unusual tastes and who kept dirty little secrets. If anything sexually "noteworthy" was going on in the eastern counties, legal or not, there was a good chance Erlene knew about it.

I'd gotten her address, on the west side of Lake Norman, from Leon, and I figured it would take me almost three hours to get there. I planned to make the round trip in one night and to get back home by three a.m. at the latest.

I was about fifty miles into my drive when I realized I'd forgotten my phone. Damn! I'd charged it and placed it near my keys so I couldn't possibly forget it, but somehow I'd done so anyway. Now I faced a dilemma. I could drive back home and get it, which would add ninety minutes to my time away from home and to an already long night of driving. Or I could drive on, knowing that would put me out of touch with my family for the next five or six hours.

I proceeded to make the worst decision of my life.

CHAPTER 14

Caroline waited until she heard the door to Lilly's bedroom close, muffling young Joseph's chattering voice. She knew Lilly would now be reading her son his bedtime story, a nightly ritual that took at least fifteen minutes. Joe had left the house an hour earlier to conduct some vague "out-of-town business," and Jack and Charlie had said their goodbyes.

The house was quiet and unattended at last.

Caroline swung her feet onto the floor and waited for the blast of pain to strike. Good grief! These days, the pain didn't even seem localized anymore. It was as if it belonged to her whole body. She was on a regular schedule of morphine now, which helped some, and she was also permitted an extra dose for "breakthrough pain." She planned on taking that extra dose just as soon as she got back to bed. She allowed the fusillade of pain-bullets to shoot through her, then she pushed herself to her feet. God, it shouldn't hurt so much just to stand.

Using the walls and furniture for support, she made her way out to the kitchen. There it was, on the counter where she'd asked Lilly to charge it: her iPad. Caroline snagged the device and returned to the bedroom. She took a morphine pill, drank some water from the wheeling tray table, and settled back into bed, letting the waves of pain crash on her, hoping they would ebb soon.

She opened the floral-patterned iPad case, revealing the screen within. Lilly had left the power on, as Caroline hoped she would. Caroline looked for the icon for the Voice Record app and tapped it. *Yes, it was still recording!* She pushed stop. The recorded file was nearly five hours long, but she was only interested in the section that began at 3:45.

Joe had been acting strange all day, which meant he was hiding something. As usual. No matter how many times in their marriage she had asked him not to keep secrets from her, he still insisted on withholding things, in efforts to "protect" her. Lilly had been acting odd too, and when Caroline overheard that a "family meeting" was planned, she took matters into her own hands. Knowing she wouldn't get the whole truth from her family directly, she decided to record the meeting without their knowledge. It wasn't the most ethical thing she had ever done, but then, neither was keeping family secrets from a dying woman.

With a tap of the screen, she selected the newly recorded file and pushed play.

***

"Joseph J. Dillard at my Old North door, I swan." Erlene seemed surprisingly unsurprised to see me. She was wearing a robe over a *very* low-cut leopard-print negligee. At 60-plus years of age, I don't think Erlene had ever bought a single article of clothing that didn't reveal more of her ample cleavage than the world was asking to see. "Does this mean you and I are finally going to surrender to the siren's call of our long-simmering passions?"

"It does not, Erlene. May I come in?"

Erlene and I spent a few minutes catching up and smoothing over a recent rough spot between us. She dropped her stagey flirtations long enough to express genuine concern for Caroline, and for my family, before I got down to business. "Erlene, between what happens at the Mouse's Tail and what goes on in your side business…" In addition to running the bar, Erlene operated an escort service that skirted the edges of legality. "You probably know the sexual proclivities of half of Dixie Alley."

"Half? That's being modest, sugar."

"You must occasionally come across customers whose tastes in female company run to the… er, 'south' side of the legal age divide."

"If you're saying what I think you're saying, honey, you better proceed on tiptoe."

One thing I've learned in my years of practicing criminal law is that no one likes to admit any knowledge of—much less direct involvement in—sexual transactions involving minors. The very topic makes people skittish. Erlene tried to dance around my line of questioning, but I didn't have the time or patience for coyness. I pressed her. She insisted that she never tolerated underaged activity in any of her various "employment opportunities." Still, I refused to believe she didn't know *anything*. We finally got down to brass tacks.

"I did have this one gal at the Tail. Tabitha. Little pixie of a thing, dark hair, bangs. Twenty-four—I checked her out, believe you me—but looked like she was barely in high school. Now, most of my dancers, they got a half-decent set of hooters on 'em. But not Tabitha. Flat as a run-over Ring Ding on the Texas Panhandle. But she did attract a certain… clientele. She worked for my escort service too, and there was this one fella who'd refer her out to his little 'club.' These were the type of johns who liked it when the gal brought along a lollipop and wore pigtails and pretended she was a seventh grader. I think most of 'em woulda preferred it if she didn't *have* to pretend. You pickin' up what I'm puttin' down?"

Erlene claimed not to know the name of the "referrer" in question, but I didn't believe her. When I told her about Abby Pruitt's disappearance, she gave up his name readily. Terrence Keene. A prominent surgeon and political contributor out of Knoxville.

Terrence Keene and I were going to have a talk.

***

Lilly was in the kitchen brewing herself a cup of bedtime tea when she heard her mother's faint voice from her parents' room. "Lilly, could you come in here?"

"What is it, Mom?" Lilly entered the room, shutting the door gently behind her.

Caroline made a weak *come closer* gesture, and Lilly approached.

"I'm going to sleep now," Caroline said with a tired slur in her voice, "but here, take this." She handed Lilly her iPad in its floral case.

Lilly assumed her mother was done with it for the day and wanted it charged again, but Caroline said, "I want you to hold on to it, Lilly. It's very important that you keep it and protect it. Only you. No one else."

"Why? What do you mean, Mom?"

"There are two files on there." Caroline's eyelids drooped heavily. She forced them open again. "You'll see. One is called, 'for Joe.' I want your father to play it in private, but only after he finds that missing girl. Do you understand? Only *after*. The other is called, 'for Jack and Charlie.' I want you to play it at your brother's wedding."

"Why are you giving it to me now, Mom?"

Caroline ignored the question and took her daughter's hand. "And I want to say this to you while I still can. You're my good, good, strong girl, Lilly, and I love you so much. I love you with every bit of my heart, and I will always be with you. I want you to promise you'll keep this family together. Only you can do it. Promise me."

"I promise, Mom," Lilly said, choking back tears.

"Okay, then." Caroline's head bobbed as if pulled by an invisible cord. "I think I want to sleep now."

***

My conversation with Erlene took longer than planned, and it was a little after two a.m. when I finally began the long drive home. It had been a long, difficult day. I was tempted to accept Erlene's offer to get a few hours' sleep in her guest bedroom, but I just couldn't stand the thought of being away from Caroline any longer than I needed to be.

It was still dark as I neared home, my headlights sweeping across the spring-green trees. And so, the sight that met my eyes as I turned into the driveway made no sense. Jack's car. Why was it still here at this hour? He hadn't planned to stay the night. And whose car was parked behind his? As I drew closer, I saw the magnetic sign on the Prius's door: Nolichucky Hospice Services. My heart jumped into my throat. Before I could put the mental pieces together, Lilly came running out the side door. Her eyes were ringed with red.

"Dad!" she cried in a raw, shaken voice. "Where have you been? You forgot your phone! We couldn't call you!"

"What? What is it, Lilly?" I said, leaping from the truck.

"It's Mom! She's gone, Dad. She passed in the night." Lilly rushed into my arms. "I'm so sorry, Daddy. We wanted to call you! We couldn't find you!"

Gone? Passed? What? My Caroline? My best friend, my soulmate, my guardian angel?

Time thickened to paste. As I thundered up the steps in slow motion, I felt my strength wash out of me, as if someone had pulled a plug at the base of my spine. Ignoring the unknown woman speaking to Jack in the living room, I ran to the bedroom doorway. When I saw her lying there, I moaned like a wounded animal. Dropping to my knees, I took her face in my hands. "No. Not yet. Not now." I sensed Jack and Lilly moving in behind me, but the sight of Caroline's lifeless head on the pillow was the only thing my mind could process. "Not yet! Not yet!"

I'm not sure how long I knelt there, begging her to come back. I vaguely recall Jack taking my shoulders and pulling me away as two strange men wheeled a gurney into the room. I remember thinking I would kill them if they laid a hand on her. At the same time, I told myself this wasn't my Caroline. Not anymore. This was an empty vessel. As the men tried to wheel her past me, I blocked their path. I knelt and put my hands on her cool face one last time. "I'm so sorry, Love. I should have been here. I should have been here."

A minute later, the taillights of the funeral home van disappeared down the driveway.

I won't repeat the terrible things I said to my son and daughter as I rebuked them for not trying harder to reach me—though I'd given them no way to do so. Or the dressing-down I gave the poor on-call nurse who had never met Caroline before and whose only job was to come to the house and pronounce her dead. Nor will I repeat, worst of all, the accusations that flew from my lips when I learned Lilly had unwittingly enabled Caroline to record our family meeting and to listen to words not meant for her ears.

A wave of shame washed over me, dousing the white-hot rage. I wanted to shrink into my shoes and disappear. I apologized to my family and to the hospice nurse for my thoughtless words and behavior. And then I did what

I should have done right away—hugged my children and cried myself raw until there was nothing left inside.

Then I went out to the back porch and dropped myself onto the steps to watch the rising sun light the Tennessee sky.

As I sat there, alone on the stoop, a thought settled on me with the weight of black water on a drowning man. Our worst fears had been realized. Caroline had found out our son was a suspect in a criminal investigation.

And the news had killed her.

CHAPTER 15

A Nintendo game gave Abby the spark of an idea.

Her initial plan to escape from the truck had been to fake a medical emergency: Call her captors on the walkie-talkie and pretend she couldn't breathe. When they stopped the truck and came back to check on her, act like she was passed out. Then, when they tried to revive her—either inside the truck or, even better, outside—spring to her feet and run like the wind. She was pretty sure she could outrun two old guys in their thirties who stunk of cigarettes.

But the more she thought about it, sitting in the dark amongst the walls of boxes, the less she liked it. What if they tortured her to find out if she was faking? What if they pinned her down and she wasn't able to run? What if they killed her when they realized they couldn't revive her?

She still thought faking unconsciousness was a good idea, but it needed something more.

She wrung her brain dry searching for a better idea. Nothing came. And then, just to give her mind a break, she fired up a game on the old Nintendo DS her captors had left for her. That did the trick! There was a puzzle where you had to move blocks around in a certain way to make room for other blocks, and somehow it broke the logjam in Abby's mind.

She knew what she wanted to try. But could she pull it off? Was it even possible?

What did she know about her rolling prison anyway? She knew she was in a small "chamber" bordered by stacked boxes. The truck was masquerading as a fully loaded moving van—so that if anyone, like a cop, opened the back, all they would see was furniture and boxes. Her captors had come back to check on her, twice. When they had done so, she'd heard them moving two distinct stacks of boxes aside, one after the other, using one of those wheely things. Then the men had walked through the open gap like a doorway.

So, there were two walls of boxes. Beyond them, what? Empty space? Other junk?

There *had* to be some open space back there near the roll-up door, Abby reasoned, because the men were able to wheel the stacks of boxes aside. Which meant there had to be someplace to park them.

If she could get past the two walls of boxes—the inner one and the outer one—she was sure she'd find some kind of open area back there, in which she could maneuver and maybe hide. Which would give her a good shot at pulling off her scheme.

If she failed... well, best not to think about that.

Abby stood up and, using her glow-stick for light, examined the inner stack of boxes her captors had wheeled aside to get to her. She could barely reach the top box—certainly not well enough to grab hold of it. But the second box down was grabbable and had just enough space on either side for her to slide her fingers around it. Holding the glow-stick in her teeth, she tried to move it, but it wouldn't budge. It was too heavy, combined with the weight of the upper box.

It took Abby nearly an hour—and several panicky moments—but she finally managed to slide the two top boxes from the inner stack and drop them to the floor without making a huge noise. Then she was able to climb on top of the shortened stack, push the top box off the *outer* stack (with a sickening thud), and climb down a five-foot bookcase that fronted the boxes on the other side. She now found herself in the open area between the boxes and the rear door.

The green glow-stick light revealed there was indeed some room to move around back here, amongst the piled pieces of furniture. There was also a big mattress leaning against the wall, which she planned to crawl behind to hide.

Abby sat on a low shelf of the bookshelf and pulled out the walkie-talkie she had slipped under her waistband. She gathered her nerve, trying to intuit the right time to make her move.

She quickly realized how hot and stuffy it was outside her "cell," without the cooling unit. The air felt thick to breathe. Musty and oppressive.

She knew she couldn't stay in this area long or she'd pass out from the heat and bad air. Luckily for her, it wasn't long before she felt the truck slow down and take a long, slow curve. A highway exit?

The vehicle began cruising along at a slower speed. It held to its reduced speed for several minutes, and Abby noted it wasn't stopping and starting. That meant it was probably driving on a country road, not a city street or highway.

It was time for action.

She lifted the Motorola walkie-talkie, which she'd been instructed to keep turned on at all times, and prepared to deliver the performance of a lifetime. She pressed the talk button.

Abby pulled in a loud, gasping breath then wheezed it out. On her next inhale, she said, "Can't… breathe." The tight air in the back of the truck was actually *making* it hard to breathe; she merely had to exaggerate the effect. "Help! Help!" she said, again on the inhale. Her panic sounded genuine to her ears. "Can't breathe…"

She collapsed to the floor, hoping the mic picked up the thud of her body.

A voice with a slight accent—Russian? German?—came through the little speaker. "What's going on back there, kid? Over." Abby didn't reply. "Kid, what the hell is going on? Over." A pause. "Kid, you better not be screwing with us, or you will die! And your mother will die! Do you understand? Over."

Abby pushed the orange emergency button on the walkie-talkie and held it down. The device began to beep. She stood and tossed it through the opening created by the boxes she'd moved. She heard it bounce off the wall of her former prison cell, rattle onto the floor, and continue beeping. Then, with great effort, she replaced the fallen box at the top of the nearest pile so that the facing stack of boxes looked undisturbed.

She made her way to the mattress. Shoving the glow-stick into her pocket to douse its light, she wormed her body backwards into the narrow space between the mattress and the wall.

Abby waited in the stuffy darkness, facing toward the back door. The truck kept moving, and at first she thought it wasn't going to stop for her, but then she heard the engine wind down and the tires grind to a gravelly halt. A twenty-count later, the back door of the truck rolled up with a metallic rattle, flooding the cargo area with daylight. Abby was far enough back, in the space behind the mattress, to remain in shadow.

She heard footsteps in the truck and the sound of the bookcase being slid aside. She slithered closer to the now-open back doorway. A slice of green landscape became visible.

Timing was critical. She waited until she heard the guy slide the wheely thing under the first stack of boxes. And then, not knowing where the second guy was, she wriggled out from behind the mattress and jumped off the back of the truck.

She hit the ground, rolled, and leapt to her feet, taking quick stock of her surroundings. The second guy was nowhere to be seen. Good! But the truck was stopped in a terrible location: a two-lane rural road with nothing but open fields and rolling hills on either side. No trees, nothing. Just green grass and sunshine. Nowhere to hide. Not a single place.

Escape was going to mean a foot race, plain and simple.

The left side of the road was bordered by barbed-wire fence; the right side was unfenced. Beyond the left-side fence, more than a mile in the distance, lay what appeared to be a farmhouse. Abby's legs decided for her. She ran to the left.

Praying the fence wasn't electrified, she ducked between two of the wire strands and planted her feet under her. She knew the men would surely spot her in the open field, but she launched herself like an Olympic sprinter toward the distant red house.

And then she ran as if her life depended on it. It probably did.

Did Abby think she could outrun her captors? Yes.

Did she know if anyone lived in the house? Or if they were home? Or if they would help her even if they were? Or if her captors would simply kill them and drag Abby back to the truck?

No. She didn't know the answers to any of those questions. All she knew was that her only hope lay in her ability to run. To run like she was stealing home in game seven of the World Series.

Run, Hawk, run! the voice of Coach Jack shouted in her head. *Steal home, you can do it! Home, Abby! Home! Home! Home!*

CHAPTER 16

For me, the math was simple. Whoever had taken the girl was the person trying to frame Jack. The framing of Jack had killed my wife. Therefore, whoever had taken the girl had killed my wife. I believe it's called the transitive property.

Not that Caroline would have lived long anyway. She wouldn't have, I know that. But she might have had weeks, even months, left on her clock. Time I could have spent with her. And someone had robbed me of that time and the opportunity to say goodbye to her—in addition to whatever terrible things they'd done to that child.

My rage felt like a wild animal living inside me.

I felt guilty leaving Lilly and Jack alone and saddling them with arranging Caroline's final rites, but I was no help to them anyway in the state I was in. I think the kids were relieved when I told them I had a job to attend to. I think they were also relieved to have a project to focus on. I left them my credit card, to pay the funeral home, and made my exit.

As I drove out into the incongruent sunshine of the Tennessee morning, I felt rudderless, anchorless. With Caroline gone, my reason for living had evaporated. I had no role in life anymore. I no longer even knew who I was. All I had was my anger and a single-minded imperative: find the Pruitt girl and set things right. As quickly and directly as possible.

***

Thus did I find myself, later that morning, sharing a parked Chevy Camaro with Ronnie Barlowe, nephew of Gus Barlowe, Erlene's late husband. We were parked outside a seedy talent agency near downtown

Knoxville. Ronnie worked for Erlene, and when she learned about my efforts to find the missing girl, she offered to lend me his "services." I'd never met Ronnie before, but his reputation preceded him. He sometimes managed The Mouse's Tail in Erlene's absence, but Ronnie's true value lay in performing duties that were "off the books." Ronnie possessed a serious criminal record as well as a brain modified by years of former drug usage, which enabled him to inflict high levels of pain on his fellow man without the slightest elevation in his pulse. Not the kind of person I normally chose to associate with.

But nothing was normal anymore.

This was our second stop of the day. Our first stop had been the multimillion-dollar waterfront home of Dr. Terrence Keene in Farragut, Tennessee, outside of Knoxville. Keene was the surgeon and political contributor Erlene had told me about—the one who liked to share youthful-looking call girls, as well as, perhaps, underaged kids, with his pals. To corroborate Erlene's claim, I had called a friend of mine in the DA's office, who told me, confidentially, that Keene had twice wormed his way out of "solicitation of a minor" charges. That was enough for me to feel confident going after the guy.

We'd been fortunate enough to find Dr. Keene's Land Rover in the driveway, which meant he was home. As soon as we parked, I seized the Camaro's door handle, priming to deliver a beating to this guy. Ronnie grabbed my arm and warned me that my loose-cannon brand of physicality wasn't going to be helpful in this situation.

"You gotta understand, Dillard, that when it comes to these guys— these cradle-snatcher types—you can beat 'em till their mama wouldn't reckon-ize 'em, and they still won't admit to it. Normal pain don't work. The things I'm fixin' to do to Dr. Keene, if he lies to us, are things you don't want to witness, as a family man. Things you can't get out of your head once you seen 'em." With that, he reached into the backseat and grabbed a small toolbox.

Message sent and received. I allowed Ronnie to lead the way as we entered the doctor's home without knocking—surprisingly, the door was unlocked. One look at Ronnie's muscular, tattooed frame caused the doc to drop his avocado toast and run for cover. But Ronnie caught him and carried him to a back bedroom as if he was an Amazon package. I don't know what Ronnie said to Keene behind that closed door, or what he threatened to do to him, or with what tools, but Erlene's nephew acquired the information I sought with frightening efficiency.

We learned that Keene was indeed part of a network of well-heeled "clients" who often paid for sex not only with underage-*looking* hookers but with actual children. Keene and his buddies were on the "demand" side of the equation, but Ronnie persuaded him to give up someone on the "supply" side: a guy by the name of Merlo Maroni. He ran a so-called talent agency in a seedy section of Knoxville. According to Keene, Maroni's "front" business consisted of recruiting talent for the adult film industry, but his "back" business was his bread and butter. He specialized in procuring underaged talent for prostitution and illegal sex videos. Word was, he'd cruise the bus stations and shelters, looking for runaways, strays, and kids in trouble. He'd tell the kid they had a future in film and give them his card. A few days, or hours, later, the desperate kid would show up at his door, and he'd begin the process of grooming them for sex work—using booze, drugs, and promises.

I couldn't wait to meet him.

Four-Star Talent, outside of which Ronnie and I now sat in his car, had its office in a commercial/industrial building just east of the Old City that housed a trucking company and a produce distributor. With its corrugated metal siding, the place looked more like a Quonset hut than an actual building. Four Star Talent was tucked around the side, a sun-bleached red awning over its entrance. When we tried the door, it was locked. A handwritten sign read, "Back in 1 hour."

An hour from when, moron? I was ready to punch the guy before I even met him. But Ronnie talked me down again, telling me to keep my fists in check and let him handle things. We waited in the car, drinking coffee and stewing in our respective juices.

I expected Maroni to fit the mold of a typical sleazeball agent—slicked-back hair, gold chain, open shirt—but was surprised to see a short, youngish man with long, shampooed hair and a neatly trimmed beard, wearing a tan three-piece suit, approach the door. If not for his darting, predatory eyes, he could have auditioned for the role of Jesus in a movie.

We waited till he went inside and turned on his lights before setting our coffees on the dashboard.

"Let's rock and roll and regret," said Ronnie, grabbing his tool kit.

Like Keene, Merlo Maroni knew right away he was in trouble. Ronnie is as large as I am and twice as mean-looking, but Maroni chose to go the wise-ass route anyway.

"Gents," he said from behind his desk, "I'm afraid I've got a surplus of middle-aged male talent in my Rolodex right now—unless, a' course, ya got a didgeridoodle you can tie in knots. But feel free to leave your head shots in the tray."

Ronnie calmly instructed me to step out to the waiting room and close the door. This time, I didn't argue. His "process" took longer than it had with Keene. There were defiant shouts and threats of retribution and yelps of surprise until the only sound coming from behind the door was a high-pitched keening that might have been a wounded dog.

"You can come in now," Ronnie called to me. "He's ready."

I stepped into the office and addressed the kneeling man. I didn't want to know what Ronnie had done to enlist his compliance. "So… you're going to tell me everything you know about child sex trafficking in East Tennessee. You're going to explain what your involvement is. You're going to give me names, dates, places. And if I'm not pleased with the information I'm receiving, my colleague here is going to 'work' with you until you are craving death the way a fat kid craves cake. Shall we begin?"

We learned, as Keene had asserted, that Merlo was indeed a "talent procurer" for a child sex-trafficking ring that operated both nationally and internationally. "But the way things are set up," Maroni protested to me, "nobody knows more than they need to know. You gotta believe me!" Despite his disclaimer, he knew quite a bit. He knew, for example, that kids who were acquired in one locale were immediately shipped to another, far away, in order to isolate them and reduce the danger of anyone recognizing them. He knew that the trafficked kids lived in supervised group residences, and that there were residences in Texas, Arizona, California, Michigan, Illinois, and Maine, as well as one here in Knoxville. Kids were rotated, Merlo said, from location to location, to keep the "product offerings" fresh and to prevent the kids from getting too familiar with any area. Most, if not all, of the kids in the ring were lost souls who were groomed with drugs and lies until they became semi-voluntary participants.

"This whole idea of kids being kidnapped in the night by sex rings," he said, "is pure Hollywood. It sells popcorn, but things don't really go down that way."

My hackles went up when he said that. I sensed he was trying to pre-emptively steer us away from that line of questioning.

"What do you know about a girl who was taken a couple of nights ago up near Johnson City?"

Something flashed in his eyes, but he claimed ignorance. I asked him several more times, and he strenuously denied any knowledge of the missing girl. But I still saw something in his eyes I didn't like.

"I think our friend is lying," I said to Ronnie. "He knows something."

Ronnie told me he would sort it out and asked me to leave the room again. "In fact, take a walk around the block and come back in ten minutes." I balked. "Do it, Joe."

I did as Ronnie asked. I left the building and took a short walk. When I came back, Ronnie was walking briskly toward his car, toolbox in hand. His eyes were darting from side to side, and he had a sheen of sweat on his face.

"Get in the car," he told me through clamped teeth, not moving his lips.

I complied, and Ronnie pulled out of the driveway with a burst of speed. After we'd turned a couple of corners, his tension seemed to ease a bit, and I asked him, "You mind telling me what just happened back there?"

"Things didn't go so good with Maroni."

"What do you mean?"

"I mighta been overly... persuasive. His own damn fault. Guy's got a high pain threshold; I'll give him that."

"Jeez, Ronnie. You didn't kill him, did you?"

Ronnie didn't answer. My stomach twisted into a knot. "I didn't ask for killing. Tell me you didn't kill him."

"I'm ninety percent sure he'll be good as new in hardly no time at all. Here, this oughtta cheer you up."

Ronnie tossed me a cellphone. Maroni's, presumably. He also handed me a beat-up little spiral notebook. "Found that in his jacket pocket."

I thumbed through the notebook. It contained passwords to websites, apps, online accounts, devices.

"Do we need to go back there?" I asked. "Do we need to call an ambulance?"

"Like I said, I'm eighty percent sure he'll be right as rain. Soon enough."

I didn't ask Ronnie to turn back. But as we merged onto Route 40 East, the skin on my face felt as hot as the phone in my hand.

CHAPTER 17

Charlie was grabbing her things to leave the house when a knock sounded at the door. She dashed to open it, figuring it was probably FedEx or UPS.

The man and woman standing in the doorframe wore TBI baseball hats and "TBI Agent" windbreakers. Behind them, on the steps, stood another man and woman whose vests read, "TBI Police."

"Ma'am, we're with the Tennessee Bureau of Investigation," said the lead agent. "Does a Jackson Dillard reside here?"

Jack. "Yes, but he's not home. What's this about, please?"

"We have a warrant to search the premises." The TBI woman held a paper up.

Charlie stepped aside in shock, allowing the uniformed squadron to stream into the farmhouse. Three seconds later, her lawyer brain kicked into gear.

"Whoa! May I please see that warrant?" The lead agent handed her the document. Charlie studied it. "What is your probable cause for executing this search?"

"That evidence was presented to the judge who signed the warrant."

Two of the team members snapped latex gloves onto their hands and marched straight for the bedroom. A third headed into the kitchen.

"And what exactly are you searching for?" said Charlie. "You're not allowed to just turn our place upside down in a random hunting expedition—"

"The items in question are listed on the attachments page, ma'am."

Charlie flipped to the second page of the document, where a boxed section stated that agents were authorized to search for and seize "any and all: cellular telephones; computers; pornographic materials; materials used for binding and/or torture; photographic, physical, or written evidence of sexual activity with a minor; clothing and/or other possessions belonging to Abigail Pruitt; any and all correspondence between suspected party and Abigail Pruitt," and finally, sending a chill to Charlie's bones, "dead human bodies."

Charlie didn't know what to do. Caroline's burial service was slated to begin in less than two hours, and she was supposed to meet Jack at the Dillards' beforehand. He had gone there early to sign some papers. She refused to leave the TBI in her house unsupervised; they couldn't be trusted to conduct their search properly. And she couldn't tell Jack this was happening. Not yet. He had a right to bury his mother in peace. One thing was clear, though: she wouldn't have time to meet him at the Dillard house now. She took her phone from her purse.

"Ma'am, we'll need to seize that," said the head agent, pointing to Charlie's phone.

"*My* phone? Why?"

"Read the warrant. '*Any and all* cellular telephones.'"

"Jack's mother is being buried today," Charlie said, trying to contain her anger. "I need to communicate with him. May I send him a text first?"

"We'll have to view it before you send it."

Charlie made up a story as her fingers flew over the tiny keyboard: *Jack, emergency situation with the Daley case. Need to deal with it. I'll meet you at the cemetery instead of the house. I love you!*

She showed the text to the agent, who read it twice then hit send and stuck the phone into an evidence bag. Before Charlie could protest further, a voice shouted from the bedroom, "Found a hiding place under the floorboard!"

***

We didn't hold a funeral for Caroline, because Caroline didn't want one. She wanted a "life celebration," so that was what we gave her. Lilly organized it. We held it on the beach, and it turned out to be one of the biggest parties Boone Lake had ever seen. We stopped counting guests at five hundred. There was music and dancing and drinking. Food and song. Impromptu performances by former students of Caroline's. Stories, speeches, remembrances. I had trouble putting my rage in a box, but eventually I let myself get caught up in the spirit of the thing and even smiled once or twice. The party went on for hours, the energy transmuting from one form to another but never waning. The highlight of the night was when hundreds of guests lit paper lanterns and released them into the night sky. I felt the same awe I'd felt at Bioluminescent Bay. Caroline's spirit was the spark that lit the evening from beginning to end.

But today was a different story. Today we were gathered at the Highland Church cemetery—family members and a few close friends only—to lay my wife's body in the cold ground. Caroline had never given much thought to what would happen to her earthly frame after she passed. "I'll be done with it; what do I care?" was her attitude. She was fine with cremation, but I chose burial for selfish reasons. I wanted a physical place where I could visit her.

The graveside service was as uplifting as it's possible to be in the presence of a coffin and a six-foot hole in the ground. I stood with my arms around my kids, trying to feel gratitude and peace, but failing utterly. Rose Chapman, a friend of Caroline's who taught part-time at the dance school and also served as a minister at the non-denominational Christian church, gave the talk. Rose had also been kind enough to secure a plot for Caroline in the cemetery, which was usually reserved for church members or their family. As she spoke, I noticed Leon Bates parked in his cruiser nearby, watching the service with his window rolled down.

When the casket was being lowered into the ground, I remembered my grandmother's burial when I was a kid. A freak snowstorm had blown up, and an aunt I didn't know threw herself onto the coffin, clutching it with clawing fingers as it descended into the earth. It was horrifying. Today I had to stop myself from doing the same thing.

The service ended, and the gathered guests began to disperse. That's when Leon stepped from his car and walked toward me, looking like death in a khaki uniform.

"In about thirty seconds," he said to me, "you're going to want to punch me in the face. And I will let you do that if it will help." Before I could ask what he meant, he pointed down the dirt road at two approaching vehicles. They were marked with TBI insignias. "I got them to agree to wait until the service was over, but that was the best I could do."

The TBI cars stopped, and four agents, two men and two women, exited the vehicles. They marched straight toward Jack. The bottom dropped out of my stomach.

"Jackson Dillard, you are under arrest for suspicion of kidnapping and sexual conduct with a minor under the age of 13. You have the right to remain silent…"

I didn't hear the rest. My rational mind dissolved, and my hands clenched into fists. My eyes locked like a tractor beam onto the largest of the TBI agents. Leon must have sensed what I was about to do. He leapt forward and wrapped his arms around me from behind in a bear hug. "Joe! It won't help anyone if you get arrested too." My old friend Bo Hallgren, who'd flown in for the celebration and graveside service, moved in to help Leon.

I was forced to watch, restrained by the two men, as the agents marched my son toward the TBI cars. Jack turned his head once and looked at me with a pleading expression. My friends tightened their grip on me until Jack was safely in the TBI car and I stopped my thrashing and straining.

"Listen to me, Joe." Bates spun me about, grasping me by the shoulders and looking into my face. "I hate, with every cell in my body, to tell you this, but you need to hear it. That phone that turned up in the ground search you were part of? It was damaged, but when they got into it, it contained some text conversations of a… sexual nature. The parties used fake names, but they weren't careful enough to disguise the fact that one of them was a minor and the other had a… coaching relationship with her."

All the strength drained from my muscles.

"The phone, along with those photos that were uploaded and the testimony of the kid on the team," Leon went on, "was enough to get a search warrant for Jack's place." His face paled. "They found the matching phone there, Joe, hidden under the floor. Along with some other things. Things that look very, very bad for your son."

I turned toward the road where the TBI cars were parked. Jack looked at me again, through the window of the back seat where they'd placed him. What I saw in his eyes was not the strong, capable man he had become but a boy in trouble, asking for the kind of help only a father can provide. I wanted to fold him in my arms and pull him to my chest.

But I also found myself wondering, for just a flickering moment, if Jack was as innocent as I was blindly assuming him to be. How well did I really know my son, after all? Hadn't there always been a pocket of darkness in Jack, one he didn't allow anyone to glimpse too fully?

No! I banished such thoughts from my mind.

"You can take that swing at me if you want," said Leon.

I had no interest in punching Leon Bates. The only thing that interested me now—the *only* thing my world now consisted of—was saving my boy. And avenging my wife. Nothing else mattered. And nothing ever would. Until that job was complete.

I strode off through the trees without a word of goodbye to anyone.

PART II

CHAPTER 18

"**R**emove all your clothing and underwear."

Jack did as the corrections officer ordered. He'd already surrendered his shoes during the booking and fingerprinting procedures.

"Place it on the table beside you."

No "please" or "thank you." The days of southern hospitality were over. Jack was an animal now, an object. Worse, he was an accused child abductor and molester, the lowest of the low. He was fighting panic with every nerve in his body, but he knew the rules. Don't show weakness, don't show fear.

Buck naked, he dropped his socks on top of the clothes-pile, setting his jaw muscles like a game-day pitcher's and putting the "hundred-yard stare" in his eyes.

The corrections officer switched on a small tactical flashlight and said in a mechanical tone, "Spread your feet apart, shoulder distance. Bend forward and shake out your hair."

Jack obeyed, and the officer examined his hair quickly with the flashlight.

Jack complied further as the officer conducted the rest of the body-search routine, instructing him to move his genitals to the left, then the right; tilt his head back and flare his nostrils; open his mouth and roll his tongue around; show the undersides of his lips; wiggle his toes; and, finally, bend over, spread his cheeks, and cough.

"You will now shower and put these on."

The officer handed him a folded orange jumpsuit, a towel, and two sets of prison-issued underwear. He marched Jack down a short hallway, then another, and into a bare room with tiled walls and floor, a drain in the middle, and a row of shower heads on one wall. The officer pointed to a specific shower unit and exited the room. Jack set his clothes-pile down, then turned the squeaky valves on the twin pipes, but only cold water came out. Figured. Everything in his life was going to be cold for the foreseeable future; might as well get used to it. He let the chilling water plunge down on him. The pain felt strangely reassuring. Something he could count on; something that made sense. Unlike everything else.

As Jack's flesh adjusted to the liquid assault, he took a few deep breaths to tamp down the fear that was threatening to grab hold of him and squeeze his chest flat. Then he replayed the conversation he'd had thirty minutes earlier, trying to digest all its facts and implications.

During the booking procedure, he'd been allowed one phone call. He called his dad's cell. He knew his father would help him with the practical stuff—like getting a lawyer—but, above and beyond that, he'd wanted to hear his father's voice, assuring him that everything was going to be okay. The call had been light-years from reassuring.

First, his father had told him, with an oddly emotionless voice, about the "evidence" that had been found at Jack's house. According to his dad's contact at the DA's office, the TBI had found, in a hiding space below a loosened floorboard, a cellphone with an incriminating text-message conversation on it that paired with one on a phone found behind Abby Pruitt's house. They had also found a stack of pornographic photo printouts featuring pre-teenage girls. Two of them had Abby's face cut out and glued over the face of the actual girl. Worst of all, they had found a blood-spattered set of girl's underpants, which Verna Roy had identified as belonging to her daughter, and which were presently being DNA-tested. A second stain on the underwear, as well as several on the printouts, were believed to be semen.

As his father talked, Jack's mind fully wrapped itself around the depth of trouble he was in. Whoever was setting him up was an expert. His father had tried to set his mind at ease, telling him that Jim Beaumont, a highly talented defense attorney the Dillard family knew, had agreed to represent him.

But then his father had dropped another bomb. "I may not be seeing you at the jail, son, and I probably won't be present at your arraignment. I have some things I need to take care of. I made a promise to your mother, and I intend to keep it. Time is critical, and I can't afford any distractions. I'm not abandoning you. The opposite. I'm trying to help you. Know that."

Upon hearing he might not see his dad for an indefinite time, Jack had been struck by a wave of lightheadedness. He was a grown man, but his father was his rock—his employer, his mentor, his confidant. The idea of facing jail time and a court arraignment without either of his parents on hand for support made him feel untethered, like being cast off in a hot-air balloon with no pilot. His father had only worsened the feeling when he said, "Before I go take care of business, I need to ask you one question, son. I will ask it only once, then you'll never hear it from me again: Do you know anything—anything at all—about Abby's disappearance that you haven't told me?"

The question had hit Jack like a haymaker. He knew what his father was really asking, behind the words. He also knew why he had to ask it. But still.

Swallowing his indignation, Jack had replied, "Nothing at all, Dad. If you see or hear anything that suggests otherwise, it's a lie. I swear it on Mom's grave."

"I knew that would be your answer, Jack. And I know it's the truth. But I had to ask, and I had to hear you say it. All right, then. I'll visit if and when I can, but don't count on it. Be strong. Your mother may be looking down on you. If she is, make her proud."

"I will. Tell Charlie I'm okay."

"Joy Boy!" shouted the guard from outside the shower room, snapping Jack's mind back to harsh reality. "Clean enough. Let's move it."

Jack dried off and plucked his prison underwear and orange jumpsuit from the tiled ledge where he'd stacked them. He put the items on, glad there was no mirror to reflect his ignominy.

"Hang on to your towel and come with me," the guard said.

Jack followed the officer out to the hall, where a second guard joined them, and then down two more corridors, pausing twice to allow heavy metal doors to unlock and allow them through. The guards led him up a set of stairs, through another locked door, to an upper tier, lined with cells, that overlooked an open area containing several metal tables.

One of the guards moved in front of him on the walkway, the other stayed behind. As they passed the first cell in the row, the lead guard cut his speed to an old man's shuffle, forcing Jack to do the same. Jack knew what was going on. He was being given the "walk of shame" in front of the other inmates. The guards were letting everyone in the cells get a good look at the new guy. The one accused of abducting and raping a kid.

"Subtle, guys," Jack said to the officers. "I'll hold still if you want to paint a bullseye on the back of my pants."

The cell doors were solid, with a narrow window in the middle—not barred like in the old days. As the three-man group paraded past the cells, Jack was aware of faces, one after the other, pressed to the glass rectangles. He didn't turn his head or make eye contact with them.

An inmate sitting at a table below yelled up at him, "Well, if it ain't Mr. Chick-fil-A. He likes that *tender* young chicken."

"Hey Chester," shouted another guy from below, "I got a question. Did her braces hurt when she was goin' to town on ya?"

"News travels fast around here," said the guard behind Jack, as they marched him past more cells. "Especially when it comes to inmates with your particular... *inclinations*."

"But don't you worry none," said the guard in front. "Our job is to protect you."

"'Course, try as we might," added the rear guard, "we can't be every-where at once."

They came to another locked door. When it was opened by remote control, the guards pushed Jack through it and perp-walked him down an inner corridor lined with cells on both sides. "Last one of your kind we had in here," the rear guard continued, "a couple of the fellas figured out a way to..." He trailed his voice off, shaking his head ruefully. "How they got that gas can past us—you can only wish they'd show that kind of resourcefulness on the outside."

"Say, Officer Jenkins," said the front guard, stopping halfway down the corridor and patting his pockets, "I reckon I forgot my breath mints back in the control room. Would you keep an eye on our new guest for just a minute, while I go grab 'em?"

"Why I'd be glad to, Officer Meriwether."

Meriwether, a beefy, red-faced guy with a marine crew cut, flashed a toothy smile at Jack and strode off, leaving Jack alone with the one called Jenkins, a slightly older African American guy with a ring of dark hair around a gleaming bald head.

Jenkins stood wordlessly behind Jack, allowing the silence to grow more uncomfortable.

Jack knew the guards were messing with him somehow. He just didn't know what game they were playing. He stood impassively, feeling eyes from all the cell windows boring in on him, but refusing to turn his head to meet them. Jenkins whistled an airy tune. A minute passed. Two. At last, Jenkins seemed to tire of waiting for Jack to do what was expected. He placed his hands on Jack's shoulders and forcefully turned him to the left, until Jack was facing directly toward one of the cell doors.

A man's face glared out the glass rectangle at him, smiling the iciest grin Jack had ever seen in his life. It was the face of Gregory Pruitt.

CHAPTER 19

I peered out the window of the Muddy Fork Motel for the dozenth time. I couldn't escape the feeling of being watched. It was probably just my conscience surveilling me, trying to make sure I didn't cross any lines I couldn't come back from.

I'd chosen this fleabag motel on the banks of the Muddy Fork, a stream outside of Jonesborough, because it was set back from the road and had a rear parking lot. Not that anyone would recognize my car anyway; I'd rented a nondescript sedan at the local Alamo. I didn't know where I'd be going or what I'd be doing next, but I didn't want to use my truck. I didn't want it being spotted and remembered.

As far as I knew, no one besides Lilly was looking for me. And that was the way I planned to keep it. I didn't want to talk to anyone. Didn't want anyone trying to reason with me or warn me not to "take the law into my own hands." I didn't want to be Joe Dillard, attorney-at-law and family man, anymore. I wanted to be a machine. A focused, manhunting cyborg that answered to nothing but its prime directive: find the girl. Contact with people I loved would only trigger my emotions, and emotions would get in my way. For that reason, I was glad I'd left Rio behind. I had considered bringing him along, for companionship and a set of teeth, but decided that taking care of an aging dog, on the road, would be a hindrance.

I wandered back to the tiny desk/table against the wall, where I had Maroni's cell phone laid out, along with the pages of notes Stony and I had written when she was here earlier. Yesterday, I'd taken the phone to Stony, along with Maroni's password collection, and she had unlocked it. She had also helped me unpack the wealth of data it contained—emails, calendar items, texts, contact lists, notes, photos, voicemails, call history, and more.

Tonight, the job I'd assigned myself was to monitor Maroni's phone for activity and pore through his old emails and text messages—thousands of them—hoping to find something useful. A couple of calls had come in on his phone. I let them go to voicemail in hopes the callers would leave messages. So far, no one had.

The fact that Maroni's phone was still receiving calls meant people still thought he was in possession of it. Which meant Maroni hadn't been in touch with his contacts. He hadn't canceled his accounts or passwords either. I didn't want to think about the implications of those facts.

I had enough problems to deal with.

Tonight, I was wrestling with a dilemma. The details of the case just weren't adding up in my mind, and I needed to view things from a fresh angle. The problem was this: the "facts," as I knew them, seemed to be leading me down two separate roads headed in divergent directions. On road one, someone was setting Jack up and doing a thorough job of it. That was personal. Motivated. Carefully executed. On road two, if I could trust my gut about that look of alarm I'd seen in Maroni's eyes, Abby had been snatched by a sex-trafficking ring. That was economics-driven. Impersonal. In that case, why go to all the effort of setting Jack up? That wasn't how these organizations worked. They called as little attention to their actions as possible.

I was missing something.

Everything. That's what I was missing. I didn't know a damn thing.

I growled and sat at the desk again. One thing I *had* discovered from studying Maroni's phone messages was that he had a second phone—a burner, or series of burners—which he used for the more sensitive aspects of his business dealings. I'd found a couple of guarded text conversations in which he told the other party to contact him on his "other line." Maroni seemed to conduct most of his business on the main phone, though. The reason he was able to get away with this was because his sleazy "porn agent" persona made a great cover for the even sleazier things he was involved with.

Another thing that caught my eye about his phone was the high number of calls and texts coming in from the 979 area code. Southeastern Texas. This was potentially significant, because I recalled Maroni telling us the trafficking ring maintained a "residence" in Texas. A couple of the voicemails and texts from that area code lent credence to that claim. One voicemail mentioned that a girl named "LT" was "not working out" and telling Maroni to call. A text message spoke of a "transfer" occurring ahead of schedule and a need to speak to him.

By eight o'clock, my head was exploding from thinking too hard and looking at the little phone screen too long. My eyes and brain needed a break.

And my throat needed a drink. Pocketing Merlo Maroni's phone, I headed out for Curly's, a country roadhouse a couple of miles down the road.

***

Curly's was a dive, plain and simple—wall-paneling from 1972, crooked floors, smell of urinal cakes steeped into the woodwork. I'd only been here once before, and that was to meet a supposed informant who ended up trying to sell me a case of prescription cough syrup. The place suited my mood, though. I wanted to stay low. In more ways than one.

I ordered a shot and a beer from the bartender, who looked like a street alcoholic, and settled into a creaky wooden booth in the corner.

As I tossed the whiskey back, a thought occurred to me. The reason I needed a drink tonight—and might need a couple more—was not the work I was doing. It was Jack. In my mind, I knew I was doing the right thing by putting all my focus on finding the girl, instead of on helping Jack directly. But my heart hadn't gotten the memo. When I'd talked to my son early in the day, he'd told me not to worry about him. I knew he was putting on a tough-guy act for me and that he was scared to death. I'd immediately gone against my own decision and driven over to the Washington County Detention Center in hopes they'd let me see him. I was told I'd have to register as a visitor and schedule my visit for another day.

Fortunately, while at the jail, my lawyer creds permitted me to meet with Badger Daley and conduct a piece of business I hoped might help my son. When I was finished with that, I walked over to see Leon Bates, whose office is on the same grounds as the jail. After a bit of wrangling, Bates also agreed to do me a favor regarding Jack. As sheriff, he was top dog of the jail. I hoped both of my actions—neither of which Jack would ever know about—would help my son in the days to come.

But still, I couldn't get my mind off the fact that Jack was sitting in a six-by-eight-foot cell right now, facing his first night in jail. Alone. Confused. Terrified.

I grasped the handle of the beer mug and swigged. The sour draft had barely grazed my lips when Maroni's phone chimed. A text: *Heard someone was ?ing about girl from E'ton.*

"The girl from E'ton"? My heartbeat sped up. This must be a reference to Abby. Was this the break I was hoping for? I looked at the "Sender" box. It contained a random-looking set of numerals that didn't even look like a phone number.

I needed to craft a reply, fast. If I played my cards right and came off as Maroni, perhaps I could extract more information from the other party. Borrowing some actual words from a couple of Maroni's old texts, I typed into the text box: *Not to worry. Everything fine. Call me on second line in ten min and I'll explain. All ok on other end?*

I held my breath for what felt like two full minutes. Finally, a text arrived: *Had some trouble, but handled. Grl should be in Sealy by now.*

I didn't want to press my luck, so I just typed, *OK, talk in a few.*

I gulped the rest of my beer and stood up from the table. Sealy? Sealy, Texas?

Everything was coming up Texas.

Sealy was a tiny city just west of Houston. It seemed like an odd location to be running a sex trafficking ring, but as I thought about it, it made sense—*near* the big city, but well out of town. Rural, private. Close enough to Austin and San Antonio to "service" those cities as well.

As I drove along Pleasant Valley Road, heading back to my motel room, I thought about Maroni again, with a chill. He hadn't reached out to his contacts yet. Did that mean he hadn't survived his "session" with Ronnie? Or…

Another possibility dawned. Was *I* being played right now? Did someone know I was in possession of Maroni's phone? Suddenly, I felt sure in my bones that the text conversation I had so "cleverly" faked my way into had actually been engineered by the other party to lure *me*. The mention of Sealy had come too fast, too conveniently. Hadn't it?

Was I being *herded* toward Texas?

I didn't know. In truth, it didn't really matter. Because one way or the other, I was already mapping out the route to Sealy in my mind. The only question remaining was whether I would start the long westward drive tonight or sleep a few hours at the Muddy Fork first.

CHAPTER 20

Two Days Earlier

Abby ran for two hundred yards without stopping or looking back. But eventually the uphill slope of the land took its toll. She stopped in the overgrown grass and put her hands on her knees, pulling in three deep breaths. Then she turned to look behind her.

There they were, the men, still back at the truck! The one with the white shirt was leaning off the rear platform, waving his arms at the one with the red shirt, who stood in the road with his arms folded.

Wait. Was that a rifle strapped to his back?

A rifle. That would be bad. Very, very bad.

She sharpened her eyes, trying to discern a weapon. Big mistake; people could tell when they were being looked at. Her mother always said that. "A gal can feel it when a guy's lookin' her over." She stared a second too long. And sure enough, Red Shirt felt it. He turned his head, looked in her direction, and pointed. And the two men were off and running. After her.

Abby bolted. She still had the advantage, she told herself. She was faster than these guys, and she had a big lead on them. Fixing her eyes on the distant red house, she poured all of her strength into her legs. Her feet pounded the grass, and she visualized her lead widening.

But then she *felt* it—that same kind of sensation Red Shirt must have had when she stared at him. Only worse. This was the feeling of being in a gunsight. Like someone was taking aim at her. Abby knew there were rifles that could plug a deer from more than half a mile away; her father owned one. And running in a straight line was making her an easy target. For a moment, she could almost *feel* the bullet ripping into her back and boring, red-hot, through her back muscles and into her heart.

Make yourself a trickier target, her inner voice screamed. She began to run in a jerky, side-to-side manner, like a running back trying to fake out tacklers. But it was harder to find her footing on the uneven ground that way. And she was losing her lead.

Abby planted her left foot to zig around a tall sumac sapling and felt the ground give way beneath her. A gopher hole! Her foot plunged into the earth. Her ankle twisted sideways as the full weight of her body pistoned down on it. She toppled to the ground, and the pain shot through her like an electric shock. White light filled her vision field. She'd heard of people "seeing stars" when injured but didn't know, until now, it was a real thing. She rolled back and forth on the ground, screaming and holding her ankle. Her escape bid was over, and she knew it.

***

"Nothing's broken, just a sprain," said the Amish-farmer-looking guy with the scraggly gray beard, "but I reckon you should take her to a real doctor."

"Advice noted, Doc," replied a dark-haired, olive-skinned man in designer pants and expensive sweater, smiling tightly and adjusting his orange-tinted glasses.

"I'll put an Ace bandage on it. All I can do," murmured the farmer-type.

Abby was sitting on a crate in a huge barn, not far from the fake movers' van that had been her roving home for the past two days. She'd arrived here—wherever *here* was—about five minutes earlier. The guys driving the truck must have called ahead to report her injured ankle, because the bearded farmer dude was already waiting for them when the truck arrived.

Farmer Bob wrapped her ankle in a long, stretchy, tan bandage, gave her a single crutch to use, and made his exit with a sullen nod.

The dark-haired, olive-skinned guy then turned to Abby and spoke to her in a voice with a slight accent. "Congratulations, the alcoholic ex-veterinarian says you're going to live." He adjusted his orange-lensed glasses. "My name is Mr. Paolo. You must be Abby. I hope you've gotten the rebelliousness out of your system. Because it won't be tolerated here. Welcome to the great state of Texas. Follow me."

Abby used the crutch to get to her feet, then hobbled after Mr. Paolo. He walked out the back door of the barn toward a white house. The sun was blinding, and the air felt summertime hot.

A black girl, about 14, hair in a top-bun, trotted out of the house with a smile and greeted them on the dirt drive before they could enter.

"Deja here will show you the ropes," said Paolo. "I'll be in the office, and we can talk later."

Abby's heart hammered. She felt like she had just stepped onto a foreign planet. She didn't know what kind of place this was, why she was here, or what was going to happen to her next. Her ankle screamed, her stomach growled with hunger, and her tailbone ached from the long truck ride. But at least Deja looked like a friendly face.

As Deja showed her around—kitchen, living room, bedrooms, bathroom—Abby felt overwhelmed and confused, but she tried to take in everything Deja was saying. There were four bedrooms, which the girls shared, two to a room. Abby learned she'd be rooming with a girl named Isabella, who was "working" today. According to Deja, the residence was a pretty awesome place to live, and the girls—the "associates," she called them—were allowed to drink all the beer and wine coolers they wanted. *No, thanks,* thought Abby. You couldn't have a phone, Deja explained, but there was a PlayStation 5 and an Xbox Series X, and the TV had all the premium movie channels. The food was good, and when you weren't working you could do whatever you wanted. No school, no homework, none of that garbage. It was like being an adult.

Missing from Deja's orientation was any mention of exactly what the girls did for "work." Abby thought she knew but dreaded finding out for sure.

After a humorless female staff member with bowl-cut bangs gave her a bag of toiletries and secondhand clothes and showed her to her bed, Abby found herself alone, her head spinning. She shut the door of her new room and sat on the bed hugging her injured ankle, feeling lost. She thought about how she would do anything in the world to be back in her little rented trailer with her crazy-ass mama.

Her "alone time" didn't last. Deja and a petite blond girl named Hope barged into the room to grill the new recruit. They wanted to know all about Abby: where she came from, what music she liked, what her story was. Abby gave them deflective answers, then asked them directly the question that was gnawing at her mind: why had she been brought here?

"You mean you don't know?" Deja asked. "Girl, what rock you been hiding under?"

The two young teens explained the "job description" to Abby and had a grand time laughing over her shock and sexual naivete. But when Abby broke down in tears and told them she was only 11 and had been abducted involuntarily, the girls softened and sat on her bed beside her.

"It ain't so bad," said Deja, putting a hand on Abby's back. "You just gotta... *be with* a few old dudes. It's gross if you think about it, but you try not to think about it. It's usually over pretty fast. Just have a couple of beers first and one of them pills Mr. Paolo gives out. It'll get you through."

"Or think about the money," Hope said. "That's what gets *me* through. Every time we go out on a job, they put, like, a hundred bucks in our account. Sometimes even more."

"Where else can you earn them kind of chalupas, Girl?" said Deja. "Not at Taco Bell. And you don't need to *spend* much, 'cause they take care of all your day-to-days. So them figgas add up fast! I got over four grand in my account already. Cha-ching, cha-ching!"

"Yeah, I got almost seven," said Hope. "I'm just gonna keep working till I have enough to move back to Montana and buy myself my own trailer." She lay back on the bed, staring at the ceiling with faraway eyes. "And then I'm gonna declare myself an Emancipated Freakin' Minor and become a country singer. Woo!"

"How come you don't just take your money now and run away from here?" Abby asked.

Silence followed for a few seconds. "Where would we go?" Deja replied at last. "Besides, you can't just 'take your money.' They hold it for you."

"Till when?"

"Till you fu'filled your contract."

"When's *that*?"

Deja shrugged. "It's different for everybody. They tell ya."

Only a few minutes earlier, Abby had felt like the greenest girl on the planet. Not anymore.

The female staffer with the severe bangs poked her head into the doorway. "You, new girl. You're working tonight. I don't know what the girls have been telling you, but Mr. Paolo wants to see you. He'll give you your *real* orientation."

CHAPTER 21

The Present

I had the old dream again tonight. The one I'd had a hundred times over the years. It usually showed up when I was feeling anxious or out of control.

The dream is based on a real memory. It always goes the same way.

It starts with the ballgame. Staticky and fuzzy. Old antenna TV. Tommy Boggs is on the mound for the Braves, and there's a runner on second for the Reds. He's got about a four-mile lead off the bag, but Boggs won't turn around and look. He could have the guy out with a snap of his wrist, but he won't look. Anxiety overwhelms me. "Look! For crying out loud," I scream at the TV. "Look, Boggs, look!" And that's when I fall asleep within the dream.

Sarah's voice cries out, awakening me. Still within the dream. Sarah's a kid, and so am I—eight years old. I'm in my grandmother's house, and I've fallen asleep watching the game, just as I did in real life. Sarah's voice shouts again, muffled, "No! Stop! You're hurting me!" I go to look for my sister, but in the maddening way of dreams, my grandmother's house turns into a maze. Halls lead to more halls; rooms open in impossible ways to other rooms. I can't find my way to her. Sarah's voice keeps crying, "Stop! It hurts!"

I know her voice is coming from my grandmother's bedroom, but I can't find the room within the twisting, shifting labyrinth.

Somehow, eventually, I enter the room from above, through a passageway in the ceiling. I'm looking down at my grandmother's bed. My uncle Raymond, 16 years old, is naked, on his knees. He's raping my sister, as he did in real life. He moves his head, and I see her face.

Here's where the dream takes a detour from its normal script. This time, when Raymond moves his head to the side, the face of the girl sprawled on the bedspread beneath him is not that of my sister Sarah. It is the face of Abby Pruitt.

I hauled in a breath and sat up fast, driven from sleep in an instant. Where was I? The drone of trucks on the interstate and the bleachy smell of the bedsheets supplied the answer. I wasn't home. And I wasn't at the Muddy Fork anymore. I was at a chain motel off Route 40 near Nashville.

After leaving Curly's roadhouse, I'd realized I was too wired to sleep and decided to get a jump on my trip to Sealy. I'd made good time, reaching Nashville in less than four hours. But then the exhaustion hit me like a sack of birdshot, and I decided to rest.

The red numerals on the bed-stand clock now blared 3:30 a.m. I'd slept for only two hours, but I was wide awake.

The bottle of Kentucky bourbon on the dresser, still mostly full, called my name. I would need to be careful about that. I'd never been a big drinker, though I enjoyed a few beers now and then with friends and family, especially on holidays. Watching Sarah's struggles with booze and substances had kept me on the straight and narrow. Suddenly, though, almost overnight, I had acquired a taste for the hard stuff. It didn't take a psychoanalyst to figure out why.

I poured a finger's worth into the motel-room glass. ("Never drink straight from the bottle," was Sarah's sage advice. "It turns into one big shot-glass.") As I rolled the slightly sweet amber nectar around on my tongue, I replayed the dream. It was only then I realized how much the Pruitt girl reminded me of Sarah. Why hadn't I noticed that before? The human brain has an astonishing ability to hide things from us until we're ready to see them. Now that I was committed to a course of action, was I perhaps getting a glimpse of the real reason—beyond avenging my wife's premature death and saving my son—I was so fixated on finding that girl and punishing whoever had taken her?

I tried to take a walk outside, but the roar of the highway and the lack of sidewalks in the concrete maze of roadside motels, gas stations, and closed-for-the-night chain restaurants chased me back to my room within minutes. I undressed, lay on the bed, and stared at the reddish glow on the ceiling from the bedside clock. I knew I probably wouldn't sleep, so I gave myself permission to simply rest. If sleep came, fine; if not, so be it.

I'm not sure how much time passed, but at some point I found myself in a strange mental state that didn't seem like another dream, though it probably was. There was no transition; suddenly I was just *there*. Standing on the shore of Bioluminescent Bay, on Grand Cayman. Staring out at the water and sky, both of which were glowing with impossible brightness. It was the scene Caroline had described on the last day I spent with her. She, too, said it didn't seem like a dream. It felt real in some way. As I looked out to sea, I couldn't tell where the horizon lay because the ocean and sky both glowed so fiercely. But then I saw something against the brightness. A silhouette. Tiny and black. I held my breath as the dark shape drew closer. Finally, I could make out what it was—a woman rowing a kayak.

Caroline.

She stopped about twenty yards out, paddling in place, still too far away to be seen as anything but a shadow. I tried to call out to her but couldn't find my voice. I could feel her eyes on me, though. After a minute or two, she lifted her arm in a small wave, then turned her kayak around and started rowing out to sea again.

"Caroline!" I shouted, breaking my muteness. "Come back! Caroline!"

She continued rowing, and as she disappeared out to sea, I felt a knife of horror slip into my gut, tearing me open again as if her death had just occurred. I rushed out into the water after her, screaming, "No, no! Come back!"

When I came to, I was pacing the floor of my motel room. If that had been a dream, it was unlike any other I had experienced. It felt like a visitation, a real one, from Caroline, but I had no context for explaining such a thing. Had she come in response to my dream about the rape? If so, what was her message to me?

Wide-awake, I sat in the chair by the window and watched the minutes tick by on the red clock numerals, conscious of every breath. At 5:00, I concluded sleep was not in the cards and decided to hit the road again.

While ordering an extra-large coffee-to-go at the nearby 24-hour roadside cafe, I found myself hoping the eyebrow-studded barista would say or do something to tick me off and give me an excuse to rip into him. That was when I realized my night's "rest" had done nothing to calm me. It had only wound me tighter.

Anger had me in its grips, even more powerfully than the night before. I was angry at my lack of sleep. Angry at my uncle Raymond, dead these forty-plus years. Angry at Abby's kidnappers. Angry at all men who think they have a right to use girls and women like objects. Angry at whoever had set up Jack and cut Caroline's life short in the process. Angry at the wild goose chase I was on. Angry at the possibility I was being played.

Most of all, angry at myself, for being angry. Why the anger? Why always the anger? Fifty years old and I was still a stranger to myself. Would it always be this way?

I didn't know. But I didn't envy anyone who crossed me today.

CHAPTER 22

"**M**ore coffee?"

Sarah stood at the end of the table, holding a hot carafe of fresh-brewed Colombian.

"Please," said Charlie, lifting her mug. Lilly echoed the request.

The three women—Lilly, Charlie, and Sarah—had arranged to meet at Granny's, Sarah's diner in Jonesborough, at 8:00 on this Saturday morning to share information and strategize. Gracie, Sarah's eight-year-old daughter, sat at another table with five-year-old Joseph. The kids colored with crayons, keeping themselves busy.

Sarah filled the younger women's cups, then placed the carafe on the counter and took her apron off, leaving the other customers in the capable hands of Marla, her young waitress, and Lester, her weekend short-order cook. She joined Lilly and Charlie at their table.

"So, update me," Sarah said. "What has anyone heard?"

Lilly shook her head. "I haven't seen Dad since the service. He disappeared at the cemetery, and no one has laid eyes on him. I did get this, yesterday evening." She held up her phone, displaying a text message: *I'm okay. Just taking care of some business. Might not be home for a few days. Don't call or text. I won't pick up. Have faith. Love, Dad.*

The women exchanged dark looks and sighed, almost in unison. The reality of Joe's absence settled on the table like a rain cloud. Joe was Charlie's boss and soon-to-be father-in-law. He was Lilly's father and now sole parent. He was Sarah's brother and emotional rock. Joe was the guy they all counted on as their anchor. And now he was gone. And for who-knew how long. The void was palpable.

"I haven't been able to visit Jack yet," Charlie said, "but I talked to him this morning. He used his phone call during the booking process to call his dad." She explained what Jack had told her—that Joe said he had a job to finish and wasn't planning to visit the jail till it was done.

"You know what's going on, don't you?" said Sarah.

The two younger women halted their coffee mugs mid-air.

"He's trying to find that girl. That's what he's doing. And he's not going to stop until he finds her, dead or alive. I know your father, Lilly. Once he gets locked in on a thing, he's *locked in.*"

"But what about Jack?" Charlie said. "He needs his father's help right now. These people who are framing him aren't messing around. Is Joe just going to turn his back on—"

"Joe *is* helping Jack right now," said Sarah. "At least in his mind, he is. He knows the clock is ticking, fast, and he's done the math. He knows the sooner he finds that girl, the better the chances of finding her alive and the quicker he can prove Jack's innocence. And he knows he can only run full steam on one track at a time, so he's chosen the Abby Pruitt track."

The young women said nothing. Their silence endorsed Sarah's theory.

"I just wish I felt better about where that train was headed," added Sarah at last.

"What do you mean?" Lilly asked.

Sarah's face flushed red, and she leaned back, studying her hands. "I don't know how much your father has spoken to you about… what happened to me when I was a girl."

"That… incident with your uncle? What was his name—Raymond?" Sarah nodded.

"I found out from Mom," said Lilly.

"So did Jack," added Charlie. "At least the basics of it."

"I'm sorry, Aunt Sarah, we probably had no right to know, but—"

"No, no, I'm glad your mother told you. After all, you saw me acting pretty reckless for a lot of years, and my antics hurt your family. And you, Lilly. You had a right to know what was at the root of 'em. That's no excuse for my behavior, but…" Sarah trailed off, her gaze retreating to an inner place. After a few seconds, she pulled in a breath and gazed at

Lilly. "But anyway… your father has carried a heavy burden all his life. He blames himself for not stopping it, even though there was nothing an eight-year-old kid could have done. That's why I'm worried about him; about what's driving him right now, and what might happen if he finds that girl or the men who took her—especially if, God forbid, she's been…" Sarah didn't need to finish. "I'm afraid your father will end up in prison. Or worse."

"We have to stop him, then," said Charlie. "Or at least pull the reins in on him."

"How? We don't even know where he is, and he's not answering calls or texts."

The women looked at one another in silence, and then Lilly's eyes lit up. "I just thought of something!" She dug a phone out of her purse, entered the passcode and flipped through a couple of screens. "Yes, here it is!" She explained: "This is Mom's phone. When she bought it, about a year ago, she downloaded this app called Family Circle. It's a phone tracker your friends and family sign up for, and everyone can see where everyone is, all the time. She made Dad sign up for it—Jack and I refused—but you know how he is with apps. I bet he's never used it. I bet he doesn't even know it's on his phone."

Lilly tapped a series of buttons on the screen. "Yes! I'm looking at him right now."

"Your father?"

Lilly placed the phone on the table so everyone could see. The screen displayed a flashing blue dot on a GPS map. She stretched the map to show a wider view. The dot was flashing from a location on Route 40 in far-western Tennessee, near the Arkansas line. "Memphis?" Lilly said in shock. "What in God's name is Dad doing in Memphis?"

Sarah: "Probably not visiting Graceland."

"Looks like he's still moving," Charlie said, "heading west. Where could he be going?"

"Should we try to… I mean, should one of us try to…?"

"What? Go after him?" Sarah said. "Chase him down by car? He's got a five-hundred-mile head start. And what would we do if we found him? Talk him out of whatever idea he's got in his pig-iron head? That dog won't hunt, and you know it. Nope, Joseph Dillard is AWOL, at least for the time being. And we'd better accept that and deal with it."

"I guess that means if Jack's going to get help, it'll have to come from us," said Lilly.

Heavy looks shot around the table.

"Well, we have our work cut out for us," Charlie said. She broke the news to the others about the evidence that had been found at her and Jack's house. Lilly's and Sarah's faces went bloodless, and they all sat wordlessly. The only sound was the clink of silverware on plates from other tables. "It's purely circumstantial. And it was planted, obviously."

"But by who?" Lilly said.

"That's what we need to figure out. We can't count on law enforcement to be much help; they think they've already got their man. So… like you said, Lilly, it's on us, I guess."

"Terrific. So where do we start?" The three women slumped in their seats.

The door to Granny's burst open, and an older woman with dyed red hair, huge sunglasses, and a low-cut, leopard-spotted blouse bombed through the door and strutted across the room. She stopped at the table where the women were sitting and lifted her shades.

"Sorry I'm late," she said.

"Oh, ladies," said Sarah. "I forgot to mention: a guest is joining us this morning. Lilly, you know Erlene, but Charlie, I don't believe you've met. Given the nature of what we may be dealing with, Erlene might be able to shed some light on things."

"I swan, I don't know where people get such ideas." Erlene batted her eyelashes in a theatrical way. Then she sat at the table, and her voice took on a more businesslike tone. "Joe had the same notion. That's why he came to see me the night your mother died, Lilly. I told him what I knew, but, of course, Joe *is* a man, so… I may not have told him absolutely everything."

***

The women talked for forty minutes, brainstorming, strategizing, and committing to work together as a team.

"Okay, roles and responsibilities," Charlie said at last, taking charge by default. "I'll start with myself. I will coordinate with Jim Beaumont; he's the attorney Joe hired for Jack. We'll work on tearing holes in that so-called 'evidence' and getting ready for Jack's arraignment. I'll give Jim the green light to use whatever resources he needs, and I'll have him hire our firm as partners. That way, I can interview potential witnesses and participate fully in his investigation. I'll also call all my contacts—and Joe's—in the TBI, the sheriff's office, and the local PDs to see if anyone will talk to me, find out what else they know. Lilly..."

"Aye, aye, sir?"

"You work on the Joe front. Keep tracking your dad, keep trying to contact him. See if you can figure out what he's up to. Otherwise, since you're the one with a young kid, you can just hold down the home fort in case any calls come in or—"

"No. Sorry, Charlie. I'm not sitting at the house, twiddling my thumbs. I need to do something. I'm coming to the office. With you. I'm your new employee. Just point me to a job, and I'm on it. If I can't find a babysitter for Joseph, he'll stay with me. That's final."

"Okay, then," Charlie said with a crooked smile. "Sarah, what about you?"

"I'll provide the meeting place and the grits 'n gravy. And there's something else I'd like to do. Talk to the Little League kids and parents. Jack brings the team here after games sometimes, and I load those young-sters up on shakes and fries. Danged if I don't forget to charge 'em most of the time. I've gotten to know some of the parents, and they like me. I think they might open up to me if they've seen something suspicious."

"Good," Charlie said. "I'll clear it with Jim first, and maybe we'll 'deputize' you as an employee too. Erlene?"

"Ladies," said Erlene, "in addition to the... leverage I'm able to exert on certain male members of our community, ahem, I also have a nephew who happens to be a talented conversation starter. In fact, he helped your father with a job recently, Lilly. I think Ronnie and I are going to make some 'social calls' around the county, see what we can learn."

"Sounds good... I think," said Charlie. "I probably don't want to know more."

"Can I just ask you something, Erlene?" Lilly inquired. "Why are you helping us?"

"Well, sugar, maybe it's because I think your father is an honest-to-God good man, and I don't meet too many of them in my line of work. Or maybe it's that poor girl. This prob'ly won't surprise you, but I didn't exactly make it out of childhood *unscathed*. It's too late to get justice for some of us…" She locked eyes with Sarah across the table. "But maybe not for everyone."

"Hear, hear," said Sarah.

"Hear, hear," said the four women together, clinking coffee cups.

"Well, what are we waiting for? Let's roll."

CHAPTER 23

"**C**ome in, Ms. Abigail. And please, close the door behind you."

Abby hobbled over the door jamb with her crutch, closed the door, and sat in the chair across the maple desk from Mr. Paolo. He smiled at her from behind his orange-tinted glasses.

"Would you like a Coke? Beer? Wine cooler?"

"No."

"No, what?"

"No, thank you, Mr. Paolo."

"That's better. So… Abigail—such a classic, old American name; makes me think of candle-making and codfish pie and women being burned at the stake—how is your ankle feeling now?"

Abby, thrown by the curveball in his question, answered honestly. "Better. A little."

"Better, Mr. Paolo," he corrected in his lightly accented voice.

"Better, Mr. Paolo." She wanted to tell him to go stick it, but she knew caution was the wiser course. For now.

"I'm so delighted to hear that, Abigail. We want our associates to be healthy, wealthy, and wise. Toward that end, what have the girls told you about our little operation? Have you been getting a thorough orientation?"

Before Abby could reply, Paolo's phone rang. He looked at the screen with a rumpled brow and excused himself from the room. A few minutes later, he returned and sat again, lacing his fingers and staring across the desk at Abby.

"You've been saved by the bell, Ms. Abigail. You won't be going out on assignment tonight after all."

A wave of relief washed through Abby from the top of her head to the base of her spine.

"Yes, it seems that someone out there," Paolo continued, "has... *taken an interest* in you. And so, for now, no outcalls for you. That means you have one job and one job only. To heal that pesky ankle of yours and get yourself in tip-top shape, all sweet and pretty. Why? Because a few days from now, you will be attending a very special event, with some very important people, in a very special location. Doesn't that sound exciting?"

"What kind of 'event'?" Abby ventured to ask.

"What kind of event, *Mr. Paolo*?" he amended. "I don't want to spoil the surprise. But before we finalize the arrangements, I need to ask you one very important and very personal question. Have you ever been... *with* a man? Or a boy? Down there? By that I mean—"

"I know what you mean. No!"

He didn't press for the "Mr. Paolo" this time. "That's excellent news, Abigail. Of course, we'll need to have the doctor verify that. By that I mean the alcoholic ex-veterinarian you met earlier today."

Abby's stomach flipped as she imagined scraggly-bearded Farmer Bob looking at her private places, or, God forbid, *touching* her there. She wanted to kick the desk over on Paolo and run. But, of course, she couldn't. Escape would have to wait.

"That's all, then, Abigail. You may go back to your room now. Oh, one last thing. What do you like on your pizza?" Abby shot him a double-take. "It's pizza night!"

***

It was almost six thirty in the evening when I passed the sign, "Welcome to Sealy, Texas. History of Excellence—Future of Progress." I'd been on the road since five-fifteen a.m. and had stopped only twice, for fast food and coffee, so I'd made pretty good time. I needed to find myself a motel room, a shower, and a meal, and then... I didn't know what. I'd come here on pretty flimsy premises and was now feeling like an impetuous amateur.

Sealy was a flat expanse of farmland and trees punctuated by a brick-façaded downtown that smacked of a bygone era—old theaters and five-and-dimes, abandoned or converted into title shops and tax service centers. The city's claim to fame was that the Sealy mattress was invented here—though none were manufactured here. I felt a rush of urgency as I idled at a stop sign, staring at the plain brick clocktower that dominated the downtown. Time was everything, the clock seemed to say, and I needed to spend mine wisely.

I booked a room in a chain hotel that looked like it hadn't been upgraded since 1979, took a much-needed shower, then went out for a walk and a meal. I wanted to get a feel for the place, see if my instincts led me anywhere. They didn't.

I grabbed some dinner in a rundown "family restaurant" that seemed to feature canned peas and mashed potatoes with every meal, and then walked, in the cool evening air, to a small unoccupied park. I wanted to give Stony a call. When we'd been working together on Maroni's phone, she told me she had contacts at a couple of the phone carriers, who, for a small "gratuity," could track the real-time location of a cellphone by its number only. My hope was that we could trace the exact origin of one of those frequent 979 callers to Maroni's phone. But right now, Stony wasn't picking up *her* phone. It was 8:45 p.m. in Sealy, which meant it was 9:45 in East Tennessee. Stony was an early-to-bed type. I'd try her in the morning.

In truth, I was eager to get back to my hotel—partly because I was exhausted from the long drive and last night's lack of sleep, but partly for another reason.

I stopped at a bar called Sonny J's and had one drink, then returned to my room. Before retiring, I checked in the bedside drawer. My gun was there, where I left it. Good. I wanted it close by as I slept.

I got ready for sleep, then dug the bottle of bourbon out of my suitcase and sat in one of the room's two chairs. I knew exactly what I was up to: trying to recreate the conditions of the previous night. The conditions that had preceded my Caroline "dream."

It was a ridiculous idea, of course. You can't force a dream to show up on demand.

But to my surprise, it did. Just as I was drifting off to sleep in my chair, I found myself, once again, standing on the shore of that Grand Cayman bay, looking out at the glowing water and sky. Again, I had that sense that the experience was more than a dream. Fixing my eyes on the horizon line, I spotted what I hoped to see. Caroline's kayak.

I waited, holding my breath, as she rowed closer and then stopped, twenty feet from where I stood. I could see her face this time, and I wanted to weep with joy and sadness.

"Joe," she said, speaking over the gentle swish of the surf. "Don't doubt yourself. You're doing the right thing here. ... Just don't do it the wrong way."

"What do you mean, Sweetie?"

"Don't let anger cloud your mind, the way you've done so many times. Jack needs you to stay clear and focused."

"I hear you, Darling. I'll do my best."

"Know that I'll be with you the whole time, though you won't always see me. Make me proud, like you told Jack to do."

She nodded once, and then paddled her kayak around, facing out to sea.

"Take me with you," I cried out to her.

She turned her head once, looked at me as if to say, "You know I can't do that... yet," and rowed out toward the horizon. I wanted to call out and beg her to stay, but I knew that would be futile.

When the "dream," or vision, or whatever it was, ended, I found myself standing on the hotel-room carpet as I had last night. Like a sleepwalker.

What was happening to me? Was I losing my mind? Or was I *finding* something new?

CHAPTER 24

"**B**oth numbers are with the same national provider," Stony told me as I wolfed down an egg sandwich on the same park bench where I'd tried to call her last night. Earlier, I'd texted her the numbers of the two most frequent 979 callers on Merlo Maroni's phone. "I had my contact run them both," Stony continued, "and both phones are in the same basic location right now. Probably on the same property."

She texted me two sets of geographic coordinates that were almost identical.

"How accurate is this location?"

"Ballpark, not pinpoint. My contact had to use triangulation, not GPS, because neither of these phones are running any GPS-enabled apps. What they do is measure the time it takes for the phone's signal to reach multiple cell towers in the area. Out in 'God's country,' where you are, there are fewer cell towers, so the readings tend to be less accurate."

I thanked Stony and hung up, then opened the map app on my phone. When I figured out how to enter the coordinates she'd given me, a location popped up on the little map. It was in a rural-looking area consisting of trees and farmland, out along a winding waterway called Irons Creek, around seven miles northeast of downtown Sealy. Odd. Or maybe not, if you're running an operation you want to keep off the radar.

I ran the same coordinates in Google Earth and was shown roughly the same location. Zooming in and out, I could see only three houses within a square-mile area. They were about half a mile apart, and each was more than a mile from the nearest "neighborhood."

After stopping in a department store and purchasing a pair of binoculars, I headed out onto Route 10. Next, I drove northeast on

Farm-to-Market Road 1458 toward Irons Creek. I was already regretting my decision to leave Rio at home.

***

Jim Beaumont had always looked larger than life to Jack, but here against the plain beige walls of the jail's small "attorney room," he loomed even larger. Jim was a good friend of Jack's dad, who often referred to the old lawyer as Wild Bill Hickok. In his sixties, Jim Beaumont still wore the fringed buckskin jackets and rawhide string ties that had earned him "character" status in the local legal community for over forty years. With his long mustache covering his mouth and his low drawl, he reminded Jack a bit of the actor Sam Elliot. But he was as sharp a lawyer as you'd find anywhere on Earth.

Charlie, now an official member of the defense team, walked in behind Jim. She and Jack exchanged a quick kiss, and they all sat at the tiny round metal table. Charlie turned toward Jim, deferring to the veteran lawyer.

"Thanks for coming on a Sunday, Mr. Beaumont," said Jack.

"Please, it's Jim now. You're not in high school anymore, and I'm not a guest at your paw's house for dinner. I'da come sooner, but I was out of town when he called. I do believe you have an arraignment tomorrow, so we'd better get our ducks lined up and ready for that. What do you know about the so-called evidence that's been gathered so far?"

Jack repeated everything he'd been told by his father and Charlie about the items that had been found at his house. He also told Jim what he knew about the prior "evidence."

"That's a pretty good summation," Jim said, "but there have been some further developments. Hate to be blunt, but are you a condom-wearing man, young Mister Jack?"

Jack shot an embarrassed glance at his fiancée. He was thrown by the question but had an idea where Beaumont might be going with it. "Charlie and I aren't ready to have kids yet, so…"

"I'll wager you don't employ a high-security system for disposing of your used prophylactics," said Beaumont in his trademark drawl.

"You would win that bet, Mr. Beaumont. ...Jim."

Beaumont looked sidelong at Charlie, then lowered his voice. He explained that the semen stains on the photo printouts and the girls' underwear had been DNA-tested on a fast track, and the semen was Jack's.

The news caused Jack's heart to turn a somersault in his chest. He looked to Charlie to get her reaction to this, but she was busy studying the tabletop.

"Here's what you need to understand very thoroughly, Mister Jack. People tend to think framing a person for a crime is a Hollywood movie thing, and jurors are disinclined to believe it as an explanation. Good framers, like these guys are, know this. That's why they stack the deck from ten different directions—to make it preposterous for a defense attorney to try to explain how anyone but the defendant could have done it all. Framing is our best defense, make no mistake, but it'll be a tough sell."

Jack hadn't thought his spirits could sink any lower, but he was wrong. "You mentioned 'further developments,' in the plural," Jack said. "Was there something else?"

Beaumont reached for his phone and laid it on the table between him and Jack. "I just received this an hour ago, courtesy of the district attorney's office." He clicked the play arrow on a video. It showed, in the curved view of a fish-eye lens, a section of a driveway and country road at night. A man and a girl walked past, the camera capturing them mostly from behind. The man wore a baseball hat and a "Tigers" team jacket identical to Jack's and was about Jack's size. The girl wore a pink sweatshirt like the one Abby wore in the damning car photographs. A truck drove past on the road, and the girl turned her head to watch it, allowing the camera to glimpse her profile. It was Abby Pruitt, no question.

"That video was captured by a home security system on Possum Hollow Road in Elizabethton. Unlike the date on the photos, which could have been fudged, this one can be firmly established as having been shot the night of the girl's disappearance."

"That's Abby in the video, but it's not me," said Jack, sounding more defensive than he intended. "I know my own walk. Convenient that you never see the guy's face."

"Indeed. But it's yet another thing we'll be asking a judge and jury to believe was elaborately staged. Listen, Jack, we've got an uphill battle here, but we will get through it. We'll start strategizing our defense right after the arraignment. But for now, *that's* my biggest worry."

"The arraignment? Why? We show up, I plead not guilty, they set a trial date, and then we work our butts off to make damn sure a trial never needs to happen."

"You're omitting one trifling detail, son: bail setting. I happen to know that Gwen Neese will be sitting on the criminal court bench tomorrow. You know Judge Neese?"

"I've argued in front of her. Fair, knowledgeable. Right, Charlie?"

Charlie shrugged agreement. She was being unusually quiet.

"Do you know anything about her background?" continued Beaumont. "She came up through the foster care system. From what I hear through the rosebush, she hit a rough patch in one of those homes. Rose above it, full scholarship through Ivy League college, top of her law school class. But she never forgot what happened to her. And unlike those two geezers who ran the criminal court for years before her—Glass and Green—who thought every underage sex crime was just 'boys bein' boys,' hoo-wee, Judge Neese takes them quite seriously."

"And you're afraid she'll set an unreasonably high bail to send a message."

"No, it's the other possibility we're worried about," said Charlie.

"Meaning?"

"That she won't set bail at all."

CHAPTER 25

It was 10:45 a.m., and for the last four-plus hours I'd been engaged in an activity I thoroughly deplored: watching and waiting. Stony tells me surveillance is sixty percent of private detective work—which is why I'll never be a real PI. The spot I was watching now was an isolated stretch of private dirt road about an eighth of a mile from the rural property's gate. I had a rough plan in mind, which might be better described as a hope.

Yesterday I had spent the whole day finding and surveilling the property itself. And I was confident this was the place the phone calls were coming from.

The way I found it: Using the coordinates Stony gave me, I narrowed my search down to the three properties that seemed likely candidates. I didn't want to be seen snooping around in a car with Tennessee plates, so I ditched my rental in a wooded turnout off a "main" dirt road. Then I headed off on foot, armed with my gun and binoculars, using the GPS and map on my phone to navigate. Dressed in jeans, work boots, plaid shirt, and hunting cap, I hoped no one would give me a second look on the road. I needn't have worried; I didn't spot a single human being. After walking more than half a mile in the steadily warming Texas sun, I arrived at the first property, which I quickly identified as a working farm and dismissed.

Another half-mile walk took me to a smaller dirt road that led to property number two. Rather than walk on the access road itself, I snuck through the woods, keeping the road in sight. After about a quarter of a mile, I spotted an electric gate blocking the road. On a nearby tree was a small black box I guessed was a camera of some sort. My pulse started racing. *Maybe* a Texas farmer would employ such security measures, but I doubted it.

I made my way through the woods to the backside of the property. Forest surrounded the entire "farm," no fences. A white farmhouse with an attached garage, a large gray barn, and a couple of smaller outbuildings sat toward the front of the lot, backed by an expanse of open field, maybe three or four acres. Small for a Texas farm. And no crops had been planted for some time. Just grass, which someone was cutting for hay. Not a working farm.

I crept up close to the tree line and looked across the field toward the house with my binoculars. Two cars and a van were parked there. No pickup trucks or farm machinery. I was tempted to try to get closer to the house but didn't want to cross the open field. Examining the perimeter with my binoculars, I spotted a four-inch white rectangular device on one of the trees, and then a second one on another tree. Motion detectors? I hoped I hadn't set them off.

Staying well back from the clearing, I maneuvered through the woods to a spot where I could safely observe the house and the electric gate from closer range. I "camped" there and watched the place through the binocs as the temperature steadily rose, glad I'd brought along a bag of gas-station trail mix and a big bottle of water.

Over the course of a long day, I watched the van come and go four times from the garage but couldn't see its occupants. Twice the electric gate was remotely opened to let in commercial vehicles, one an Amazon delivery van, the other a spring water vendor. Both times, the drivers were instructed to leave their deliveries on the porch by a woman with dark hair and bangs.

As dusk drew nearer, I was still unsure I had found the right place, but then at around six thirty, I heard girls' voices and a radio. Moving to a spot that afforded me a better view, I saw, in my twin lenses, four girls sitting around a picnic table with a boombox, eating sandwiches. They looked like young teens, but I couldn't be sure. Two of them were drinking from red-and-white cans. Budweiser. Two were Caucasian, two were darker skinned. I felt certain I'd found the place, but I was wary of the motion detectors. I decided to leave, while I still had enough daylight to find my way out of the woods, and make a plan for the next day. And then the mosquitoes—Texas's state bird—descended, cementing my decision.

Now here I was, the next day, staking out the small dirt road to the farm. About two hours earlier, a large movers' truck had exited the property. It must have been parked inside the barn. I had a strong instinct to follow it, but I couldn't be in two places at once. I opted to stay put.

At 10:53, I heard tires grinding in dirt and looked down the road to see a supermarket delivery truck approaching the property. I had picked this spot in the narrow, curving road because it couldn't be seen from the main road or from the house.

The truck moved slowly on the rough ground. I waited till it passed, then dashed out onto the road and ran up behind it, hoping to stay out of sight of its rear-view mirrors. It didn't stop, so I guessed the driver hadn't spotted me. I took a running jump up onto its rear platform. Landing on the metal grating as softly as possible in my work boots, I grabbed onto the door handle for support. The truck rolled on.

It stopped after a hundred yards or so, and I heard the hum of the electric gate opening. The truck moved forward, then stopped a few yards further ahead. The gate closed behind us.

I sidestepped off the platform and landed in a thick patch of greenery, scraping my arm and side on sharp branches. Hiding in the bushes, I scoped out the house.

The truck stopped near the house to unload its delivery. As it did, it gave me some good cover, so I took the opportunity to run like hell and hide behind the barn. I froze, hoping I hadn't been spotted or triggered any alarms.

All was quiet. Now what to do? I had no idea.

Looking in a back window of the barn, I saw its big front door was open, letting in a massive swath of sunlight. But I also saw plenty of shadowy corners in which I might be able to hide until I figured out my next move. I slid open the wobbly rear window, listened for movement, and then climbed over the sill.

I had barely taken three steps toward a row of dark old horse stalls when my phone rang! The opening licks of Chuck Berry's "Johnny B. Goode." At full volume. Somehow, I must have turned the ringer on! I fumbled the phone out of my pocket. The incoming call was from Jim Beaumont—might be important—but I just needed to shut the damn ringer off. I was all thumbs, couldn't remember how to do it.

I finally managed to silence the phone, and then a firm voice behind me said, "I have a gun. Hands up. Don't turn around."

CHAPTER 26

"I know you're in shock, Charlie, but we'll get through this," Lilly said. The two women sat across from each other at their now-regular table at Granny's. It was lunchtime on Monday, and they were waiting for Sarah and Erlene to join them for their scheduled gathering.

"Murder," said Charlie, her face slack with disbelief. "I still can't believe he's been charged with murder."

During Jack's arraignment, the judge permitted the prosecution to introduce new evidence that had come to light that morning. Jack's computer, seized during the home search, had been forensically examined, and a hidden Word file was found. It was a first-person account, written in grisly detail, of the abduction and killing of Abby Pruitt. The DA's office decided that, coupled with the blood on the underwear, which was indeed Abby's, they now had enough evidence to seek murder charges. Judge Neese allowed the new charges to be filed.

"Given the new charges, Neese had no choice but to deny him bail," Lilly said.

"And now Jack has to rot in that awful place for the next five months," Charlie replied, "until the trial date. And I've got to try to keep the firm afloat with both your dad and your brother *in absentia*, while also working full-time to prove Jack's innocence."

Lilly looked into Charlie's eyes, but Charlie wouldn't hold her gaze—she drummed her fingers on the tabletop, biting the corner of her lip.

"But that's not all that's bothering you, is it?" Lilly said.

Charlie shrugged and shook her head.

"Come on, out with it."

"Well… I mean, it's all a bit… damning, isn't it? The written 'confession,' the video footage, the text messages, the blood, the semen, the—"

"Are you having doubts, Charlie? About Jack's innocence?"

"Aren't you? Just a little? I mean, there must be some tiny part of you that wonders…"

"No!" Lilly snapped, surprising Charlie and several customers at other tables. "No, there isn't. Jack is innocent, period. I know that in every drop of my blood in my body. And if you don't feel the same way, then maybe you shouldn't—"

"Whoa," Charlie said, taking Lilly's hand and looking her in the eye. "No, you're right. There's no place for doubt here. Not even a shred of it. I'm sorry. You won't hear anything like that from me again. I promise. I'm just feeling… so overwhelmed."

"I get it. Sorry for unleashing the kraken." Lilly squeezed her hand, as Sarah and Erlene slid into seats beside them. The four women regarded one another with tight smiles.

"The meeting of the Jonesborough Women's Investigative Committee is hereby called to order," Sarah said. "Food is on its way, let's start. Okay, so we've just had some terrible news about Jack, but all it means is we need to double down and work faster and harder."

"Right," said Charlie. "So, what have you got, ladies? Lilly, why don't you go first?"

"Okay, I'll start with Dad. He's in Sealy, Texas, as I told you in my texts. God knows why. Been there the last two days. Spends his days out in the boonies, northeast of the city, his nights in town, probably at a hotel. Still won't answer my calls. On the Jack front: I finally found a guy at the DA's office who likes Dad and got me the serial numbers of those two phones with the creepy texts on them. Same brand, same lot number, probably sold at the same store at the same time. I'm trying to track down who bought them. I'm sure the cops are doing the same. Oh, and a weird thing: last night, Rio was acting strange all evening, snarling and roaming from window to window. I think someone might be watching the house."

The women exchanged dark glances. "Aunt Sarah, what about you?"

"I've been on the horn all weekend with those Little League parents. *Trying* to be, anyhow. Amazing how people's attitudes have changed. I'm no longer the kindly diner lady who gives free food to their kids, I'm the aunt of an accused child molester. And accused equals guilty, apparently. The few who would talk to me were already 'revising history' the way folks'll do. 'I had a bad feeling about him all along,' or 'I always thought there was somethin' fishy about the way he acted with that girl.' Bull-crap. If they felt that way, they wouldn't have let their kids near him. I did get a call-back from one mom, though, who said she'd talk to me, but only confidentially. Said there's something I should know about the Osborne kid, the one who came forward with those stories about Jack. I'm trying to set that call up for today."

"Great," Charlie said. "Oh, and just a reminder: don't talk to the Osbornes directly. As an attorney, I'll handle that.

"Right."

Charlie turned to the red-haired woman in the low-cut blouse. "Erlene, do you have anything for us?"

"Too early to say, ladies. But Ronnie and I have been making our 'social calls,' as promised. We paid visits to two gentlemen here in Washington County and another down near Knoxville—a 'man of medicine' Ronnie and Joe had already visited. These men are all customers of mine who have given repeat business to my most tender-aged-looking employee, a gal goes by the name of Tabitha. She delivers a particular kind of service. And so, believing as I do that you catch more flies with honey than with vinegar, I approached each of these men with a sweet lil' ol' proposition. Call it 'Erlene Immunity.'"

"What's that?" asked Charlie, wincing in anticipation of the answer.

"It works very much like legal immunity, though I s'pose you couldn't hardly call it legal. I simply tell them, *Give me dirt on a bigger fish than you and I won't use the dirt I have on y'all.* Works like a charm. What I am learning is that there seems to be a 'club' of very wealthy and prominent fellas—globe-hopper types—who gather occasionally, on yachts and private islands, to enjoy the company of underage females. Such a shock to discover. One of the members of this informal club may be a very high elected official in our state government. I won't mention his name until I know more. Another is a *very* well-known multibillionaire. An international real estate investor who has been photographed with princes, presidents, and popes.

"These men don't get their hands dirty procuring the 'talent,'" she went on. "They rely on a supplier for that. A supplier that happens to operate locally. Thanks to the opioid epidemic and the poverty here in these beloved hills, we've become a goldmine of lost young souls. Talk is, they may have nabbed the Pruitt girl, but I don't know. So, I've brought Leon Bates in on the situation. He and I are 'old friends.' I'll keep you posted on anything we find."

"That could be huge. What have you got, Charlie?" Sarah asked.

"Not much, unfortunately. Jack's trial's been set for September twenty-first. Jim is filing motions to move the trial date up and to reconsider bail, but he doubts he'll succeed. Jim and I are meeting today—along with Susan Stoneman—to start deconstructing the 'evidence' and brainstorming alternative theories. But Jim is pretty sure whoever's framing Jack is a big-time pro. The quality and quantity of evidence they're fabricating... These people are no amateurs."

"Which raises the question," said Sarah. "Why Jack? Why such elaborate measures? Who would have such a strong motive to target him?"

"Right," said Charlie. "He hasn't been practicing law very long, and he hasn't dealt with any real high-profile clients or crossed swords with anyone super-dangerous, that I know of."

"But his father has," said Sarah.

The four women looked at one another in charged silence.

"Oh my God," said Charlie. "This isn't about Jack, is it? Never has been. It's about Joe. Purely Joe. Of course. How did we not see that?"

Lilly spoke up. "As far as I know, no one has approached him with any extortion demands. No one's trying to get something from him."

"That means payback," Charlie said. "Someone wants to see Joe suffer, plain and simple. Someone who knows that the best way to do that is to cause pain to his family."

"But who?"

Another silence ensued.

"I can think of one person," Sarah told the others. "Because *I* was the family member he chose to target. John Lipscomb." She explained that John Lipscomb was a powerful businessman and drug merchant whom Joe had accused of a triple murder back when he was D.A. Lipscomb's men had invaded Sarah's home, cut off her clothes, bound her to her bed with razor wire, and soaked the bed with gasoline as a warning to Joe. "And he certainly would be vindictive and powerful enough to do something like this to Jack. There's only one problem... He's dead."

Erlene muttered something beneath her breath that sounded like, "You can take that to the bank."

The younger women didn't ask her to repeat herself.

"There was something in the papers about it just a year or so ago," Lilly added. "A hiker found his body, right? If not him, then who else?" asked Lilly.

"That's what we need to find out. Come on, Lilly." Charlie rose from her seat. "Let's get back to the office and start digging through Joe's old case files. We'll take our lunch to go."

And with that, Charlie was out the door, leaving Lilly to collect the food.

CHAPTER 27

"I repeat: hands up and don't turn around."

The human brain, I've discovered, can perform an astonishing number of calculations in a very short time when its survival is at stake: *The guy's voice sounds fairly high and young. It's coming from below my ear level—he's shorter than me. There's a slight wobble of fear in it. He's stalling; he hasn't had time to prepare his next actions yet. He doesn't want me to turn around because he doesn't want me to see he's smaller than me and unarmed. He's standing about three feet behind me.*

Before I was consciously aware of any of these thoughts, my body launched into motion. Pivoting with my right foot, I propelled myself backwards, then spun around with lightning speed, driving my left elbow into the side of the man's head and plunging my body into his.

My size and weight were too much for him, and he toppled backward to the dirt floor. I landed with one knee on his belly and one on the ground. I pulled my gun from my waistband and put it to his head.

"Don't shoot! Don't shoot!" the mustachioed young man with the bad teeth screamed. "Tell me what you want!"

One thing I learned long ago—back in my Army Ranger days—was never to ask the enemy an open question. It betrays uncertainty and gives them wiggle-room to lie. Always act like you already know the big stuff.

"I know you have the girl," I said.

With my free left hand, I pulled my phone from my pocket. I tapped on "Photos," as Lilly had taught me to do, and brought up Abby's picture. "Her name is Abby Pruitt. Tell me where I can find her. If I don't believe your answer, I will fire a bullet through your rotten teeth."

"She's not here! Not anymore. She left this morning, with three of the other girls."

"Liar. I've been watching the road all morning." I pointed the gun into his mouth.

"They were in a moving van! That's how we transport them!"

Damn. That truck. I'd had a feeling I should follow it.

I lifted the guy to his feet by his shirt collar. "We're going to walk. Don't speak unless you're spoken to. Understood?"

He nodded. I punched him in the stomach, just to establish dominance. Marching him in front of me at gunpoint, I explored the barn, looking for materials with which to tie him up. Luckily, the place had a workshop area with lots of tools and supplies. I tied the guy to a barn post, using weed-whacker cord, then found some duct tape in a crate of junk.

I placed the gun barrel against the immobilized man's cheek and asked him where the moving van was headed. To a residence in Arizona, he informed me. Like Merlo Maroni, he claimed employees of the organization, such as himself, were never told more than they needed to know. All he professed to know was that the residence was somewhere near Phoenix and that a couple of the girls who had lived there referred to it as Black Canyon.

I duct-taped his mouth shut and made my getaway.

***

Augustus Paolo—aka "Mr. Paolo"—picked his phone up from his desk and flipped through his contacts until he came to a name that caused the hairs on his neck to bristle. El Espectro. The Ghost. He took a deep breath, held it, then hit the dial button. "He was here, sir, asking about the girl. He was told about Arizona, as you instructed, but was given only hints. He is driving a rented, new-model, dark red Toyota Camry, Tennessee license plate 2G6-11A7. I will. Yes, sir. Thank you, sir."

***

The first thing Jack learned upon returning to the jail after his arraignment was that he was being transferred from the "holding unit" to one of the long-term units, where inmates serving sentences or awaiting far-off trial dates were housed.

A guard escorted him briskly to the Deputy Warden's office, still in handcuffs, for his pre-placement meeting.

"Inmates of your stripe…" Deputy Warden Cyrus Clark said to Jack across his desk. "That is to say, inmates with a sexual component to their crimes or charges, are given an option. They can choose to reside in PC, protective custody, or they can choose Gen Pop. If you choose PC, you will not be 'exposed,' so to speak, to other inmates during rec time or church time. If you opt for Gen Pop, you will be accorded no such protection, and it is entirely possible you will receive a *welcoming* of sorts from your fellow residents. However, opting for PC does not guarantee the same thing will not occur down the line, via slightly more creative means."

"So, you're saying I can get my ass kicked now or later."

"Your words, inmate, not mine, but I believe we are aligned in that regard."

"Then why put off till tomorrow what can be accomplished today?" said Jack with a cold smile. "I'll take Gen Pop. Preferably a non-smoking room with a view."

Clark shot an icy smile back at Jack. "You might change your mind about that, inmate. This meeting is over. We'll need a bit of time to prepare your 'room'—mint on the pillowcase, that sort of thing—so you may go join the others for rec time now. After rec, you'll meet your new roommates."

Jack hadn't had time yet to digest what had just happened in court, but as the guard led him out into the bright afternoon sunshine of "the yard," both his pulse and his mind were racing. Questions tumbled in his mind like clothes in a dryer. *Is Abby Pruitt really dead? Do they really believe I murdered her? Who is doing this to me? Why? Will Charlie stick with me? Does she believe in my innocence? How will she run the business without me? Where did my father go? Why isn't he here? Is this place really my home for the next five months? Will Jim Beaumont get me out of this?*

Will I ever practice law again or is my reputation ruined forever? Did Mom know about any of this? Did the news about me hasten her death?

Jack didn't know what to do with himself in the yard. Blending into the "scenery" was what he *wanted* to do, but he knew, as the new guy in the unit, he was the deer in the wolf pen. He surveyed the dusty lot, trying to look steely-eyed and bored. Some of the inmates were playing basketball at the netless hoop, some were working out with weights, some were playing chess or Scrabble, and some were just jogging or walking around. Jack fell in with the walkers, keeping his distance from the others.

Two minutes hadn't passed when a greasy-looking, wild-eyed guy in his forties with a huge spider tattooed on his neck and face approached Jack and began walking beside him. "So, here's the deal, Chester. You're *gonna* get the livin' snot beat out a' ya, that's a fact. We call it your 'pullin' in.' But we employ a democratic system here, so you get a choice. You can take your whuppin' peacefully, in private, in one of the cells, or you can take it right out here in the yard. What's it gonna be?"

The two men stopped and looked at each other, eye to eye.

Jack hadn't expected this to happen so quickly. He did the calculus in his mind. A private "pulling in" would probably involve fewer men. There wasn't room in a cell for a crowd, after all. On the other hand, fighting out in the yard might give Jack a chance to show the others that he wasn't to be taken lightly. At 6'2", he was built even more thickly than his father, and anyone fighting him would pay a price, win or lose. And truth be told, Jack was so keyed up right now, he almost *welcomed* a fistfight, even one he would almost certainly lose.

"Bring it," said Jack, spreading his arms to signify a public battle.

"Your funeral, hoss. Follow me."

Spider Tattoo led Jack toward the building, where four men in orange jumpsuits sat in a row against the wall in a small strip of shade.

"Chester don't want to go inside," said Tattoo to a heavy, bald guy.

Baldy *tsk*ed, shook his head, and muttered, "Dumb-ass." He stood up and walked off around a corner.

A minute later, Baldy returned, followed by four other men of mixed races and ethnicities. Whatever was about to happen was to be delivered at the hands of a racially diverse committee. A rare cause for inmate unity, apparently. The men sitting against the wall joined the new men to form two lines of bodies with a "corridor" down the middle. The two men on the end nearest Jack, both with arms the girth of legs, grabbed Jack in an iron-strong hold and turned him so that he was facing down the "corridor."

Jack had erred. This wasn't going to be a fistfight; it was going to be a defenseless beating. A man stepped into the open end of the corridor—the man who would deliver the beating, presumably.

"Hello, *Counselor*," growled the inmate, eyes ablaze with animal fury. Greg Pruitt. Of course. He must have been denied bail too. "You're about to wish your mama died before she ever coughed you out of her whoring body."

Pruitt stepped into the human corridor. From his sleeve, he pulled a length of metal, sharpened to a razor's edge, with a cloth wrapped around its base as a handle. A shank. Jack's guts went cold.

Pruitt took a step closer to Jack, almost ceremonially. Then another. And another. His eyes were locked on Jack's.

Jack strained against his captors but couldn't budge. Pruitt stood two feet in front of him. He held the blade upright, midway between their two faces, and stared into Jack's eyes.

"Did you kill my little girl?" he said to Jack in a voice barely above a whisper. Jack didn't answer. "I asked you a question, Dillard. Did. You. Kill. My. Little…"

Pruitt lashed out with the blade. Jack felt his skin rip open, from beneath his right eye down to the middle of his cheek. The pain was sharp and instantaneous.

"…Girl?"

"That's enough!" shouted a voice from about three yards away. Jack hoped it was a guard, accompanied by about ten others.

But no, it appeared to be an inmate—short and stocky—flanked by two other inmates on either side of him. The sun behind them cast them in shadow, making their features hard to see.

A staring contest went down between the two groups of men, and then the musclemen released Jack, and his tormentors began to disperse. Whoever this new guy was, he commanded some authority. Greg Pruitt spat out, "We'll finish this job another day, Dillard, you can count on that," as he walked off.

Jack's rescuer stepped forward, allowing Jack to get a better look at his mutton-chop sideburns and tattooed-on widow's-peak. "The things you gotta do around here to get a meeting with your lawyer."

"Hello, Badger," muttered Jack, ignoring the searing pain in his face. He recognized Clovis "Badger" Daley from his booking photo and had spoken with him by phone after his father's initial interview.

"Welcome to the Washington County Hyatt, Couns'lor Dillard. Come on, let's get you to the infirmary."

CHAPTER 28

Tommy liked to spend time with his scorpions in the morning, after his chores were done and before the toolshed got too hot from the Arizona sun. He kept them in a big, clear-plastic tub set up like a terrarium: dirt, rocks, a plastic cactus, some palm tree bark for the little fellas to hide under, and a couple of cholla branches for them to climb on for exercise. The cool thing about bark scorpions was that, unlike many other scorpion species, they were communal. They liked to huddle together with others of their kind; the more, the merrier. Last count, Tommy had put seventy-two of them into the bin, but he wasn't sure if they were all still alive. Some of them might have got eaten by other ones. They did that sometimes. But then again, some of them might have had babies. And when scorpions had babies, watch out.

The scorpions didn't need a lot of care. He'd punctured the bin-cover with hundreds of tiny holes to give them air, and every couple of days he sprayed some water on the inside wall of the bin and tossed in a few crickets and roaches. Of course, he couldn't leave the bin out in the open. He stacked it in a corner with some boxes of junk, and nobody ever noticed it. But every day, he took the lid off to let in some fresh air and to talk to his pets.

The things Tommy said to the scorpions wouldn't make sense to anyone who heard them. But they made sense to Tommy.

Every day he started his talk the same way, reciting his words in a rhythmic beat, almost like a chant or prayer. "List of residents," he said. "Year one, June second: Priscilla Ann. Blond hair. Fourteen years old. Red nose ring. Flower tattoo. Born in Boston. Loves Hawaiian pizza. Left August fourth. June twelfth: Rosalita. Curly hair. Big hips. Parents from

El Salvador. Brother killed by gang…" Tommy proceeded to recite the names of every single "associate" who had lived in the residence since the day he arrived, along with the dates of their arrivals and departures, their physical descriptions, and any facts he'd been able to collect about them during their stay. The list grew longer over time, but every day he recited it from the beginning, adding any new names at the end.

When he was finished reciting all the shorthand facts he knew about every kid who'd lived at the place for the past two and a half years—a feat that currently took about fifteen minutes—he moved on to "List of staff members." Tommy narrated every piece of data he knew about each and every staff person who had worked at the residence since his arrival. It was a shorter list, but a more detailed one.

After doing that, Tommy moved on to "Facts and Observations." He listed aloud everything he knew about the house itself, the surrounding area, the daily living routines, the outcall procedures for the associates, the drugs and alcohol consumed in the house, and all the noteworthy incidents he had witnessed, including two deaths and several beatings.

Tommy didn't think of himself as smart—he was never good at math or English—but he was smarter than *they* thought he was. A lot smarter. And one thing Tommy was *very* good at was remembering. His mind could hold onto things like a bug grabber holding a scorpion.

Tommy memorized his facts, instead of writing them down, for three reasons: One, he didn't want the staff to know he *could* write—anything more than TOMMY and words like CAT. Two, he didn't want anyone to find his writings. And three, he wanted to keep his mind sharp. When people treat you like you're mentally deficient day in and day out, you start to believe it. Tommy worked hard at staying mentally acute beneath his dull eyes and vacant smile.

But the primary reason he held on to facts was this: The people who ran this place—and the other places like it—had done something terrible to Tommy, and he was never going to forget it. Someday, his chance would come, his chance to take these people down and make them pay. And when that happened, he wanted to have all the facts at his fingertips that would put people behind bars and help the police find some of the missing kids.

Tommy recited his facts to the scorpions, not because he thought they could understand his words—he wasn't stupid—but because it felt good to say them aloud to another living thing. It might be the only chance he would ever get.

"Year three. April 19," Tommy droned on, now nearly an hour into his daily recitations, "Luka dies. Body buried behind the big rocks…"

"Hey Goof-tard!"

Tommy went silent. Shane. What did he want this time? Tommy quickly covered the scorpion bin and stacked it in the corner where it always went. He stepped out of the toolshed holding a rake and watched Shane approach, shielding his eyes against the morning sun.

"There you are, Goof-tard. Quit screwing around out here and come with me!"

"What's going on?" Tommy asked. He thought Shane sounded upset.

"I'll tell you what's going on. We're about to be put under the microscope, that's what. We gotta get this place spic and span and running like a Swiss watch." Shane marched toward the house, wiping his brow, and Tommy followed him. "Do you understand what I'm saying?"

"Yah. We gotta make things super nice and clean. How come?"

"Because a new batch of associates are on their way, and Mr. Paolo's coming."

"He comes here lots of times."

"Yeah, but this time someone else is coming too. *His* boss. And that don't make me very happy."

"How come?"

"Because of who this guy is. 'The Ghost.' I didn't even know this dude was real. I thought he was just made up. A story, like. To keep people in line."

"Sounds spooky."

"You don't know the half of it, Goof-tard, you don't know the half of it. Move!"

***

"You callin' me *stupid*, trailer trash?" Deja shouted. "Say that to my face, and I'll put you through that wall of boxes!"

"Calm down, Deja," said Hope.

"I'm not calling you stupid," Abby explained to Deja. "I'm saying they're lying to you. They're using you. It's *them* you should be mad at, not me."

Four girls from the Sealy residence—Deja, Hope, Abby, and Selena—were seated in the back of the moving van, en route to Arizona. The three older girls were being transferred there as part of their "rotation"; Abby was being sent for reasons not yet fully explained. The cargo space had been arranged more comfortably than when Abby had ridden solo. The whole front half of the freight area was opened up, a space about eight by ten feet. A carpet was laid out on the floor, a padded air mattress had been allotted to each girl, and two battery-operated lamps had been provided, along with a cooler full of soft drinks, beer, and sandwiches. A porta-potty sat in a corner, blocked off for privacy by a sheet hung between the two adjacent walls.

"You keep saying the money isn't real," said Deja, "but what does an eleven-year-old baby who still rides a pink bicycle know about it? They show me my bank account every week. It's on a real banking app."

"But why don't they let you *have* your money?"

"They *do* let you have it, just not all at once! A couple weeks ago, I asked for two hundred dollars to buy some new clothes and undies. They gave me the money, took me shopping, no prob."

"That's because they want you lookin' nice and pretty for their customers. But if you asked for a thousand dollars in cash money, I bet they wouldn't give it to you."

"I told you, they can't hand us a big bunch of cash. They want us to save for the future. And they don't want us runnin' off till we fu'filled our contract."

"Let me ask you something, Deja," said Abby. "Have you ever met anyone who's 'fu'filled their contract' and got their money handed to them, all tied up in a pretty bow?"

The three older girls' eyes met darkly in the light of the battery lamps. The only sound was the churning of the a/c unit and the truck's transmission.

"They're lying to you," Abby said again. "To all of you. The money isn't real. You'll never get any of it. You're working for nothing!"

"Shut up, trai-trash!" Deja snapped, her face twisting in rage. She grabbed a beer from the cooler and popped it open. "You think you're so frickin' smart, but you don't know jack. You don't even know what's about to happen to your own ass."

"What do you mean?"

Deja laughed, low and menacing. "You think you dodged a bullet back there when they didn't send you out on a job. That just means they're just saving you for something worse. Something way worse. You got no idea, Miss Smarty Pants."

"Don't be mean, Deja," said Hope.

"She might as well hear the truth. Here's what you don't realize, little girl," Deja said to Abby. "You got the 'money look': face that says sweet sixteen, body that says thirteen, still got your virgin's veil. There's dudes out there that pay BIG bucks for a chickadee like you." Deja paused, taking a slug of her beer. "Wanna know what's going down? I'll tell you. They put your face out on the web—the dark web; these pervs have a network—and somebody liked what they saw. Someone with a boatload of cash. And they *reserved* you."

"I know someone that happened to," said Selena, a Mexican-American girl with long braids. "She was a virgin too. The guy who paid for her was super rich. He had something he called a 'breaking-in party.' He did her in front of all his rich buddies, while they all watched. Then they all got their turn."

A lightning bolt of terror shot through Abby.

She *hated* the men who had taken her. She hated Mr. Paolo. She hated the man who had "reserved" her, whoever he was. She hated her father and his leering friends. She hated every man who'd ever looked at her like she was something on display at a meat counter. What gave them the *right*? She was just a kid. A kid who wanted to play baseball and maybe get into a decent high school, and, who knew, maybe even go to college one day. Why was she suddenly in this horrible grownup world? What had she done to deserve it?

"I'm not going to let them do it to me!" she shouted, jumping to her feet, startling the others. "I'm not going to let them keep lying to you and stealing your lives. I'm going to stop them. Somehow. Are you with me or not?"

CHAPTER 29

"Sarah? Sarah Dillard?" the voice on the phone whispered. "This is Tammy Stanton. Can you talk?"

"Just a sec," said Sarah. She slipped into the pantry at the back of the diner, closed the door, and sat on a stack of tomato-juice cases. "I can now."

"Here's the deal, Miss Sarah. I shouldn't be calling you, but my conscience won't let me stay quiet. You can't tell the police we talked. Understood? If you do, I will call you every kind of liar. If you're gonna use what I tell you, you gotta do it in some way that don't involve me. Agreed?"

"Agreed," said Sarah. "I appreciate your call. I won't make you regret it."

Tammy Stanton spoke in a rushed whisper. "Ginny Osborne is my best friend." Ginny Osborne was the mother of the boy on the Little League team who had come forward with the stories about Jack and Abby Pruitt. "She called me a week or so ago scared plumb out of her mind. Said her and her husband came home from a movie date—Billy, their boy, was sleepin' over at a friend's—and there was a man in their house. Just sittin' at the kitchen table, no lights on. Tall, blond-haired, missing most 'a one ear, look in his eye that'd freeze your blood, she said. He told 'em he'd been looking into Ted's background. Ted, that's Ginny's husband. Said he knew stuff that would get Ted fired and destroy the Osbornes' lives. Then he said worse stuff. Stuff about what he would do to Billy if they didn't cooperate. Real specific things."

"What did he want from *them?*" Sarah thought she knew but wanted to hear it from Tammy.

"For Billy to lie. Well, to exaggerate. You see, Miss Sarah, it wasn't all that hard to make it seem like Jack, your nephew, *was* doin' something a little off. The truth was, he *did* spend a lot of time with the Pruitt girl, and he did touch her sometimes—ruffled her hair, put his hand on her shoulder. But it wasn't like *that*. It wasn't, you know, icky. It was just him trying to give her something she wasn't getting at home. Some guidance and encouragement. …But Ginny told Billy to say he saw that touching turn into something more. I think she somehow talked the boy into believing it really did happen. Don't judge her, Ms. Sarah, she had no choice. She was trying to protect her son. From the devil."

"Do you know who this guy was? This tall, blonde guy? Do you know what he—"

"That's all I can say right now, Miss Sarah. And remember, you and me never talked."

The call went dead, and Sarah knew better than to redial Tammy Stanton.

***

I was getting that feeling again, the feeling I'd had back at the Muddy Fork Motel, that I was being watched. But as I drove west on Route I-10 in my rented car, I didn't see any cars behind me.

I thought back on my Caroline "dream" back at the hotel room in Sealy. She told me she would be with me my whole journey. Was that what I was feeling? The presence of Caroline?

Or was that just what I wanted to believe?

Maybe the "watched" feeling was just a general sense that I was being hustled by someone, lured to Arizona like a bass chasing a spinnerbait through the reeds.

Mentally reviewing my encounter with the guy in the barn, I couldn't help feeling he'd parted with his information a little too easily. That stuff about the sex-trafficking residence in Arizona, the place the girls called Black Canyon. He blurted it out without much prodding.

"I've got a bad feeling, Sweetheart," I said to the empty passenger seat of the rented Camry. I should have felt foolish uttering the words aloud. But I didn't. Rather, I sensed my words had been *received* in some way. Just wishful thinking, I supposed. But I felt emboldened to speak aloud again. To attempt a "conversation."

"Do you know where I'm headed, Love?"

No reply. But *something* maybe. A slight charge in the air?

"To Arizona. I know you always wanted to see Arizona, and I'm so damn sorry I never took you there. That was the plan, remember? Back before you got sick? I was going to retire at forty. Ha. We were going to buy a Winnebago. Spend six months driving around the country, seeing every place we hadn't seen. Arizona, that was one of the places you talked about the most. The red rocks of Sedona, the Apache Trail, Grand Canyon."

I listened for a response. Nothing but road noise. Glancing at the speedometer, I realized I'd dropped my speed to fifty. I gave the car some gas and looked in the rear-view mirror. Empty road behind me, no followers. "I hate that I'm going there without you," I continued. "I hate *why* I'm going there. And I'm getting a very bad feeling about the whole thing." I paused for a moment. "What's that all about, Sweetie? What is it that I'm sensing?"

No reply again. Why would there be? But then a crazy idea struck. If I was going to consult my deceased wife about my plans and activities, I should at least consult her in a way she could respond to. Maybe ask a yes/no question instead of an "open-ended" one like Lou Anne, the hospice worker, had trained me to do.

"Am I walking into a trap, Sweetheart?" I said to the empty passenger seat.

A waft of her smell drifted past my nose. I was sure of it. That familiar mixture of her sweet breath, her favorite soap, and that drugstore shampoo she liked to buy.

My breath froze in my throat.

Easy, Joe. Don't get carried away. A smell is a subtle thing. Easy to conjure in the mind.

"Am I in danger right now?" I asked, again aloud.

Her smell hit me a second time.

At least I thought it did. I couldn't swear to it in a court of law.

I couldn't swear to anything anymore.

***

Gracie rode Pepper, her black pony, around the big rock formation she called Skull Mountain. It looked kind of like a monkey skull when the sun hit it just right. Grace had names for all the landmarks along her looping, three-quarter mile trail in the woods—Grandpa Willow, Wheat Field, The Rapids.

The trail was the only place Gracie was allowed to be alone. Her ninth birthday was still four months off, so her mom didn't usually let her out of her sight. Grace went to school in Jonesborough, and every day she took the bus to her mother's restaurant and hung around there until it was time for Mom to leave. Then they drove the seven miles together to their country home in southwestern Washington County. Whenever she wasn't in school, she was with Mom.

But her mother did allow her to ride alone in the woods behind the house with Pepper a few times a week. It had taken Grace a while to talk her into it. Sarah had finally relented, saying, "I guess I don't want to be one of those 'helicopter parents,' always hovering around."

When Sarah had said that, Gracie pictured a bunch of parents wearing helicopter backpacks, hovering like hummingbirds over their kids as they played outdoors.

There were three rules Grace had to follow if she wanted to keep her trail-riding privileges: (1) she could only go riding when her mom said so, (2) she had to stick to the trail, no detours, and (3) she had to take a phone with her. Her mom even made a special Velcro holder for the phone, so it could rest on Pepper's neck and Grace could grab it quickly in an emergency.

As Grace urged Pepper around the rear of Skull Mountain, a bullfrog croaked in the bright spring growth choking the creek. It sounded huge. She wanted to go check it out, but she didn't want to break Rule Number 2. Maybe just a quick peek, though. From the edge of the trail.

She put her phone in her pocket, slid off the saddle, found the stirrup with her boot, and landed on the rocky ground. She pulled on Pepper's reins to lead her in a walk, but the pony refused to budge. Instead, she did a funny sideways step and lifted her nose in the air.

Pepper was spooked; Grace knew the behavior. Sometimes her pony could see and smell things Gracie couldn't. Grace looked around, didn't see anything. But then a chill tickled her spine. She looked toward the creek and listened.

A twig snapped in the woods behind her. Grace almost whipped her head around to look, but something told her to play this more cautiously and artfully.

"Wait here, Pep," she said in a deliberately loud voice. "I want to get a picture of these flowers."

She slipped her phone from her pocket and walked toward the overgrown creek. Her thumb found the camera function and put the phone in selfie mode. Holding it at a low angle, she surreptitiously studied the woods behind her.

Something moved back there! She stifled a gasp. Angling the camera for a better look, she saw a figure step out from behind a tree.

A man. Tall, blond, something wrong with his ear. The cold expression on his face made her almost pee herself with fear.

She crouched before a tangle of purple flowers and aimed the camera toward it. But she was aiming the *lens* at the man behind her. She snapped a photo.

That might be the last thing you ever do was the dark thought that struck her eight-year-old mind.

CHAPTER 30

"Let's meet in the conference room," Charlie said to TBI agent Anita White, who was right on time for their 7:30 a.m. meeting.

Lilly and Charlie had spent the previous day combing through Joe's files and case notes. Joe wasn't the best record keeper, and he wasn't big on writing down his thoughts. His records didn't contain any major revelations. Yes, Joe had made some enemies, both in his many years as a defense attorney and in his brief stint as D.A. But the women could find no evidence of anyone with a strong enough vendetta against him, or a lawless enough nature, to warrant the extreme actions taken against Jack.

They'd even checked into the John Lipscomb character Sarah mentioned. Lipscomb had disappeared years earlier, not long after his attempts to have Joe and his family murdered. But then, about fourteen months ago, a badly decomposed body was found by a hiker in the Cherokee National Forest. It turned out to be Lipscomb, as proven by DNA testing.

As the two women dug through the files, they had continued to monitor Joe's movements. He was now headed west out of Scaly, Texas, to parts unknown. Sarah had dropped by the office, midday, to discuss her call from Tammy Stanton, which only added to their sense that a jigsaw puzzle was forming around them with huge pieces missing.

At the end of their day, Charlie and Lilly had gone for a beer. Feeling frustrated, they decided to call Anita White, SAC of the Johnson City office of the TBI. They knew Anita was a person Joe liked and respected, and they believed the feeling was mutual. Maybe the three women could help one another. Joe had her cell number in his computer.

After a bit of "feeling out" on both sides, the women had agreed to meet on an unofficial basis to share information—pool their knowledge, try to get closer to the truth. Because the conversation was to be off the record, Anita suggested she come to the Dillards' law office in Jonesborough, rather than having Charlie and Lilly visit the TBI, and that she come early, before her workday officially started.

And now here she was, at 7:30 sharp. After cordial introductions, the three women entered the small conference room together, coffees in hand.

Charlie and Lilly showed their cards first. They told Anita about Joe's disappearance and westward journey, and their belief that Joe was hunting for the girl and perhaps possessed some key information. They shared their theory that Jack was being framed as revenge against Joe. They hinted about Sarah's conversation with Tammy Stanton, while keeping the details vague in honor of Sarah's promise to Tammy. They also told Anita about the rumors Erlene had heard about Abby possibly being snatched by a sex ring.

Now it was Anita's turn. "It's my job, as a law enforcement officer, to continue gathering evidence against your brother, Lilly, and I have to tell you: most folks in my office believe he's their man. But if I'm being honest, I don't buy him as a child killer. Never have."

Lilly and Charlie sighed in relief.

"First of all, knowing your father's character and knowing what I do about your family, I can't picture your brother being that kind of person. Second, this thing smells like a frameup to me. Just a vibe I get. It's a little too pat, the way the evidence is coming together. Everything fits a bit too neatly. Third, and this is a biggie, we're getting some intel that your friend Erlene might be right. The Pruitt girl may have been taken by a trafficking ring, and I think her father may have been paid off to facilitate it. An informant swears he saw Abby Pruitt's photo show up on a dark-web site where sex rings 'advertise their wares.' But it was taken down soon afterward. We've been talking to the FBI, and they've picked up some other stuff too." Anita sipped her coffee thoughtfully. "I'm telling you things a law enforcement officer should never tell a civilian, especially a defense attorney. And I'm doing so because of my relationship with your father. I hope I don't need to emphasize how stone-cold confidential this conversation is." She paused again. "But if Abby was taken by a ring, then Jack is innocent, period."

"But why would a sex trafficking ring go to such elaborate measures to frame him and turn this into a public lynching?" Charlie asked. "That's not their M.O., is it? They try to fly below the radar, I'd imagine."

"You're right," Anita said. "And that's the puzzle here. Those two pieces don't go together: high-level framing and sex-ring snatching. But I find that whenever two things don't *seem* to go together, it's often because I'm not looking through a wide enough lens. So I step back and ask myself, 'What's a scenario where these things *do* go together?'"

"And…?"

"I'm not sure yet. But think about this: Whoever is framing Jack has criminal connections and, apparently, plenty of money. Let's say, hypothetically, he's got ties to a trafficking ring that's already in operation. In that case, the easiest way to disappear the Pruitt girl—and make some money on her to boot—is to have the existing operation snatch her. *While* framing Jack. Have your cake and eat it too. Which suggests an organized crime angle to me."

At the mention of organized crime, gooseflesh erupted on Charlie's neck and arms. She thought back on the gold that had been found on her land a few years earlier—the gold she had buried via dynamite blast. It had been originally owned by an organized crime family, hadn't it? The Russos.

Damn. Maybe it wasn't Joe who was being targeted for revenge after all, maybe it was her, Charlie. Maybe the Russos were seeking payback for the family gold—and family *member*—entombed under Buck Mountain. Was that possible? Was that cursed gold reaching out to infect her life once aga—

"Earth to Charlie," said Lilly.

Charlie snapped to attention. How long had she been lost in thought?

"Agent White was asking if we knew of a high-level member of a criminal organization who might have a score to settle with my dad."

Before Charlie could reply, the front door to the law practice burst open and slammed shut. Footsteps pounded across the floor, and Sarah

Dillard appeared in the doorway of the conference room. She looked as pale as if a vampire had been feasting on her. Her eyes locked onto Charlie and Lilly. She didn't even seem to notice Agent White, sitting across the table.

"A man was following Gracie," she said. "Out on the trail yesterday. Scared the living daylights out of her. Thank God Pepper has a good gallop."

Sarah reached out with a phone in her hand, the phone Gracie had used to photograph the man. It was only then she seemed to notice Agent White.

"May I see that phone, please?" said White.

CHAPTER 31

Verna's heart raced as she ran her hand over the red Ford's finish and pictured herself driving it. Was she really going to do this? Was she going to pull the trigger?

A drop of perspiration ran down her side. The car was four years old, it was Ford's lowest-priced model, and it had sixty-eight thousand miles on it, but it still looked and felt like a new car. It would be the newest car Verna Roy had ever owned, that was for sure. Also, the most money she'd ever spent at once.

"Sweet set of wheels, Ms. Roy," said the salesman, "for a sweet price. I can promise you one thing—if you don't buy her today, she'll be gone tomorrow."

Verna bit her nails and grimaced. She wanted the car badly. But it wasn't just the price-tag that was making her sweat. The agency guy had told her not to do anything—what was the word he used?—*conspicuous* for a couple of months. That was why she had driven all the way to Knoxville to shop for a car. To avoid prying eyes. But it wasn't like she'd be buying a Rolls-freaking-Royce. Candy-apple red or not, it was still a used Ford.

"Tell you what, Ms. Roy, I'll give you seven-fifty for your trade-in, 'stead of five. Final offer."

Seven-fifty for my *old beater?* thought Verna. *Is this guy nuts? I better grab this deal before he changes his mind!* "I'll take it." Verna felt her underarms tickle.

The dealer did the paperwork to switch her old plates over to the Ford, and she was driving off the lot in less than an hour. Her first destination in her "new" car was an apartment she wanted to check out in Greeneville.

She'd need to do it on the sly; she was pretty sure if the agency guy knew she was thinking about moving out of her rented trailer in Elizabethton, he'd tell her that was a very "conspicuous" move. But Verna didn't care.

She couldn't stand the thought of spending one more night in that godforsaken trailer. It was like living with Abby's ghost. Everywhere she looked, every corner her eyes landed in, everything she touched, it was Abby, Abby, Abby. Her daughter's stuff was everywhere. And she couldn't very well get rid of any of it. Not yet; that would *really* be a conspicuous move.

She pulled out onto Route 40 East, toward Greeneville, and couldn't believe how smoothly the car accelerated. It held nice and steady in its lane, too, and you could hardly feel the road. The steering was tight, and the tires felt like they all had the same tread.

But as nice as the car was, it didn't make her feel the way she thought it would when she was drooling over it on the lot. Nothing about her new life felt the way she thought it was going to feel. Being kid-free was supposed to make her feel lighter. Verna had birthed Abby when she was still a kid herself and had never known a moment's freedom. Now here she was, footloose at last, Greg locked up for a while, Abby with her new family somewhere.

And Verna still had her looks—more or less—and now some money in her pocket too. She could finally live the single life she'd always dreamed of.

So why did she feel so numb and empty?

She gave the car some gas and zipped over to the fast lane, trying to ignite a spark of excitement. It didn't work.

Alone in the car, with only her thoughts, her mind sunk to that shaky place she hated, that place that made her breath get all shallow and fast. The Anxiety. The agency guy had promised Verna that Abby would go to a good family, one that could better provide for her and maybe even pay for some private athletic coaching, so Abby could get into a top high school. True, it was an "off the books" transaction, he explained, but that was because sometimes good parents had blemishes on their records and couldn't adopt legally. But even though the agency operated outside the law, it had good intentions: matching loving homes with kids in need.

Verna couldn't bear to tell Abby what was being planned for her and hadn't wanted any involvement in the "transfer." All she'd been asked to do, to earn her fee, was pretend to be passed out drunk on the couch, so the agency people could walk in and take Abby quietly and without a fuss—and then report Abby missing in the morning and act like she didn't know how it happened.

She had done the right thing, damn it! Verna knew she was no kind of mom. She could barely take care of *herself*. Abby deserved better. And although things would be tough for a while, Abby would be happier in the long run with real, responsible parents. And without Verna.

Verna had nothing to feel guilty about.

She sped up to pass a semi in the middle lane, trying to enjoy the car's pick-up. It was *so* much nicer to drive than her old beater. Then why the flat feeling?

If everything the agency guy had told her was true, she had absolutely nothing to feel guilty about.

...*If* everything he had told her was true.

But was that what she really believed, deep down in her belly? Did she really believe Abby had been adopted by a new family? That was a question she wanted to avoid like a raw nerve in a bad tooth.

An idea struck Verna like heavenly inspiration. Even with the cost of the car, the down payment on an apartment, and the fund she'd set aside for furniture, she still had plenty of cash left over for something extra for herself. To kick her mood into gear. She made a spur-of-the-moment decision to add another stop in Greeneville before checking out the new apartment.

At an address she'd visited before.

***

Godfrey Edelberg pressed his thumb to the security plate at Red Rock Cottage, his 7,500-square-foot, multi-level home nestled among the rust-colored peaks of Sedona, Arizona. The nine-foot-high Brazilian rosewood door swung open, and he stepped inside. Because of all the traveling he did, and all the larger homes he owned, he didn't get to spend as much time as he liked at some of his favorite little getaways, like this one. It had been over a year since he'd set foot in Red Rock Cottage, but the place smelled fresh, and the glass walls sparkled. His staff was doing a fine job; he'd have to give them a nice bonus at Christmas.

He stepped to the glass wall of the foyer and looked out at his post-card view of Cathedral Rock. Magnificent. Breathtaking. If scenery was everything, he might even consider making Red Rock one of his primary residences.

"Good afternoon, Mr. Edelberg."

"Ah, hello, Quentin," Edelberg said, turning to greet the trim man with the salt-and-pepper hair and three-piece suit. "I've told you a hundred times, call me Godfrey. Or just call me what my friends do… God."

"Yes, Mr. Edelberg," said Quentin Fox with a small smile. "Will you be having a cocktail in your office?"

"In about twenty minutes. First, I want to do my walkthrough and freshen up a bit."

Edelberg struck off at a brisk march, the pace he always used when touring a property—of which he owned dozens. Quentin Fox, his West-Coast property manager and executive assistant, stayed abreast of him step for step.

"How are plans coming for the Golf Weekend?" Edelberg asked as they crossed the massive Great Room with its cathedral ceilings, exposed beams, and multiple entertainment centers. Every room had floor-to-ceiling windows that looked out on the red rocks.

"Excellent, sir. Tee times are set for eight a.m. Saturday and Sunday at Seven Canyons. Chef Matignon is coming a day early to begin his preparations, and the guest quarters are being freshened as we speak."

"Perfect."

Godfrey Edelberg's Golf Weekends were legendary amongst an elite group of regular invitees that included a former president, an A-list movie star, CEOs of Fortune 100 companies, high-end real estate investors, royalty, and several top government officials from around the globe. Edelberg always called them Golf Weekends and took great care to ensure that the weekend's prime activities revolved around golf. But it was the evening entertainment—which Edelberg always presented as a minor afterthought, a bit of boys' fun and games—for which the Golf Weekends were famous. Or infamous. And for which the men really came.

Edelberg and Fox toured the dining room, the chef's kitchen, the spa, the screening room, the multiple outdoor decks looking out on various stunning vistas of Sedona, and the six guest rooms in the bottom-floor Guest Wing. Everything was in tip-top shape.

Edelberg concluded the walkthrough at his office. After showering in the all-marble *en suite* bathroom, donning his bathrobe, and receiving his Absolut Crystal martini from the help, he closed and locked the door. Edelberg's sprawling office was more than a workspace. It featured a large lounge/entertainment area with an 80-inch TV and a wet bar, a putting green, and an extra bedroom to the side. The "office" was the only room in the house that didn't have windows. These days you had to think about things like drones and high-powered telephoto lenses.

And what happened in Edelberg's office needed to *stay* in Edelberg's office.

Edelberg fired up the iMac on his dining-table-sized desk. He brought up the picture of the girl—*one* of the girls—he had reserved for the weekend. Hair falling over one eye, provocative half-smile. This one was special, a one-in-a-million find. She had the exact look that drove him wild, and he hadn't hesitated to offer a six-figure fee to retain "exclusivity rights" on her until the party. He couldn't believe she'd be here in this room in just a few days.

Godfrey Edelberg untied his robe.

CHAPTER 32

Phoenix, Arizona is half the size of the state of Rhode Island. Five Knoxvilles would fit inside it, a dozen Johnson Cities. And yet I'd shown up here on nothing more than the word of Merlo Maroni and some low-level lackey that the sex ring had a residence in or around the city, and that it was referred to as "Black Canyon."

What was my plan to find it? Start knocking on doors?

It was early afternoon as I arrived in the Valley of the Sun. I wanted to use my time well, but I had no direction to go in except the results of a web search Stony and I had done this morning while talking on the phone. We'd turned up four main "black canyon" hits for Phoenix:

1. Route 17, the main north-south highway through the upper part of the city, was known as the Black Canyon Freeway. So, if the residence was located anywhere along that main artery, that might be the reason for its nickname. That narrowed my search down not at all.

2. Black Canyon Trail was an eighty-mile wilderness trail that ran roughly parallel to the Black Canyon Freeway for a big chunk of its length. According to Google Maps, the trail didn't seem to go near many houses, but it did cross inhabited roads in a few spots.

3. There was an apartment community in north Phoenix known as Black Canyon Heights. But if the Sealy residence was any indication, it was unlikely the trafficking ring would be running its operations out of a densely populated urban neighborhood.

4. And finally, there was an unincorporated rural community north of Phoenix known as Black Canyon City. It didn't look like much of a city on the map.

I'd spent the previous night in El Paso after a long day of driving. My hope, when I checked into my Travelodge digs, was that I'd be able to recreate my experience of the previous two nights and that Caroline would visit me again in her kayak, maybe stay longer. But third time wasn't the charm. I sat in the motel-room chair for two hours, nursing a tumbler of bourbon, but the only visitation I received was from a drunk hooker knocking on the wrong door.

Yesterday's experiment of talking aloud to Caroline, however, had blossomed into a full-blown habit. All day long, as I carved up the miles on Route 10, I'd been chatting with the love of my life as if she were present in the car. Anyone observing me from a passing vehicle would conclude I was either talking on a Bluetooth or out of my damn mind. As for the latter possibility, the jury wasn't in yet, but for some reason I didn't *feel* crazy talking to Caroline.

I felt comforted. Calmed. And I needed all the calming I could get.

"Look at this sign, Sweetheart. 'Caution: Water on Road During Rain.' Who knew?"

Talking to Caroline was the only thing preventing the tension in me from exploding.

Every now and then I would ask a yes/no question and see if I caught her smell again or felt any other kind of response. And sometimes I'd swear I would. Not the smell anymore, but maybe a little firing of the nerves. Of course, it might have been just my own sixth sense at play, the thing Stony calls the *ping*. She says she couldn't do her job without it. The ping tells her when she's following a promising lead, not just a dead end.

But this felt like something more. It felt stronger. Was Caroline really communicating with me from the Great Beyond? Doubtful. But I clung to the possibility that she might be.

As I drove past South Mountain, in the southern end of Phoenix, heading north, an idea struck me. Maybe the ping—the Caroline ping—could actually help me in my search.

I exited Route 10 and parked in the lot of a fast-food joint under the bright Phoenix sun. I ran inside to grab a meal and use the mapping app on my phone. As I scarfed down a Hatch chile burger, I studied the map and plotted my experiment. First, I would drive to the half-dozen locations where the Black Canyon Trail intersected roadways. Then I would drive the full length of the Black Canyon Freeway, up and down. I would also explore the Black Canyon Heights neighborhood. All the while, I would feel for the ping. If I sensed it at any point, I would stop and focus my searching on that area. If I didn't sense the ping anywhere within Phoenix proper, I would drive north to Black Canyon City.

It was a plan, I guessed. A bad one, but the best I had.

Maybe Stony would call me with a brilliant idea. I hoped so.

***

"Grab an end," said Shane, taking hold of the dresser and tipping it toward Tommy.

"Why do we gotta move all this furniture?" Tommy asked, stepping around to the other side of the wooden piece. "Why do I gotta give up my room?"

"Because Mr. Paolo said so, that's why," Shane replied. "And because the workmen are here, and they need room to… *work*."

Tommy looked around the back bedroom where he and Shane stood—Tommy's room—and put on his work gloves. He didn't understand why all these changes were happening and why he had to share a room with Aaron now. Yesterday, a carpenter and a locksmith had been here. They'd replaced Tommy's door with a thick, heavy one. Replaced the door frame too. The locksmith had installed three heavy-duty locks—one at the top of the door, one in the middle, and one near the bottom—that locked with a key from the outside, not the inside. Workmen had removed the ceiling fan, too, and installed a plain bulb socket. And now they were coming in to do something to the walls. It looked like they were turning his former room into a jail cell.

"I don't like it," he said to Shane.

"Well, I'll let Mr. Paolo know. I'm sure that will inform his decision-making process. Come on, grab your end."

"Does this got anything to do with that new guy that's coming? Mr. Paolo's boss?"

"Goof-Tard, if I knew anything, I wouldn't be working here. Lift, let's go!"

Tommy and Shane hoisted the dresser and walked out of the room, passing two guys carrying a large panel of sheet metal toward the bedroom.

Tommy had a bad feeling, a feeling that things were changing for the worse. Even though he didn't like the people who worked there and *really* didn't like the stuff the kids were forced to do, he did like the freedom you had inside the house. Things were peaceful, in their own way. If you didn't have a job to do, you could just hang around or play video games. Now locks were getting put on inner doors and people were acting all keyed up and nervous.

As Shane rounded the hallway corner, gripping the dresser, his phone rang. He set his end down to answer it. The call lasted about five seconds.

"Okay," Shane said, turning to look at Tommy. "The new associates are going to be here in about an hour. After we clear the rest of the crap out of the back room, go hit the two middle rooms with some Endust and the vac. Chop, chop! Let's go!"

***

The moving-truck stopped, and the engine shut off.

"We have arrived at our destination, ladies," said the driver's voice on the walkie-talkie. "Thank you for choosing Southwest."

Abby found no humor in his "joke." She looked at the other three girls in the cold, battery-operated lamplight of the makeshift travel chamber they'd been riding in for days. "So, we need to decide now," she said to them. "Do we stick together or not?"

"What does that even mean?" asked Deja with a sneer.

"Just what it sounds like. We watch out for each other. Have each other's backs. Share stuff we hear. If things go bad, we work together as a team."

No one spoke for a few moments.

"I'm in," said Hope. "I care about you guys. Let's watch out for each other, you know. Try not to let anything bad happen to our sisters."

"I'm in too," said Selena. "We stay friends. What about you, Deja?"

"I say we got enough to do, watchin' our own backs."

"Come on, Deja, we need you," said Abby. "All for one, and one for all. What do you say?"

Before she could reply, a swath of daylight flooded the chamber as a column of boxes slid away from the wall of packed cargo. The girls turned to see the driver silhouetted against a rectangle of sunlit desert.

"Welcome to Black Canyon."

CHAPTER 33

Leon Bates parked his cruiser in a no-parking zone in front of the federal building on Market St. in downtown Knoxville. He figured no one would ticket a Sheriff's Department's vehicle, even one from a different county. He grabbed the file folder from the seat, locked the door, and marched toward the sprawling, cupola-topped, Georgian-style edifice that housed the Howard H. Baker federal courthouse. It also housed the field offices for Tennessee's U.S. Senators and members of the U.S. House of Representatives.

His destination? The office of Senator Todd McGinty. Bates had been told by phone that McGinty couldn't see him today, but he didn't intend to miss this opportunity to catch the senator in person. McGinty spent at least half his time in Washington, D.C., and then divided the rest of his time—when he wasn't golfing—amongst five Tennessee field offices. And today was his rare day in Knoxville. Bates hoped that showing up in uniform might be enough to convince the senator to squeeze him in. If not, he would simply make a nuisance of himself. And if that didn't work, Leon Bates had other forms of persuasion at his disposal.

He passed through the entry door flanked by white columns, talked his way past the security station using his law-enforcement status, and strode down the long hall toward the first-floor office suite. The heels of his dress shoes echoed on the tile.

"Your appointment time, sir?" said the receptionist in the senator's waiting area.

"Don't have one, I'm afraid, ma'am. But I'm here in an official capacity, as you can infer by these fine duds I'm wearing." He gave the receptionist his most captivating smile.

"Regardless, sir. You still need an appointment. Senator McGinty is very busy today."

"You might want to tell the senator I'm here on a matter of some sensitivity, involving him, which I will be happy to discuss in front of these good constituents…" Leon swept his arm toward the seven or eight people occupying waiting seats. "…If he would prefer not to have a private conversation."

***

"Sheriff! Pleasure to meet you," said Senator Todd McGinty, rising from behind his antique mahogany partner's desk. His combed-back, salt-and-pepper pompadour looked frozen to his head like sculptors' plaster.

"Actually, we've met before, Senator. At a fundraiser in Johnson City, last winter. I don't expect you'd remember me. You were shaking a lot of hands that night."

"I imagine I was, Sheriff. Nature of the beast. Sorry about all that business out there." He nodded toward the reception area beyond the doorway. "They call them gatekeepers for a reason, am I right? Can I get you something to drink? I'd offer you some fine Tennessee corn-and-barley product, but I'm sure you don't imbibe while in uniform. Water? Coffee?"

Leon waved off the offer and sat in one of the guest seats, unbidden. He lay the file folder in his lap.

"Then how can I help you, Sheriff Bates?"

Bates took an unhurried breath and looked around the dark-wood-accented office. He let his eyes sweep across the framed photos of McGinty's family members and assorted global dignitaries and then come to rest on a shelf of trophies.

"You're a golfing man, isn't that right, Senator?"

"I've been known to shoot a round of pasture pool now and again. You, Sheriff?"

"Never much saw the point, sir. Why spend years of your life and thousands of your dollars trying to get better at something that guys like Tiger Woods will still embarrass you at, even on their worst day? Naw, I figure if

I'm going to invest my time getting good at something, it should be something I can truly excel at. In a world-class way."

"And what might that be for you, Sheriff Bates?" asked McGinty with an amused grin.

"Discovery. Sniffing things out. I like to think I'm exceptionally good at that." Bates beamed at McGinty with a warm smile and cold eyes. "I'm kinda like a dog that way. When I catch a scent of something, I can't seem to let go of it till I track it down."

"Do tell, Sheriff. And your canine activities involve me in some way?"

"I understand you have some pretty high-level golf buddies, Senator."

"As I'm sure you can imagine, being a holder of public office yourself, I prefer to keep my private life private."

"I would prefer to keep mine private, too, if it involved swinging wood with the likes of Godfrey Edelberg."

A flash of unease skittered across McGinty's eyes. "It's no secret that I've spent time with Mr. Edelberg. As have literally hundreds of other elected officials, celebrities, business figures... Mr. Edelberg is a highly influential man with a wide social circle."

"Indeed. But I often find, when it comes to social circles, that there are circles within circles. And sometimes circles within circles within circles."

"I'm finding *your* circling rather tedious, Sheriff."

"You should be grateful for my indirectness, Senator." Bates shifted forward in his seat, lifting his hat brim to show more of his face. "For there are things that once spoken aloud cannot be unsaid."

McGinty rose from his seat, closed his office door, and sat again. "I have no idea what you're—"

"Let me try it this way," interrupted Bates. "Over the years, I have developed an extensive and well-cultivated grapevine covering a fairly wide swath of our good nation." A key branch in that vine was Erlene Barlowe, who had recently reached out to Bates with eye-opening rumors, which he had vetted with great interest and diligence. "And according to what I'm hearing through that grapevine, Godfrey Edelberg has a particular circle of friends who share a particular set of tastes they like to indulge in a particular way. And when this particular circle gathers for a weekend on the golf links, golf is not, shall we say, the topmost thing on their minds."

"I think I'm ready for you to leave, Sheriff."

"Fine, McGinty." Bates stood, dropping all pretense of gentility. "I gave you a chance to play nicely. Opportunity withdrawn." He splayed his hands on the desk and leaned forward. "Here's what I know." Leon Bates didn't actually *know* everything he was about to say; he only suspected some of it. But, like Joe Dillard, he had learned that you don't betray doubt when laying out your case to an opponent. You act like you have all the facts, and then you read their reactions. "I know Godfrey Edelberg is a pedophile. I know he likes girls miles below the age of consent. And I know he enjoys sharing his 'hobby' with like-minded individuals at his homes and resorts all over the world. Individuals such as U.S. senators, I'm told."

"That's enough, Bates!" said McGinty, rising from his seat to meet Bates' eyes.

"Sit down, McGinty!"

"I want you out of here, or I will call security."

"Sit down, jagoff, or I'll open that door and yell the rest of what I have to say."

McGinty sat.

Bates went on. "I also know, as does everyone, that Godfrey Edelberg is absurdly wealthy, and so he gets away with his little pre-dilections. Barely even tries to hide 'em. But Edelberg is also a busy and clever man. He doesn't dirty his hands procuring the 'talent' he hires for his amusement. For that, he relies on the services of discreet professional traffickers. One organization in particular. This organization recruits kids from all around the country and occasionally kidnaps them outright."

McGinty gave no reaction, but Bates thought he saw something shift beneath his façade.

"When they acquire a new prospect with potentially high… retail value," Bates continued with a look of distaste, "they post a photograph on a secure dark-web site, allowing their high-end clients—like your pal Godfrey—to bid on 'first rights' to that individual."

"That's a fascinating theory, Sheriff. Are you also a fan of *Ancient Aliens*? My daughter loves that show." He folded his arms, affecting boredom. "What do you want from me?"

"What I *want* is for every grown man who has ever defiled a child for his own pleasure to writhe in the fires of Hell forever. What I'll settle for is this…"

Bates pulled a computer-printed photo of Abby Pruitt from his file folder and showed it to McGinty. "I have reason to believe this girl's photo was posted on the website and that she may have been 'spoken for' by someone. Someone of means. Here's what I need you to do. Godfrey Edelberg is hosting a 'golf weekend' in a couple of days. I want you to get yourself invited."

"Mr. Edelberg plans his events well in advance, for a limited number of guests. I can't just call him up and invite myself to his house."

"Figure it out. Promise him something. Do what you senators do. And while you're there, I want you to ask around, put out feelers, talk to your golf buddies. See if anyone has any information on this girl. I will not regard your actions as an admission of guilt. In fact, if you are helpful to me, I will do everything in my power to make sure you're painted as a cooperator, a whistleblower, an outraged public servant doing the right thing. But if anything happens to this girl, and I find out your 'circle of friends' was involved, I will destroy you."

The two men faced off again in silence.

"Here, take this." Bates handed the folder containing the printouts of Abby's photo to McGinty. "If you want the electronic version, let me know where to send the file."

Bates turned and headed toward the door.

"Cocky bastard, aren't we?" said the senator in a voice sharp enough to stop Bates in his tracks. "Blithely assuming you're the only one who keeps track of your fellow elected officials' extracurricular activities."

Bates turned toward McGinty, his brow raised.

"How do you think I got elected U.S. Senator in Tennessee as a lifelong Florida native with two DUIs under my belt and a liberal voting record in my House career? My haircut? No, Sheriff Bates. By *knowing* things. Come here, I'd like to show you something on my computer. I think you'll find it fascinating."

CHAPTER 34

Verna Roy strolled from the kitchen to the living room of her new apartment, taking in the gleaming linoleum and spanking new wall-to-wall carpeting. She was feeling *much* better, now that the Oxy had kicked in. She'd been able to score a whole bottle but had waited until after meeting with the new landlord before taking any.

The interview and walkthrough had gone as smoothly as a warm knife through Crisco. It hadn't hurt that she'd offered to pay first and last months' rent, plus security deposit, cash on the barrelhead. It also hadn't hurt that she'd taken her bra off before the meeting. That decision had sealed the deal, she believed. Especially after she dropped her car keys "by mistake" and bent over to pick them up, letting her tank-top work its magic. They'd signed the papers right on the spot, and she was given the apartment keys, along with enthusiastic offers of help with anything she needed with her move.

She felt a weight lift from her shoulders as she toured her new home. The third-floor apartment was partially furnished and included a bed, so she didn't even need to shop for furniture right away. All she needed was some sheets, pillows, towels, and other supplies, and she'd just returned from Walmart with two bulging bags full.

Off the living room was the bedroom and another carpeted room. It was more square footage than she needed, but it felt good to have some space around her after living in that cramped trailer full of Abby's stuff. Still, she'd been nervous about renting a new place until a brilliant idea occurred: she could keep both places for a while! That way she wouldn't arouse any suspicion. During the day, she could spend some time at the Elizabethton trailer, so people would still see her there now and then—if anyone was looking.

But after sundown, when the ghosts came out, she could be here in Greeneville.

As Verna unpacked her bags of new purchases at the kitchen table, a rush of euphoria moved up her spine and into her brain. Whoa. She was *really* feeling the Oxy now.

She strolled out onto the balcony off the kitchen. She couldn't believe she had her own balcony too. It looked out on the twin building next door, not the French Riviera, but still, a balcony was a balcony. One thing she loved about this place was that a few of the tenants still used those old-fashioned pulley clotheslines that ran between the buildings. Though some people thought clotheslines looked trashy, Verna liked them. They reminded her of childhood and fresh-smelling sheets. Verna wanted to set hers up right away. A clothesline said home to her.

She went back to the kitchen and found the hank of nylon rope she'd bought at Walmart, then carried it back out to the balcony. Studying the pulley on her balcony and the one on the building twenty feet away, she burst out laughing. She had no idea how to string the rope from one building to the other. This realization struck her as profoundly funny. She laughed so hard she collapsed to her butt, right there on the balcony, gasping for air and almost passing out.

And then she had an amazing idea! Using a steak knife, she cut a length of the strong yellow rope about fifteen feet long. She tied one end to the balcony railing. With the other end, she formed the special loop her cousin Brenda had taught her to make when she was only twelve.

Noose was the correct term for it, she believed.

She placed the noose around her neck, climbed over the railing, and stepped out into empty space.

***

Jack looked up when he heard the cell door unlock. The merest shifting of his facial muscles caused the new stitches in his cheek to sing out in pain. He was lying on his mattress in the "boat"—new guy always got the boat, a movable plastic shell on the floor—using the tablet device assigned to his cell. The device, though not connected to the Internet, allowed the men to read books, play games, and watch movies and videos. It was a new concept in jails.

The door opened and Badger entered, returning from his therapy session.

"What's up, Badge?" said Jack. He tried to keep his voice light, but his hand unconsciously moved to the bandage on his face.

Badger Daley was one of the two "cellies" Jack had been assigned after moving to unit D. Jack suspected Leon Bates had made those arrangements, perhaps at his father's request. And although he appreciated the protective intervention, the resulting situation was more than a little strange. An attorney and his active client housed together in the same jail cell? Jack wondered how many times in history that had ever happened. Not many, he wagered.

Badger wasn't wearing his customary brash smile today. Instead, he sat sullenly at the metal desk-table attached to the wall, ignoring Jack in pointed fashion.

"Bad therapy session?" Jack asked. "What, they didn't accept your insurance plan?"

Badger didn't laugh. Silence ensued.

"Therapy went just fine," replied Badger at last. "But you and me, we got us a problem, Couns'lor. And it's bigger than that gulch on your cheek."

"Oh?" said Jack, rising from the "boat" and approaching Badger. "What's that?"

Badger indicated the matter was sensitive, rolling his eyes toward cellmate number three in the top bunk: Julio Gomes, a placid giant of few words and fewer teeth, awaiting trial on grand larceny charges. Another gift from the cellmate gods—i.e., Leon Bates.

"Julio, you wouldn't mind watching a movie for a while, with your earphones on, would you?" said Badger.

Gomes shrugged amicably. Jack handed him the tablet, and Gomes plugged his earphones in. Jack crouched beside Badger, and Badger said in a low tone, "I wasn't aimin' to tell you this, but now I need to. Your daddy come here the day you was incarcerated. They wouldn't let him see you 'cause you didn't have your visitors list yet, but they let him see me, 'cause he's on my legal team. Me and your daddy, well, we made a deal."

"A deal?"

Badger nodded. "I would try to protect you while you was in here, and if I done my job good, he'd go the extra mile to try to get me out. Call in favors, pull strings, do whatever."

Jack wanted to protest that he didn't need protection but thought better of it.

"No offense, Couns'lor Jack," Badger went on, "but you's just my court-appointed defender. And a pretty dang green one at that. Your daddy, though, he's a boney-fide high legal mucky-muck."

"No offense taken, Badger. My father's a good man to have on your side."

"Problem is," Badger said, "I ain't been keepin' up my end of the bargain too good, what with lettin' you get your face sliced open like a catfish belly at a fish-fry. And things is about to get a whole lot worse."

A mantle of dread descended on Jack. "What do you mean, Badge?"

Badger's eyes met Jack's with a look of compassion that worried Jack by its implications. "Someone done put a hit out on you. Not to kill you, but to do things to where you wish they had. Remove a few body parts you mighta been plannin' on usin'."

Jack's heart sped up, but he did his best to appear calm. "Who?"

"Someone from outside," Badger said. "Someone big. I got no power over a situation like that. Truth be told, Couns'lor Jack, the only reason I got any clout in here at all is 'cause I been locked up so many times, I can play the system like a Fender Strat. But when someone from the outside, someone with power in the real world, orders a hit, there ain't aught I can do about it."

"Who is it? Who gave the order? Do you know?"

Badger shook his head solemnly. "Couldn't tell you even if I did."

"Where's it supposed to happen? When?"

"Sundee. Before or after—maybe *durin'*—church service."

"Well… what if I just don't go to church service?"

"You make it hard for them to get to you, they go after your people on the outside. That's the message I was gave to give you. Sorry, Jack. Don't hate the messenger."

Jack stood up, walked back to his floor-mattress, and grabbed his "chirper." In addition to the tablet device the cellmates shared, each inmate was assigned a smaller gadget, about the size of a cellphone, on which they could send text messages to preapproved family members.

Jack caught his reflection in the glass of the chirper. He wondered what the seven-stitch gash in his face would look like when the bandage came off. It would leave a lifelong scar, no doubt. Great look for a criminal; not so terrific for an attorney at law.

But it was nothing compared to what was coming next. Jack found his short list of contacts on the chirper and tapped "Charlie."

He had no intention of telling her what was in store for him. But he did text a one-word message—HURRY!—and hit send.

CHAPTER 35

Augustus Paolo felt nervous knocking on the door to his own office. As operations manager, he had offices in each of the seven residences distributed around the country, all near major cities. He'd just arrived at the Black Canyon site, fresh from Sky Harbor airport.

"Come," said the flat voice from inside.

Paolo's knot of anxiety tightened when he saw the unfamiliar figure sitting behind his desk. But he affected a pleasant smile for the tall blond man with the broad shoulders, cold green eyes, and disfigured ear. El Espectro. Here. In person. Key figure in the parent organization of which Paolo's modest enterprise was just a small part.

"Sit," ordered the man known variously as The Ghost, The Surgeon, El Espectro, and a half-dozen other monikers; the man about whom people whispered, *He can appear and disappear at will, He can be in two places at once. He kills for pleasure...*

"Relax." Paolo's skin prickled as he took a seat. The Ghost's eyes bored into him as if gazing straight into his head. "This is not a disciplinary visit. If it was, you would know it." The Ghost's voice creaked like an old coffin hinge, and he spoke in short, choppy phrases. "You have nothing to fear... yet."

Paolo pulled in a breath. If this wasn't a disciplinary visit, then why had the house been taken over by his boss in such a heavy-handed way?

"But you must have questions."

Paolo had dozens of them. Why had The Ghost descended on his operation? Had Paolo done something wrong? Why had a pair of armed men who looked like soldiers been stationed in the house? Why had one of the bedrooms been turned into a high-security prison chamber? But Augustus Paolo knew his place. "I'm confident you have good reasons for being here, sir."

"That I do. The Black Canyon site... is well-suited... for handling some... business that has come up. But as soon as my business is finished... I will be out of your hair."

"You're welcome here anytime, sir."

"That is correct, Paolo. I am."

Paolo shifted uncomfortably in his seat. "May I ask what your business is about, sir?"

The Ghost's eyes flashed, and Paolo was afraid he'd said the wrong thing. "It has to do with the new girl. Abigail Pruitt. Among other things."

"Ah yes," Paolo said, affecting distaste. "Pruitt."

"As you may know... I acquired her for a purpose. Not only for her 'marketability.' She has served my purpose already. And so, her value to me, alive... is no longer high."

"But sir, her value to the operation is still *quite* high," Paolo hazarded to point out. "She's a 'premier associate.' She can command top dollar for at least another year or two."

"Correct. That means we have a difficult decision to make. What to do with the Pruitt girl? Tell me what you know... about her."

"She already tried to escape once, in Texas, and very nearly succeeded. And here, look at this." Paolo took out his phone and located a video file. "I hid a camera in the transport truck."

Paolo played some clips of the conversations amongst the four girls, in which Abby tried to convince the others they were being lied to and urged them to work together as a team.

The Ghost frowned. "I see. Troublemaker."

"The bad apple that spoils the bunch, sir."

"What do you suggest we do, Paolo?"

"Well, sir, as you know, her services have been booked—at an all-time-high price, I might add—for a gathering in Sedona this weekend."

"Yes. Godfrey Edelberg." The Ghost leaned back thoughtfully in the office chair, then seemed to come to a decision. "The girl will work the party. Until then, she will be tightly managed. And when she comes back after the job, she will be treated as a... 'business loss.'"

"There is one other option, sir. Our Eastern European operations would be happy to take her off our hands. For a very nice fee, I'm sure. She'd never be heard from again."

"I can make better use of her... dead. In fact..." An expression vaguely resembling a smile crept over The Surgeon's face, icing Paolo's blood. "I'm expecting a guest here soon. I will make him watch as I do the job. And I will do it in my... unique way. Burn it into his brain-meat... for the rest of his days... what few of those remain."

***

All afternoon I'd been exploring Phoenix by car. I'd driven up and down Route 17 twice, stopping at random exits to look around. I'd visited all the spots where roads crossed the Black Canyon Trail, and I'd circled the Black Canyon Heights apartments multiple times. I'd even been up to Black Canyon City and driven down every desolate mountain road I could find.

Not the slightest hint of the "ping." No gut reaction to anything.

"Please help me, Sweetheart," I said to the empty seat beside me. "You promised you'd be with me all the way. But what good is it if you won't communicate with me?"

No response. I no longer had the sense Caroline was hearing my words. Perhaps that had just been temporary insanity on my part. But I continued to talk to her anyway. It helped diffuse my tension and prevented me from going even crazier.

"I'm falling asleep at the wheel here, Sweetheart," I announced, around 4:45. The endless hours of driving in the Phoenix sun were taking their toll. "Here's where you're supposed to poke me in the arm and tell me to pull over before I get us both killed."

No response again. I spotted a Hampton Inn off the freeway and decided to check in. Take a nap and get out of the "rush hour" traffic, such as it was. Later, I would hit the road again, revisiting all my Black Canyon spots and hoping for a sign from Caroline.

I found my room and collapsed, fully dressed, on the bedspread.

Sometime later, I had the dream again.

Not Caroline in the kayak. The rape.

My uncle Raymond on the bed. Me, looking down from above, as if from another dimension, unable to stop him. My sister Sarah, a kid, beneath him. Then she became Abby Pruitt. Then Sarah again. Then a blend of the two girls—fused in some mysterious way.

I awoke, gasping for air, and sat bolt upright on the bed. Rage formed into a hot ball in my belly, eclipsing the fear and helplessness. I wanted to punch a wall. Or better still, a face. I noticed my phone vibrating on the bed stand. Stony. I hit the green button and said, "Yeah?" with an unintended edge.

"Joe, I don't know why I didn't think of this earlier. Maroni had his phone backed up on the Cloud! I was able to log into his account. I've got the entire contents of his phone up on my computer." I was chilled once again by the fact that Maroni still hadn't closed his phone accounts. "I went through his web searches and found something." She directed me where to look on his physical phone, which I was still carrying. I found the page she was referring to. It was a Google Map search showing directions to a specific address in Black Canyon City.

I was out the door and into my rented Camry in twelve seconds flat.

***

Tommy seized his NinjaGrip-360 bug grabber, happy to be out of the house and to have some free time for an hour or two. He didn't like it when Mr. Paolo visited. He *really* didn't like this new guy with the blond hair and the ugly ear-stump. And he hated the changes happening in the house—the locks on his old bedroom door, the guys with the rifles...

He hoped hunting scorpions would bring him peace, as it usually did. He went to his favorite hunting place: the patch of desert trees and cacti about twenty yards behind the house. The scorpions loved this spot. There was lots of plant debris on the ground, with plenty of insects to eat, and the palm trees dropped their old fronds and chunks of bark here. Great hiding places for *Centruroides sculpturatus*.

It was a warm, dark evening. Perfect for hunting. He turned on the U.V. light, pulled the trigger to open the grabber's fingers, and kicked aside a piece of bark.

A powerful arm grabbed his neck from behind in a stranglehold, and a man spoke quietly into his ear, "Don't make a sound or I will snap your neck like a twig."

CHAPTER 36

"Let's walk," the man said to Tommy from behind, pressing something hard into his back. "That's a gun. Don't test my will to use it."

The big man loosened his grip on Tommy's neck slightly and pushed him out of the bushy area in the direction of the big rock formation about sixty yards away. "If I let go of your neck, will you do anything stupid?"

Tommy shook his head no. The man released Tommy's neck but kept the gun pressed to his back as they took the long walk to the back side of the rock formation, away from the view of the house. Tommy hated this place. This was where the bodies were buried—one body in particular. Tommy never came here on his own. He thought of the rock formation as one big tombstone.

The man ordered Tommy to sit in the dirt, facing out toward the desert, then sat behind him. Tommy still hadn't seen his face. "Tell me about the house on the hill," said the man.

Tommy gave the answer he'd been trained to give: "It's a g-group home for ad-ad-adolescents with mental, emotional, and substance abuse issues." All the trafficking ring's residences had, in fact, been designed to resemble group homes, in case uninvited company showed up, asking questions.

"Are you lying to me right now?" The man pushed the gun into Tommy's back.

Tommy's mind went blank. He had not been trained on how to deal with that simple question. "Yes."

"Let's start over, then. Here's what I think..."

The man spoke for a while, telling Tommy what he thought about the house. His ideas were mostly right. He said he thought it was a place where teenage kids were kept when they weren't being forced to have sex with people for money. He thought there were other places like it and that the kids moved from place to place. He showed Tommy a picture of a girl he thought might be at the house now, and he was right about that too—she was one of the girls who'd come in the truck today. One thing he was wrong about. He thought Tommy was one of the kids that did the sex stuff. That part wasn't true. Not anymore. But the man was right about most of it.

The man sounded angry about the house. Just like Tommy was. For a long, long time, Tommy had been hoping and praying someone from the outside would find out about the house and would come here and try to shut it down. Was this angry-sounding giant the one? Was he the answer to Tommy's prayers?

"Are you a p-policeman?" Tommy asked the man.

"No, I'm not. But I plan to tell the police, and a lot of other people, about this place once I get the girl out of here."

"M-maybe I can help you."

***

"Come in, Miss Abigail, don't be shy. Shyness is hardly a virtue here."

Abby hobbled through the doorway of the back bedroom, no longer using her crutch. She took note of the heavy door with the three deadbolt locks on its edge. The hatch in the center of the door looked like something designed for feeding a zoo animal.

Her pulse shifted into high gear as she surveyed the empty room, devoid of all furnishings. Standing in the middle of the floor were two men with their hands folded in front of them. One of them wore a familiar pair of orange-tinted lenses and an expensive sweater. Mr. Paolo. The other, a stranger with an odd-looking ear, stood six inches taller and had green eyes that looked utterly soulless. He was holding a complicated-looking pair of scissors, like you might see on a tray of hospital tools. Abby's pulse shifted gears again.

"You probably didn't expect to see me again so soon," said Paolo. "I earn a lot of frequent-flyer miles in my job. This man here—they call him

The Surgeon, but think of him as my boss. We all answer to someone, right, Miss Abigail? My boss is not happy with the things he's been hearing lately, and he thinks we need to run a tighter ship. What do you think, Abby?"

Abby was frozen with fear but knew she'd better answer. "Um… I don't know, Mr. Paolo."

"For example," Paolo continued, "he was displeased to hear that you had sprained your ankle during an escape attempt. Damaging the goods, upsetting our drivers. He was even more displeased when I told him that your friends came to me shortly after the truck arrived here. They told me all about your attempts to stir up rebellion in the ranks."

A stab of betrayal pierced Abby's heart. Her new "sisters" had already turned on her? They'd only been pretending to be her friends the whole time in the truck?

"It has become apparent," said Paolo, "that we cannot trust you out amongst 'the general population.' So welcome to your new quarters."

Abby regarded the boarded-up window, the bare light bulb on the ceiling, the hard wooden floor, and the metal-reinforced walls. Suddenly, it all hit her like a roundhouse punch: the terror, the pain, the betrayal, the confusion, of the past several days. And now this—a prison cell to live in. Her knees gave out, and she collapsed to the floor. She rolled onto her side in the fetal position and moaned, willing the world to go away.

The men watched her in silence for a full minute.

"Get up," Paolo ordered. "Up!"

Abby knew better than to disobey. Her ankle screamed as she pushed herself to stand.

"This room is not for you," Paolo said at last. "We merely wanted to get your attention. Did we succeed?"

Abby nodded furiously.

"Good. Then I expect your total cooperation from this point forward. Any further trouble from you will be handled by..." He gestured toward The Surgeon, who stared expressionlessly, giving the surgical scissors a single snip.

Abby bowed her head, cowed, and slipped out of the room.

The tall blond man turned to Paolo. "Smart. Telling her the other girls turned on her. Instead of the truth. You have potential, Paolo. I always said so."

***

I hated roughing the kid up and threatening him. He seemed like an "innocent." Not that he had an intellectual disability, exactly, but there was something about the way he spoke and processed information that told me he had mental or emotional challenges. Still, he was my best shot at learning what I needed to know, so I pressed him.

We sat behind the rock formation, talking, in the dark, for quite some time. I eventually put the gun away and let him see my face in the moonlight. We were starting to build some trust, and I wanted that to continue.

The kid was cagey with me at first—I didn't blame him—but at last the dam broke and he told me everything. Yes, this was the place they called Black Canyon, and it was part of a sex trafficking ring. It "serviced" metro Phoenix mainly, but also Tucson, Sedona, Flagstaff, Prescott, and other localities. Yes, Abby was here; she arrived today.

At my urging, the kid told me his own story too. His name was Tommy, and he was from Lawrence, Massachusetts. Though he spoke in simple, concrete language, I was able to learn that he grew up in a rough neighborhood. His parents were druggies who would disappear for long periods, leaving him and his brother, Chris, to fend for themselves. Chris was a year younger than Tommy but was a streetwise kid who took care of Tommy in a big-brother role-reversal way. Chris turned tricks to earn money for the brothers to live on. But then one day, Chris told Tommy they had to flee because the state was going to put them in a "home." That was when they hooked up with the traffickers, though Tommy was fuzzy on those details.

They had lived together in residences in Maine, the Chicago area, and California. Chris was the good-looking, high-value brother, but he insisted on keeping Tommy with him wherever he went. Not long after they arrived in Phoenix, Chris had been assigned a hookup with a sketchy john up in Jerome, an old mining town in the mountains, and had gotten stabbed. He died in the residence a few hours later and was buried out here in the desert with the others. And now the management kept Tommy around—out of some vestigial sense of duty, it seemed. He cleaned the house and did other odd jobs to earn his keep.

I believed his story; he didn't seem capable of making up such details. In fact, even though I was holding a gun on him, he seemed almost relieved to talk to me, like he'd been waiting years to find a listening ear. But when I tried to enlist his help to sneak into the house, his defenses went up. He told me couldn't help me with that, especially now, he said. There were new guys in the house, guys with guns. Things were tense. Trouble was brewing.

Was he telling the truth? Who knew?

I needed a moment alone, to think and to offload some of the road coffee in my bladder, so I stood up and walked a few yards away, telling Tommy to stand where I could see him. I put the gun in my pocket, unzipped, and commenced my business.

A tie-sack came down over my head. Two men grabbed my arms from behind, taking me to the rocky ground, face down. A third guy, with trained hands, crossed my wrists and strapped them together with a nylon band. I felt a needle jab my right butt cheek, and then another one jab my left.

Whoever these guys were, they were pros. As a former Ranger, I could usually sense it when I was about to be ambushed. Maybe my brain was tired. Or maybe I was just getting old.

The men held me down, one of them compressing my carotid artery, until my consciousness faded.

CHAPTER 37

Consciousness returned. At least partially.

My mind stirred, but my body didn't move. *Couldn't* move, I discovered. My muscles were frozen. They didn't want to obey my brain's commands.

I was lying, stomach down, on a hard surface. Even through my closed eyes, I sensed a bright light—the sun?—beaming down on me.

I tried to move, but the paralysis wouldn't break.

A hand shook my shoulder. I couldn't respond. The hand shook me again. And then a voice said, "Joe?" It was Caroline. "Joe?"

I tried to speak, but what came out of my mouth was only a cattle-like moan.

"Joe? Wake up. You need to move. The tide is coming in. It's going to be a big one."

"I ca' move," I slurred.

I wrenched my eyes open. I was lying on a flat rock on a beach. The midday sun was beating down on me. I saw Caroline's feet scurry away. Moments later, they returned, and I was doused with ice-cold water. My paralysis broke and I pushed myself off the rock.

"I need to go, Joe. I shouldn't even be here," Caroline said. She was wearing a white dress and holding a huge conch shell she must have filled with the seawater she dumped on me.

She ran off toward the water, where her kayak awaited in the sand. I staggered to my feet and lumbered toward her. But after a single step, I fell to the ground. My knees landed on hard wood. My awareness switched to a different channel. I suddenly found myself in an empty room, lit from above by a bare, high-wattage light bulb. There was one window, boarded up, and the walls were reinforced with sheet metal. The door had no handle, but had heavy locks at the top, middle, and bottom, and a hatch of some kind in the center.

"Sweetheart, are you still here?" I shouted in desperation. "Where am I? How did I get here? How long was I out?"

As if in answer to my questions, a wave of memory washed over me: Finding the Black Canyon house. Talking to the kid, Tommy. The men grabbing me, the needles in my rear. What chemical had they injected me with?

I felt my pants and pocket. My gun, my phone, and my wallet were all gone. Of course. Even my belt had been taken. My shoes too.

The harsh light from the bulb revealed that the bare room was as secure as a vault, with nothing to grab onto or use as a tool. I was well and truly screwed. And that meant so was my son. And the girl. And maybe a lot of other people. I stood up and paced like a caged leopard.

"You've got to help me, Sweetheart," I said. "You've got to help me help Jack."

***

Erlene parked her vintage red Corvette and headed from the lot toward the Vanderbilt Hotel in Johnson City, where the morning meeting was planned.

"Looks like we're both going to the same place," said a voice from a few yards away.

She turned to see Sheriff Leon Bates draw up alongside her.

"Which is fortunate," said Leon, "because you and me have a few things to discuss before the meeting."

As they walked toward the stately old hotel, Leon told her about his meeting with Senator McGinty. The surprise item on McGinty's computer turned out to be video footage of a sexual rendezvous between Leon Bates and Erlene Barlowe. "It was one of our more 'adventurous' episodes," said Leon. "Such that, if it were to become public, my career as an elected official would be over. You wouldn't happen to know how that encounter became immortalized on 4K, hi-res video, would you, darlin'? Or how it made its way into the hands of a sitting U.S. Senator?"

Erlene sighed as she bustled along. "Climb off your high horse, Sheriff. You know I'm always working both sides of a fence. You were aware of that before you decided to knock boots with me. I like you, Leon. But I also know that relationships go sour. People change. Memories change. I always like to have a little leverage I can use, just in case."

"So, you recorded us. Understood. But how did McGinty get hold of it?"

Erlene stopped and looked around the parking lot. "For 'business insurance' reasons," she said in a low voice, "I make a habit of gathering dirt on elected officials. Well... I acquired some on the good senator. Deals were made, backs were stabbed, and... things got complicated."

"Things got complicated? That's all you're going to tell me?"

"There are goings-on in my world that you don't want to know about as a law enforcement officer. If you did, why, you might not be so sweet on me anymore." Erlene batted her mascara-heavy eyelids, but her attempt at levity was halfhearted at best.

"Well, McGinty's got me over a barrel now," Bates said. "I was trying to squeeze him for help in my investigation, and he squeezed me right back. Now if I continue to pry, he'll play his card. And my days as Sheriff of Washington County will be countable on a horse's toes."

"Let's see how this meeting goes, sugar. Things are changing fast. We can talk later."

***

Sarah dropped Gracie at her school, then headed back to the Vanderbilt Hotel, where she and her daughter were living temporarily. She'd chosen the Vanderbilt because it was large, public, and in the busy downtown area of Johnson City. The last place in the world she wanted to set foot right now was in her isolated country house—a place that normally gave her comfort, warmth, and a sense of safety. The man on the trail had taken all of that away.

She had fifteen minutes till the big meeting of the "Jonesborough Women's Investigative Committee," the name she'd coined but no longer found amusing. She no longer found anything amusing, since Grace's frightening near-encounter. A couple of TBI people were coming to join them, as was attorney Jim Beaumont and Sheriff Leon Bates. They had agreed to meet in a conference room at the Vanderbilt because of its central and neutral location and because the meeting was "unofficial." At least for now.

Sarah entered the elegant, wood-accented lobby, then stepped into the elevator. She was about to press the "4" button to ascend to her suite. But just as the elevator doors were closing, she saw a man in the lobby close his laptop and rise from his seat. He was tall, blond, and broad-shouldered. She barely registered a glimpse of him before the doors shut, but her nervous system shot into high-alarm mode.

Sarah pressed the button for floor six instead of floor four, where her suite was. Heart jackhammering in her chest, she rode the elevator up and exited on the sixth floor. She half-ran down the corridor and turned left into an adjoining hallway. From there, a curved mirror offered a view of the main corridor. She watched the elevators in the mirror for two or three minutes. No one got off at floor six. Mildly relieved, she ran to the end of the hall, where a staircase led her down to the fourth floor.

Sarah unlocked her room and closed the door behind her, taking several fast, deep breaths, nearly causing herself to hyperventilate. *It wasn't him*, she told herself. *It wasn't the guy in Grace's photo. It was just some random stranger. My imagination is working overtime.*

She walked to the mini fridge, fetched a bottle of water, and plunked herself in an armchair to take a few long drinks. She couldn't relax, though. Something was still needling at her gut.

She rose, crossed the room, and peeked out the door's peephole. There, in the fish-eye view of the hall, stood the blond man she'd seen in the lobby. It was him, for sure: the guy in Grace's phone picture. His half-missing ear confirmed it. He stared at her door for several long seconds, then walked away.

Sarah crumbled to the carpet.

CHAPTER 38

"Step away from the door, Dillard. Move to the far wall."

I didn't recognize the voice, but whoever the man was, he knew my name. The gears churned in my mind, trying to assimilate the implications of that fact. My brain was still foggy from whatever knockout drug had been injected in my backside. Ketamine, maybe?

The hatch in the middle of the door slid open, and a pair of ice-cold green eyes looked in. I took three steps backward. The final lock unlatched, and the door opened.

A man I'd never seen in my life stepped in. He was tall, blond, and had the wide shoulders and narrow waist of an athlete. He might be considered classically handsome if not for the disfigured left ear and the dead, almost inhuman, look in his eyes.

"This," he said, holding up an instrument that looked like a scalpel, but much larger, "is a post-mortem knife." He did not elaborate. He didn't need to. It was a tool used to cut human flesh when survival was no longer a concern.

He turned and nodded to someone outside the door. Tommy, the kid I'd been talking to last night, entered the room carrying two folding chairs. His presence confirmed what I already suspected: I was inside the house known as Black Canyon. Tommy opened the two chairs, making brief, intense eye contact with me, then left the room. The tall man gestured me into one of the seats. He sat in the other.

He didn't speak for half a minute, simply held the instrument in both hands, staring forward with an almost dull look on his face.

"This day has been a long time coming, Dillard," he said at last. His flat voice creaked, as if he was unused to speaking more than a few syllables at a time. "The day you suffer the consequences... for your deeds."

He waited, as if for me to ask, *Who are you? What "deeds" are you talking about? What do you want with me?* I didn't give him the satisfaction.

"Pride got your tongue? You must be wondering who I am."

I didn't reply. I wasn't even sure I *could*. My mouth still felt like dry cotton.

"I will tell you, then. They call me The Ghost. The Surgeon. Other things. But who am I, really? That is the question." He lifted the razor-like post-mortem knife and trimmed a hangnail from his thumb. "Some years ago... when you were playing district attorney... you made some grave accusations... against someone important to me. A powerful and unforgiving man."

My heartrate kicked up. In my brief stint as a prosecutor, there was only one 'powerful and unforgiving' man against whom I made grave accusations.

"Do you remember who that man was?"

How could I forget? John Lipscomb. Successful businessman. Charity donor. Model citizen. Murderous psychopath.

"I see by your eyes," said the man they called The Ghost, "it's all coming back. That man was my cousin. But we were more like... brothers."

After I'd accused Lipscomb of murder, he had called my wife a whore to my face. I then did a reactive thing, as is my wont. I placed him in an unsupervised jail cell, where I beat him mercilessly with my hands. The last words he spoke to me, after receiving the beating, were, "You're a dead man, Dillard. Do you hear me? A dead man!"

And he nearly made good on those words. He sent an armed guerilla squad to my home, but I managed, against all odds, to disarm and defeat them. Was Lipscomb now making good on his promise from beyond the grave?

"John disappeared," said the blond man, "not long after your dealings. Many thought *he* had arranged it. Himself. To avoid the murder charges. Andres Pinzon... his partner... took over the company. He was glad to have John... out of the picture. Didn't follow up. Didn't investigate. Didn't do what was right. Even forbade the mention of my cousin's name. Years passed. And then... just last February... John's body turned up. Dead the whole time. Murdered."

He stared at me with unblinking, inhuman eyes.

"And Pinzon is no longer running the show." He paused, letting that fact sink in. "Did you really believe you would get away with it? Did you really believe John's death would go… unrequited? John was family. You understand the importance of family. Don't you, Dillard?"

I glowered at his alien eyes.

"Now…" The Ghost rose. He stood like a statue before me, holding the blade. Then he signaled out the door. Two beefy men in their twenties entered the room, armed with military-style rifles. They placed the barrels against my chest. The blond man sat again.

"…Let's talk about you. It would have been easy just to *take* you. And do what I do. Slice you apart. Bit by bit. While you watched. But that would not have been… enough. And so… we surveilled you. And your family. For almost a year. Listened to your calls. Read your texts, emails. Followed you. Took video, audio. What we learned… is that you are a family man. Hurting those you love… would be the surest way to hurt you. And then… your son… and his 'interest' in the Pruitt girl. Opportunity knocked. We had the means to make the girl disappear… and a profitable use for her. Setting your son up… was easy. That is what we do. And the timing of it. With your wife on death's door. Perfect."

"You son of a bitch!" I yelled, unable to keep my silence. The armed men tensed their weapons. "You put her in an early grave! You took her last days away from me!"

The blond man signaled the men to restrain me. They shouldered their weapons and put me in a lock-hold with their arms.

The blond man leaned in close to my face and said, slowly and precisely, "Your wife… was a diseased whore… who was going to die anyway."

My brain went white with fury. I tried to lunge out of my seat. The two mercenaries were able to hold me back only because of the drugs still in my system.

"Tie his hands and feet."

The men wrestled me to the floor and bound my wrists behind me with a strong polymer restraint, then lashed my ankles together with the same. They lifted me back into my seat.

"Now. An update on your son. More evidence has come forth. Home security video. Of 'him' and the girl. Also, her underpants. Her blood. His semen. A detailed diary of his acts. Murder charges have been filed. More evidence will come. It will include... the body of the girl. Or parts thereof. Your son *will* be convicted. But even if he is not…"

I knew what he was saying: the charges would stick to Jack forever.

"I will kill you!" I shouted. It was all I could come up with. "Even if I have to come back from the grave to do it, I will kill you."

He signaled for one of the men to gag me. The man pulled an elasticized rubber strap down over my head till it blocked my mouth.

"One more thing…" The Ghost said with unruffled calm. "On Sunday morning… after church services... your son will receive some 'services' of his own. A fellow inmate… armed with a tool such as this…"—he held up the razor-edged knife—"will remove... something from him. Something that will mean the end of the Dillard line."

I roared at him through the gag, feeling the blood rush to my face. He stood up and stepped toward the door, then stopped and turned around.

"The pity of it all... is the girl. That she needs to die. We could have made… a fortune on her. Lucky for us, we found a replacement... who may help make up the loss. She is a bit young for our system. But she will do well in the European market. I think you may know her. Her name is Grace. Grace Dillard."

My eight-year-old niece. I felt like I'd been kicked in the chest by a horse.

"Remember, Dillard," he said. "It is you who brought all of this down on your family."

He nodded to one of his men, who pulled a stun-gun from his pocket.

"Sleep on that."

The man fired the taser at my chest. My body ignited in pain. I fell to the floor and went blank.

CHAPTER 39

Seven grim faces ringed the conference table at the Vanderbilt Hotel. But when 9:00 a.m., the scheduled meeting-time, arrived, Sarah Dillard was nowhere to be found. She wasn't answering her cell-phone, and she wasn't answering her room phone or door. Concerned about her absence, but assuming she was just running late, Charlie called the meeting to order. Schedules were tight, and the opportunity to get heads around a table couldn't be forfeited.

Present in the meeting room were SAC Anita White of the Johnson City TBI office; a fellow TBI agent who'd recently started working the case; Lilly; Charlie; Erlene Barlowe; Leon Bates; and Jim Beaumont.

"I want to thank everyone for coming," Charlie said. "I know it was an unorthodox request, and some of you had to abandon your usual pro-tocols and policies to be here. But in the urgent interest of finding Abby Pruitt alive and well, I think it's critical we all share what we know." She handed off the meeting to Anita White, who got the ball rolling.

Information was beginning to gel, White said, and a clearer picture was emerging.

- White reported that the dark-web site on which the sex traffickers promoted their underage offerings had been forensically examined. A photo of Abby had indeed been posted briefly on the site. She said that others in the TBI, not just her, were now open to the theory that Abby Pruitt had been abducted by professionals and may still be alive. But until proof could be found, Jack Dillard was still their prime suspect.
- The evidence against Jack had begun to spring leaks, as reported by Charlie, Lilly, and Jim Beaumont. The phones on which Jack and Abby

allegedly texted each other were purchased at a store in Virginia at a time when Jack had a solid local alibi. A phony pest exterminator had spent time in Jack and Charlie's rented house, alone, two days before the evidence was found under the floorboards. The time-stamp on the photos, the writing in Jack's alleged "confession" note, and the security video were all showing stress cracks under close examination.

- Bates and Erlene shared what they had learned about the wealthy pedophiles' "club" that was believed to be a major client of the trafficking ring—including the Godfrey Edelberg piece. The FBI was reluctant to go after Edelberg, Bates reported, because he had successfully sued them twice. They would proceed against him only if and when the evidence was rock solid.

Other matters discussed:

- Verna Roy, Abby Pruitt's mother, had committed suicide. Before doing so, she had spent over fifteen thousand dollars in cash. Windfall from a payoff?
- An anonymous call had led Knoxville police to an unconscious man named Merlo Maroni, who, according to the caller, possessed information about the sex ring and, possibly, about Abby's abduction. Maroni recovered consciousness after a few days in the hospital and was cooperating with authorities to some extent. He said his main connection to the traffickers was via their Sealy, Texas, site.
- Joe Dillard was believed to have inside information about the ring and had recently spent time in Sealy, Texas, before departing for Arizona, where another of the ring's locations was believed to exist. Joe had been tracked by his family to an area north of Phoenix before his phone app stopped transmitting.

"Now here's the part I hoped Sarah Dillard would be present for," said Anita White. She informed the others about the man who was stalking Grace on the trail. "Grace's photo was vital. We've identified the man as someone called Alec Crandall. He is referred to as The Ghost and several other names. He's the top enforcer –the 'wet work' guy—for the criminal organization formerly run by John Lipscomb, which operates under the banner of an investment firm, Equicorp, and which we believe operates the trafficking ring. This Crandall character is astonishingly violent and cold-blooded, but he's been notoriously hard to prosecute. Twice he was caught for murder, dead to rights. In both cases the victims were mutilated in horrible ways while still alive, but Crandall walked because he had airtight alibis—as proven by video and DNA evidence. No one knows how he does it; that's part of his 'mystique.' If The Ghost is involved in this, as he appears to be… well, let's just say, that's not good."

As if on cue, the door to the meeting room flew open. Heads turned to see Sarah Dillard standing in the doorframe, looking pale and shaky.

"He was here. In this building. Outside my room. The man in Grace's photo."

"Crandall? Oh God," said Anita White.

PART III

CHAPTER 40

I couldn't tell how long it had been since I awoke from the taser blast. Days, for sure. It was hard to judge time in that empty room. Day and night didn't exist. The boarded-up window sealed out all outside light, and the high, bare bulb was on constantly. No mattress, no pillow. The full POW treatment.

Every now and then, not sure how often, "The Ghost" would throw a sandwich and a bottle of water through the feeding hatch and say a few words about Jack's, Abby's, or Grace's impending fate. He made me return each empty water bottle to him before giving me a new one. Didn't want me fashioning the empties into a tool or weapon, apparently.

The discomfort I could tolerate. It was the helpless ticking of time I abhorred. Every hour that passed made the safe rescue of the girl less likely and brought my son's Sunday-morning jailhouse attack an hour closer.

Though I did drift off now and then, the sleep deprivation was starting to affect my mind. I'm sure that was my captor's intent. I began to hear Caroline whispering to me from time to time. Seemingly aloud. I didn't know if it was her real presence or just the slow decay of my mental state, but it was the one thing saving me from utter despair.

The words she kept repeating to me didn't make sense at first. "Be still, Joe," was what she said. How could I be any more still than sitting motionless on the floor? And then it hit me: she wasn't talking about my body, she was talking about my mind. Telling me to stop its ceaseless churning and racing.

When I realized what she meant, I thought back on a time—during that magical vacation in the Caymans again—that Caroline and I

195

signed up for a morning meditation session on the beach. I was the only person in the group who couldn't do it. I was too restless, couldn't shut my mind up. Nor have I ever been able to. But now, sitting on the hardwood floor, I remembered what the instructor had said all those years ago: "Don't try to *stop* your thoughts. Simply choose not to engage with them. Let them pass like clouds in the sky. Be the sky itself."

I decided to try his advice, which I rejected at the time. After all, I had nothing but time to practice. I sat on the floor and observed my thoughts and worries, a new one assailing me every few seconds. But instead of following each thought down its rabbit hole, I let it pass. The thoughts kept trying to grab me, and I just kept letting them go. Eventually, I found the instructor was right. The more I refrained from engaging, the weaker the stream of thoughts became, and the more the stillness beneath them began to emerge.

I finally understood what Caroline meant. I was being still. Maybe for the first time ever.

My newfound state was quite enjoyable, despite the circumstances. It didn't fix any of my real-world problems, but it let me detach from them. Insights began to pour in. From a deeper place. I thought about the anger and impulsivity that had plagued me my whole life. It occurred to me that a single moment of uncontrolled anger—that thrashing I gave Lipscomb in that jail cell years ago—was the root cause of all the dire consequences my life was now serving up. Abby's kidnapping, the framing of Jack, Caroline's premature demise, the danger Grace was in.

I wondered how many other such monsters I had unleashed without even knowing it, how many other chains of causality I'd set in motion with my actions.

I'd always told myself my anger was righteous and reserved for "bad" people, and that beneath it I was a man of peace. But was I, really? And did it matter? Every action has an equal and opposite reaction. Period. You only control the first link in the chain. Everything else is out of your hands, both the good and the bad.

How much damage had I done out in the world with the rippling effects of my anger? Those endless chains of action and reaction?

And the bigger question was, how much more was I planning to do?

A lot was the truthful answer. I knew that if I escaped from this makeshift prison—which wasn't likely—I had every intention of loosing my rage on every person responsible for the events that had transpired.

But was that really a good idea? Setting more chains of causality in motion, *ad infinitum*? Was there a better way? Was that what Caroline had been trying to tell me all along—not only since her passing, but in the years she and I had spent together?

A metallic rattle at the door seized my attention. The hatch lifted. Feeding time? No. I heard a *psst* and saw a familiar pair of blue eyes through the hole. Tommy.

"I only got a second," he whispered. "I'm trying to help you, but I can't get you out. Not yet. Only one guy has the key to this room. That new guy, the tall one with the funny ear."

"Here's what you *can* do, Tommy," I said, crawling to the door. I'd thought about what I'd tell him if I got the chance. "Get me a phone."

If I had a phone, I could call Sarah and warn her that Gracie was in danger. I could tell my family where I was and set things in motion for law enforcement to descend on this house.

"I can't," Tommy said. "They don't let us have 'em."

I figured as much. But I also knew Tommy had become a fixture in the house. Therefore, invisible. People probably let their guard down around him all the time.

"Keep your eyes open. Figure something out," I said. "Get me a phone." The hatch closed, and Tommy scampered away.

***

"I am not putting Grace in harm's way," Sarah said to Anita White. They were seated in the living room of Sarah's hotel suite, along with two other TBI agents. "And I'm certainly not using her as bait."

"I wouldn't even suggest such a plan," Anita White explained, "except for the fact that The Ghost may be involved. The TBI can protect Grace temporarily, but we can't keep her safe forever."

The plan Anita White had cobbled together called for Grace to pretend to sneak out of the hotel to visit a traveling carnival that was in town a block away. Several agents would be stationed along the way, dressed as hotel janitors, pedestrians, carnival customers, etc. The hope was that The Ghost would make a move on Grace, and the TBI would catch him.

"The man has a reputation for cruelty and extreme violence," continued White, "which he enjoys inflicting. And also for relentlessness. If he decides someone needs to die, they die. Even if it takes a year—or five—for it to happen."

"So, you're saying Grace will never be safe if this guy has marked her for death."

"That's exactly what I'm saying."

"But we don't even know for sure it's him. And he hasn't made any actual threats. We don't know if he's planning to harm her."

"If it isn't him, then Grace won't be in danger."

"But if it *is* him… Can you guarantee…?"

"We can't guarantee anything, including her safety. Unfortunately. This guy is good at what he does. And clever. But so are our people. The one thing I *can* guarantee is that if we don't stop him, you and Grace will never enjoy a peaceful night's sleep again."

Sarah leaned back in her chair and stared at the ceiling. Her face, which usually looked a decade younger than her 51 years, was drawn into lines that made it look a decade older.

"No," she said at last. "It's too risky. I'd never forgive myself if I was the one who delivered her into the hands of the devil."

"I understand," said Anita White, but her sigh said she didn't. Not really.

CHAPTER 41

Saturday, April 29, 2:17 p.m.

"Sit still," said the black-haired woman holding the makeup brush. She stood behind Abby in the mirror of the bathroom vanity. "You'd think you never wore makeup in your life."

"I never did," Abby fired back. "Except when my maw and me used to play dress-up. I'm only eleven!" Tears threatened to flow, but Abby knew she needed to be strong. She sat up tall in the stool and looked her mirror-self in the eye.

"Eleven?" the woman said, then muttered, "Sweet Lord," under her breath. "Well, when I'm done with you, you'll look fourteen-going-on-twenty. You certainly have the goods. Head up."

Abby lifted her chin. The woman brushed some rouge onto her cheeks, just a subtle touch to bring out her cheekbones. Abby needed only a subtle touch of everything—base, mascara, eyeliner—to make her face look like that of a beautiful young woman of indefinite age.

A knock sounded on the bathroom door. Shane stuck his head in without invitation. "Her car's here," he said to the woman. "They want her there early."

"Your own car and driver, all the way to Sedona, think of that," said the woman to Abby. "And you'll be spending time in the kind of house most people never set foot in in their whole-entire lives. I hope you appreciate that. This ain't the treatment most of our gals get."

Appreciate it? Abby couldn't believe her ears. *Appreciate it?*

The black-haired woman reached for the clothes laid out on the vanity top—a sparkly blouse, cut low in the front, a set of red underwear that looked like it came from the Victoria's Secret store at the mall, and a pair of tight-looking jeans. "They've probably got their own clothes they'll want you to wear, but put these on for now. We want you lookin' fine when you step from that limo."

Limo? They sent a limo *for me? What are they expecting in return?*

"Ever seen one of these?" The woman held up one of the red undergarments. "It's called a pushup bra. It hooks in the back. Let me know if you need help with it."

The woman exited the room, leaving Abby alone.

Abby put the clothes on, then looked at herself in the mirror. A gasp filled her lungs. For an instant, she didn't even know it was *her*, looking back. And then an unexpected emotion flooded her. Pride. For the first time, she saw the woman in herself and realized why people had been making such a fuss about her. She was flat-out gorgeous.

No. The flash of vanity was flushed away by shame and fear. She wasn't ready for this. Any of this. Not by a Louisville light-year. And she didn't want to be!

She dashed to the toilet and threw up.

Rinsing her mouth out at the sink, she thought back on her last Little League game—it seemed a lifetime ago—and the way she had flaunted her premature curves to fluster the opposing team's players. She'd had no idea what kind of fire she was playing with. Was this her punishment for being such a flirt? Had she brought this on herself?

"No!" she shouted at the "woman" in the mirror. "You didn't ask for this!"

You're damn right you didn't, she could almost hear Coach Jack saying. *Bad people* did *this to you. And those people don't own you. Remember that, Hawkeye. Nobody owns you but* you!

She wished Coach Jack were here right now. To stand up to these men like he'd stood up to her father. What would he tell her if he was here?

You're the Hawk, he'd say. *You've got the best stuff I've ever seen. And when you have your stuff going for you, no one in the world can beat you.*

Her stuff. She tried to remember what having her stuff felt like.

"Well, look at *you*," said the black-haired woman, stepping back into the bathroom. "You're going to turn some heads, that's for sure. Come on, princess, your coach awaits."

Abby followed the woman out of the bathroom and down the hall, her heart rate increasing with each step.

Words arose in her mind. Not in the voice of Coach Jack this time. In the voice of a woman. She thought it might be the voice of the woman she would become someday. If she ever got the chance. *You're not in Little League anymore,* said the woman's voice, somber and steady. *You're in the big leagues now.*

Abby stepped out into the blazing Arizona sun. Two men with rifles waited outside, one on either side of the door. They fell into step behind her and followed her toward the white Mercedes limousine. Its door stood open, darkness inside. A uniformed chauffeur with gloved hands gestured her toward the black leather seat.

You're in the big leagues, and you better find your stuff. You better find it right now.

***

Same day, 5:30 p.m. Eastern

As Abby was walking to her limousine at 2:30 in Arizona, Jack was being walked to the deputy warden's office at 5:30 in East Tennessee.

Jack had requested a meeting with the deputy warden to discuss his possible protection. The meeting had been granted, thanks to Jack's standing with Leon Bates. Because it was a Saturday, Jack had to meet with the weekend D.W., a slim, goateed man named Boyd Whitley he'd never met before.

"So, I understand you're concerned about your safety," Whitley said to Jack, feet up on his weekend desk. "But here's what I *don't* understand. Why didn't you accept protective custody when it was offered to you? Lemme guess. Because you wanted to show everyone what a tough guy you were? Ain't that right, Mr. Scarface? Well, now it sounds like you want to have your cake and eat it too."

"Because I'm asking for protection against a specific threat? I thought it was a basic human right not to be tortured or killed. Or is that considered a 'frill' around here?"

"We're unaware of any credible threats that have been made against you."

"Badger Daley told me," Jack said. "And Badger knows everything. A 'hit' has been ordered. From outside. Tomorrow morning at church services. All I'm asking is that staff be watchful of the situation and ready to step in."

"Asking? Is that what you're doing? 'Cause from here it sounds like *demanding*." To Jack's surprise, Whitley broke into a quiet laugh that rocked his thin frame. "You're probably wondering why I'm chuckling," he said. Jack didn't reply. "It's 'cause I'm sittin' here looking at you with that smug face of yours." Jack wasn't feeling the least bit smug. "Thinking you've got a shoo-in with my boss, Sheriff Bates, and that I better dang-well do as you say." No such thoughts were in Jack's mind. "Well, here's the high-larious part. Not an hour before you walked in here, I got a text from a buddy who sent me the funniest durned Internet link I ever did see."

Whitley turned his laptop toward Jack and clicked on a web address. A video played. Were it a Hollywood film, it would have been rated NC-17. A highly "stimulated" Leon Bates, clad only in a cowboy hat and gun holster, approached an eyelash-batting Erlene Barlowe, clad only in a cowboy hat and boots. And things proceeded from there.

"Do I need to explain…" Whitley asked through his laughter, "that your alliance with Leon Bates is no longer a working asset for you in this jail?"

Whitley's laughter reached a higher note, and that was the end of the meeting.

And now Jack was being marched back to his cell by a guard. As he shuffled along, his mind swam with disbelief and recrimination. He wanted to blame the world—to blame God—for the injustice of his situation. But then it struck him that all his troubles could be traced to the same root cause. To a single moment in time—the moment his rage had taken over. *If I hadn't killed Sheila Self, my life wouldn't have gone into a tailspin of self-hatred. I wouldn't have tried to redeem myself by helping Self's kids and becoming a substitute father for Abby. I wouldn't have started drinking—so I'd have an alibi for the night Abby disappeared. Maybe I'd have been a better son to my mother. Maybe she would have lived longer. Maybe she'd even have gotten better…*

The guard pushed him through a door and paraded him down the walkway that ran above the sitting area. A song arose from a table below. Jack knew it was aimed at him. The singer was a decent tenor, and Jack recognized the tune instantly. An old Kris Kristofferson ballad he liked. Normally it would have brought a warm, slightly sad, feeling to his heart.

But today was not a normal day.

The song was "Sunday Mornin' Comin' Down".

CHAPTER 42

I must have fallen asleep on the hard wooden floor, because the sound stirred me from a dream. In the dream, *I* was the prisoner, chained to a jail cell wall, and John Lipscomb was beating me senseless with *his* hands.

I sat up, my neck and shoulder muscles locking into a cramp. I was still in prison, I noted. Just a prison of a different kind.

Psst came a voice from the door. Tommy's eyes, wide with fear, looked at me through the hatch. I crept up closer to him.

"Here," he whispered, and shoved a phone through the hatch. I grabbed it. "The code is 4539. I seen him use it." His eyes darted from side to side, then he whispered, "They took the new girl. Up to Sedona. A couple hours ago."

I glanced at the phone in my hand. Its clock showed 6:25 on Saturday, April 29. I instantly digested the implications. About thirteen hours till Jack's jailhouse "hit." As for Abby, she was no doubt on her way to a Saturday night assignation that would rob her of her virginity and a lifetime of emotional wellbeing, if those things hadn't already been taken from her.

"Listen, Tommy, you need to—"

Before I could finish my sentence, a voice shouted from down the hall. "Hey, Goof-Tard, what the hell are you doing? Don't talk to him! Hey, did you take my phone?"

Tommy dropped the hatch cover and ran. "Somebody grab him!" the voice yelled. Heavy footsteps charged toward my door, and a new pair of eyes looked through the hatch. "Get the keys! Fast! I think this guy's got my phone!"

I punched in the phone code. I had only seconds to place a call. I would try Sarah first. Then 911, if I had a chance. I'd already dredged Sarah's number from memory in preparation for this chance. My fingers tapped it in from muscle-memory. The call rang through.

Answer, Sarah. Answer, damn it. Don't ignore it because it's a strange number. Don't let it go to voicemail like you always do. Hurry. Pick up. Hurry.

***

When Sarah's phone rang, she and Grace were sitting at the table of their room at the Vanderbilt, playing cards with a pair of TBI agents. Sarah's caller ID read, "Unknown caller, Phoenix, AZ," and showed a 623 area code. She answered it immediately.

"Sarah, it's me." Her brother. Joe. She leapt to her feet and walked away from the table. "I gotta talk fast. Listen: Grace is in terrible danger. A man called The Ghost is planning to take her—"

"I know. We've seen him around. The TBI is—"

"That couldn't have been him. He's here," said Joe, speed-talking. "He's John Lipscomb's cousin and he's a very bad, very dangerous man. He's holding me prisoner. In Arizona. And listen: they have Abby Pruitt too. She's on her way to Sedo—"

The call went dead.

Sarah turned to the TBI agents. "Call your boss. Anita White. Tell her I need to talk to her right away. Tell her the plan is a go."

***

Shane caught up to Tommy in the kitchen. He grabbed him by the waist and flung him like a cornerback tackling a wide receiver. Tommy smashed into the beer refrigerator, hit his head, and fell to the floor. Shane and Raji descended on him, pinning his shoulders to the stone tile.

"Smart move, 'tard," said Shane, his face pink with fury. "I've been waiting for the day you'd screw up. I knew it was coming. You think you got the brains to pull one over on me? Think again. I'm going to enjoy what happens to you. The only reason they've kept you alive this long…" Shane looked around and lowered his voice. "…is because your fag brother kept Mr. Paolo happy behind closed doors. Now you're going to be as dead as him."

At the mention of his brother, Tommy's brain lit up fire-red with rage. Adrenaline spiked to his muscles. He bolted to a sitting position, shedding the two men as if they were made of straw, and swung his fists in random directions. One fist connected with Raji's jaw.

Tommy jumped to his feet and clapped his hand to Shane's face. He pushed with all his might, sending Shane sprawling backward. He ran out the back door.

***

The third door-lock opened. Before I could get my last words to Sarah out of my mouth, the door burst open. The Ghost's two "soldiers" barreled in and took me to the floor.

They grabbed the phone from me. One of them smashed my temple with the butt of his rifle. Hard. My consciousness dipped and wavered, and my vision flooded with swimming tendrils of flashing light.

The Ghost stepped through the door. I could see him only in flashes and negatives. "That was a bad idea," he said to me. "I'll be back in a few minutes to deal with you. You will not enjoy what I'm about to do to you. …But I will." He grinned like a plaster funhouse clown.

He took the phone from the guard, signaled the two men to stay in the room with me, then stepped out the door and locked the three locks behind him. I was sealed inside with the armed guards.

The swimming tendrils of light began to coalesce. They formed a circle in the center of my vision. That circle of light seemed to be pulling me. Like a magnet. My nerves tingled with the same frequency that was emanating from the light. It felt so good, I wanted to fuse with it. I just wanted to fuse with that rotating circle of light.

***

Tommy ran to the tool shed instead of out into the open desert. He knew Shane and Raji would be following close behind. But he'd been preparing for a moment like this.

Tommy stepped into the shed and grabbed the white plastic bucket with the perforated lid. For the last couple of days, he'd been transferring his scorpion inventory from the terrarium-bin to this smaller container. He was astounded by the number of tan-colored crawlers he'd managed to amass. Baby-making had surely been going on: his bucket contained hundreds of scorpions. Tommy put on his heavy gardening gloves, the ones with the long, wide cuffs that covered his forearms. He picked up the plastic cooking spoon he'd borrowed from the kitchen.

As Tommy was fond of pointing out, the bark scorpion is the most venomous scorpion in North America. When agitated, it stings instantly on contact. Victims often report multiple stings by the same scorpion as it tumbles down the inside of a sleeve or pant-leg. The venom from a single specimen causes intense pain but is not usually enough to kill a healthy adult. But venom from fifteen or twenty scorpions at once, Tommy figured, *that* might do the trick.

If not, it would certainly put the victim into anaphylactic shock or paralysis.

Tommy heard Shane and Raji running toward the shed, where he stood. He waited, facing into the shed, till they were just a few steps away. Then he turned. With calm control, he tilted the open bucket toward them. In a fanning motion, he scooped two large spoonsful of scorpions toward Shane, then two toward Raji. The two men, dressed in tee-shirts and shorts, didn't fully realize what Tommy had done. They looked at each other with amused contempt, as if to say, *What's this idiot doing? Throwing bugs at us? How awful!*

Then it hit them. Both. At once. That look of shocked confusion. That sense of something gone horribly wrong, but not knowing what it was. And then the pain. Oh, the pain. Their faces contorted into masks of horror.

"AAAAAAAH!" they screamed, in perfect stereo.

Shane fell to his knees, dropping his gun, slapping himself all over. Raji, unarmed, dove to the ground, face down, and wriggled in the rocky dirt. The men screamed as if being flayed alive.

Tommy covered his pail. He bent over and snatched Shane's keys from his pocket and his gun from the ground. He thumbed the safety off, the way he'd seen Shane do. And marched toward the house, holding the weapon.

CHAPTER 43

Tommy was almost to the screen door when he saw the inner door opening. He dashed to the side and pressed himself against the wall.

Mr. Paolo burst out of the house—responding to the screams, no doubt. Tommy observed he was unarmed. Paolo marched straight toward where his two men lay on the ground. Raji had already stopped moving. Shane was half-sitting, breathing hard, a stunned look in his eyes.

Tommy snuck up behind Paolo. In an urgent tone, he said, "Mr. Paolo!" Paolo spun around.

Tommy pointed the gun at him. Paolo's face looked absurdly surprised. "Tommy, what the hell are you doing? Put that thing down."

"No, Mr. Paolo. Get in the shed or I'll shoot you."

"Don't be ridiculous. Give me that thing." He opened his hand.

Tommy repeated, in the voice of a man, not a boy, "Get. In. The. Shed."

Paolo lifted his hands in compliance. "Okay. Easy there, Tommy," he said. A slight tone of amusement still tinged his words. But he walked toward the shed and stepped inside.

Paolo turned and faced Tommy from within the shed. "If you stop whatever you think you're doing right now," he said, "I will forget this ever happened. But if you take things one step further, you will regret your actions for the rest of your life."

"No," Tommy said, uncapping the plastic bucket. "*You* will."

He flung a spoonful of scorpions at Paolo's face. Then another. Like the others, Paolo didn't seem to understand what was happening for a few seconds. Then his facial muscles twisted into an expression of agony like Tommy had never seen. "WHAT THE FU—"

Tommy slammed the shed door and clasped the padlock.

"That's for my brother Chris," Tommy said to the closed door. "And for every kid who ever stayed in this house. I remember all their names." He turned and marched back toward the house.

"Help," Shane gasped at him as he passed. "Hospital."

"Did *Chris* get a chance to go to the hospital?" Tommy said. "Or Luka?" He heard Paolo screaming from the locked shed behind him.

***

The Ghost stormed into the office looking for Paolo. He hadn't heard any of what had happened outdoors; he'd been too busy dealing with Dillard. And the double-paned Arizona windows killed most outdoor noise.

Where the hell was Paolo?

The Ghost needed to figure out who Dillard had called. If he had managed to make a 911 call, the police were obligated to track the call and show up in person. The Ghost could handle the cops, but he needed to know if they were coming. Shane's phone had already locked up. But Paolo kept the phone codes somewhere in his office. The Ghost stepped around the desk and slid open the top drawer. A notepad page displayed a short list of names and numbers. He leaned over to read the code to Shane's phone.

He looked up when Tommy stepped into the room. "Go find Mr. Paolo right now," he ordered the kid.

The Ghost was surprised when Tommy didn't obey but rather dipped a plastic spoon into a bucket. Was the kid *throwing* something at him? Crickets? Cockroaches? What the hell?

He was doubly surprised when the pain erupted. All at once. On his cheeks, his lips, his forehead, his neck, his chest, his hands... As if he'd just dived head-first into a nest of murder hornets.

The third surprise came when Tommy pulled a gun from his waistband and said, "Sit!"

The Ghost was not accustomed to taking orders. Even from someone holding a gun. And especially not from a soft-brained kid. He marched around the desk toward Tommy, his nerves igniting in rage and pain.

Surprise number four came when Tommy pulled the trigger. The blast exploded with a loud *pow* in the small room, and The Ghost felt a bullet rip through his abdomen. Left side, near the edge. Lower rib broken, for sure.

He stumbled backward and landed in the wheeling office chair.

The kid kept the gun on him, eyes unwavering.

***

Lilly sped toward the Vanderbilt Hotel after learning about the TBI's plan to snare The Ghost—the plan that involved putting Grace in harm's way. Charlie rode shotgun, working her phone. She had her own worries at the moment.

Earlier, Jack had texted Charlie with a cryptic message. It read, "If anything should happen to ruin our wedding plans, I want you to know how much I love you, Charleston Story. I love you so much it hurts, and I always will. No matter what."

Touched by the sentiment of the text but disturbed by its implications, Charlie had immediately texted him back, asking him to call her. Jack had failed to respond.

She continued to text him, every few minutes, saying, "Call me!" or "Text me," but still Jack had not responded. She knew he was "home," in his cell. So why wasn't he answering her text or calling? Each time her text was ignored, her anxiety mounted. Was he hurt? Was he in some kind of trouble? Why would he send a text like that and then ghost her? Why?

Lilly leaned on her horn and raced around a double-parked car.

***

Don't blink, Tommy told himself, holding the gun steady. *Don't show weakness.* "Toss me the phone," he said to The Ghost, "and the keys to the back bedroom. Make any other move, I'll shoot you again."

Tommy thought he could see The Ghost's tongue swelling up already. A look of animal panic was widening the man's eyes by the second, but his teeth were gritted in rage. His breathing was becoming labored, either from the wound, the swollen tongue, or the venom. Or all the above. He pushed his keys and Shane's phone across the desktop. Tommy grabbed them.

"Get... doctor," said The Ghost in a halting voice, "Or you will die... begging for the pain to end."

Tommy backed up to the doorway, keeping the gun on The Ghost. He turned to see all the kids from the residence crowded into the hallway, looking on with shocked faces.

He knew Aaron was handy with tools. "Go find a hammer and some nails," he shouted, tossing Aaron the keys he'd taken from Shane.

Aaron ran off and was back within thirty seconds, tools in hands.

"Can you nail that shut?" Tommy asked, pointing to the inward-opening door. Aaron shrugged a maybe. "If I hear you move," Tommy said to The Ghost, "I'll start shooting through the door." Then he shut the dying man inside. Aaron was able to angle a nail through the face of the door into the doorframe. It didn't grab much wood, but a few more nails should do the trick.

Tommy left Aaron to his labors. He turned to the girls to explain what was happening.

***

When the gunshot went off in another room, it snapped me out of my trance. I'd been in danger of slipping out of consciousness. Perhaps permanently. I shook my head like a wet dog's. My temple throbbed with pain, but full awareness came flooding back.

A gunshot. In the house. That was either good for me or bad for me. I had to be prepared for either case.

My two guards looked at each other with raised hackles. But they were locked in the room, same as me. One of them stood near the door, rifle at the ready. The other guard kept his gun on me. I stared at the door, wondering what would happen next.

Tension and uncertainty flooded the room. We all awaited our next cue.

The hatch-cover flew up, and Tommy's eyes appeared. He gave me a split-second look of warning. I jumped backward in a crouch, not knowing what he wanted me to do. A gun barrel popped through the hatch and fired instantly. The guard facing the door went down, dropping his weapon.

The other guard was momentarily distracted. I took the opportunity to spring, full force, to my feet and grasp his rifle with both hands. He tightened his grip.

We wrestled for the gun.

I heard the top door-lock open.

Using a Kali take-down I'd learned in the Army Rangers, I brought my opponent to the floor. But he was strong and would not release the firearm.

The wounded guard was seriously weakened but rolled over and pushed himself onto his hands and knees. He groped for his weapon.

The middle lock on the door opened.

The guard and I wrestled on the floor for possession of his gun. Neither of us could wrench it from the other.

The wounded guard seized his rifle.

CHAPTER 44

The bottom door-lock came undone, and the door flew open with the force of a battering ram. It struck the downed guard and knocked him backward. He dropped his newly regained weapon.

What happened next shouldn't have surprised me, given the nature of the place. But it did. A mass of young females—five of them, it turned out—surged through the door like floodwater through a broken levee.

Tommy must have prepped them; they all moved into action. A blonde girl, about 15, dove on the free rifle, protecting it. Two others jumped on the wounded guard. He didn't resist much and fell flat to the floor. They pinned him down.

The other two girls rushed to my aid. They kicked at the face of the guard I was wrestling beneath me. *Stomped* is the right word. Still, the guy managed to keep his grip on the rifle. But when he saw Tommy pointing a handgun at his head from six inches away, he let go.

I now had the guard's rifle. One of the girls had the other one. I rose to my feet.

The young people looked at me as if I was in charge. Good.

"Out of this room and lock this door," I told them. "We'll send medical help when we can." I didn't think the wounded guard would make it. His problem, not mine.

We exited the room, leaving the guards inside. As Tommy relocked the three deadbolts, he quickly filled me in on everything that had happened in the house. He was more articulate than he'd let on, even in our private desert conversation. He handed me the Ghost's keys and the phone he'd given me earlier.

The first thing I did was call 911. I didn't give them details, just told them to send police and ambulances. I guessed it would take them a while to arrive. Next, I called Sarah. I'd left her hanging in our last, interrupted call. I told her The Ghost was our captive and was close to death, if not already dead. How had he been able to travel between Arizona and Tennessee so quickly? we wondered. Private jet, perhaps. No matter, he wouldn't be flying anymore. That didn't mean Grace was safe, though; his operatives might still be planning to grab her. But at least the threat of her long-term endangerment had perhaps abated.

Sarah, for her part, told me that the Dillard women had been working together and with others including Anita White, Jim Beaumont, Leon Bates, and Erlene Barlowe, of all people. She summed up everything they had learned, and I told her what I knew. One thing she mentioned was that Merlo Maroni was recovering—thank God—and was telling the TBI everything he knew about the trafficking ring. An immunity deal. I told Sarah to await further word from me.

I called my daughter Lilly, to tell her I loved her and that I'd be home soon. I told her I was no longer maintaining radio silence and to stay in touch by phone. I also told her to get ahold of Jack and tell him to hang in there; I was doing my best to help him.

Tommy gave me my shoes, which he'd found, and he and I ran out doors to check on the status of the men he had incapacitated. The one he called Raji was lying face-down. I shook him but couldn't tell if he was alive. The one named Shane lay on his back, wide-eyed, breathing hard. In shock. I knocked on the door of the shed where Tommy's boss, Mr. Paolo, was locked. No answer.

"We're sending medical help, but it might be a while," I shouted. Some of them might make it, some might not. Oh well. Actions had consequences.

Tommy and I dashed back into the house. Next: find some vehicle keys and get to Sedona. ASAP. I'd left my rented car a couple of miles away. It had likely been towed by now.

I wanted to use the fastest car, the Audi R8 parked in the driveway. I assumed it belonged to The Ghost. But the key to it wasn't on his ring with the other keys.

It didn't take us long to realize that all the vehicle keys were in the office. Which was now nailed shut. With The Ghost inside.

Damn. But maybe it was for the best. I wanted to assess The Ghost with my own eyes before leaving. "Get those nails out," I told Aaron. He'd smartly left the nail-heads protruding. The three of us holding the guns—Tommy, the girl called Deja, and I—kept our weapons poised as Aaron worked the nails out. He thrust the door open.

The Ghost was lying back in the office chair, mouth open, tongue thick, eyes glazing over. I ran in and was about to feel for a pulse when he pulled in a shallow breath. He wasn't dead yet, but he was on the doorstep. I waved the kids in.

"Watch out for scorpions!" Tommy shouted.

The girls and Tommy and I cautiously searched the room, opening drawers and cabinets, eyes alert for stray arachnids. I crushed two of the tan crawlers with my shoe-heels, Deja crushed another; no time for humane options. We found the key to the transport van and another key labeled, simply, "Truck." I found my gun, too, and my phone. But I couldn't find The Ghost's car key anywhere. I patted him down. I found his phone, which I took. But no key.

No more time to lose. I'd have to use the van.

We found some zip ties like the ones that had bound my hands. I tied The Ghost's wrists together behind his chair and strapped his ankles together. He was as good as dead, but I wasn't taking any chances. I took a photo of him with my phone, then hustled everyone out the door.

I told the kids to hang on to one of the rifles and one of the handguns. I quickly demonstrated how to use them. I would take one gun of each type with me as well.

"Here's what I want you to do," I told them. "Nail this guy inside again—I don't want any of you in the same room with him—and guard the door. Guard the three guys out back, too, until the cops get here. I don't think they'll give you any trouble. The two guys I locked in the back room won't either. Don't let the ambulance take anyone until the cops clear it. Okay?"

Everyone nodded.

I called Anita White—she'd already talked to Sarah, she said, so I didn't have to explain everything—and texted her the Black Canyon location from my phone. I also sent her the photo I'd taken of The Ghost, incapacitated. I told her I'd already called 911 and asked her to work out all the chain-of-command details with the various law enforcement agencies that might show up.

I ran outdoors. Darkness had arrived. I tried the door of the Audi, just in case. Locked. I ran to the van, which was parked behind the fake moving truck—still on premises. Tommy came running up behind me.

"Here's where we say our goodbyes," I told him. "Listen, Tommy—" I was about to quickly thank him for everything he had done, but he cut me off.

"I'm coming with you," he said.

"No, you're not. It's too dangerous. You've done more than—"

"I'm coming. You might need help. I can do more than you think. And I know things. Lots of things."

"No, Tommy."

"Yes. These guys got my brother killed. And did terrible things to other kids. And to *me*. I *need* to help stop them."

We exchanged stares. He looked five years older and five times more capable than the kid I'd talked to in the desert two or three days ago.

"Get in," I said. "But I'm driving."

No argument from him. I threw the van in reverse, turned it around, and we tore out in a cloud of desert dust.

CHAPTER 45

"**D**o the line dance, Sweetie, you'll feel better," said the older brunette girl.

Abby looked at the five lines of white powder laid out on the black stone tabletop. She knew what it was. She'd seen her father and his friends snort it. She wanted no part of it.

She wanted no part of any of this.

Abby and three other girls had been ushered into the "girl-party room" of the Sedona home a while ago and told to wait there and "enjoy" themselves.

The room featured four huge leather couches and dozens of throw-pillows. Fresh fruit, little sandwiches, and sweets were laid out on side tables, and two bottles of Veuve Clicquot—whatever that was—sat in a silver bucket of ice. Hip-hop music blared.

Two of the other girls looked like older teens, but still only 15 or so. They seemed like they had done this before and were having fun. Sort of. The third girl looked younger. Her eyes said she felt the same way Abby did, but she was pretending to be cool about it all.

"You're gonna need *something*," the older brunette said to Abby. "This is your first time, and you're the, ah, featured attraction. Believe me, you're gonna need something."

Abby studied herself in a wall mirror. She was dressed in an outfit that looked like it belonged on a Victoria's Secret *runway*, not just in a store. It amounted to a tiny, jeweled bikini with a sheer robe of sorts draped over it, made of shimmery material.

A middle-aged woman leaned her head into the room. "Woo! Party on!" she said to the girls, then added, "They're finishing dinner now, so be ready for your call. It won't be long."

Abby's whole body felt like it had broken out in a rash. *No, no, no!* a voice inside her shrieked. She almost vomited into the iced jumbo shrimp.

***

"There goes your chirper again," Badger said to Jack, responding to the electronic *bloop*. "Ain't you gonna answer it?"

Jack paced the floor of the cell, front to back, back to front, front to back. He stared straight ahead, his hands clenched into fists.

"Sweet pretty thing like your wife-to-be," Badger persisted, "and yer just gonna keep ignorin' her?"

Jack paced. He didn't respond.

"Ignore a lady and she won't be your wife-to-be for long. Here, lemme answer it for ya." Badger started toward Jack's floor mattress, where his text-chirper lay.

"Don't!" snapped Jack in a voice that caused Badger to raise his palms and step back toward the bunkbeds.

Jack didn't want to talk to Charlie tonight. He didn't want to open his heart. He wanted to close it. Seal it off. Weld it shut. After he'd found out the guards were not going to offer him any protection in the morning, he realized he was on his own. He returned to his cell, grabbed his chirper, and sent Charlie his love.

Then he reset his inner gears. Now he needed to channel his hate. Only his hate. Until the deed was done. He needed to be like his father. Focused. Deadly. A weapon, cocked and loaded.

Heartless. Mindless. Soulless.

Jack paced the cell, back to front, front to back. Badger and Gomes stayed out of his way.

He might lose tomorrow's battle, but God help the men who tried to rob him of his future with Charlie. God help them. Because they would pay. Whatever happened, they would pay.

***

"I thought you knew how to drive," Hope said.

"I drove cars before, not a beast like this." Deja ground the transmission every time she shifted and couldn't find the gear to make the huge moving-truck go faster than 40.

After Joe and Tommy left, Abby's three Texas travel companions decided they needed to do something to help her. They cooked up a quick idea. And a very bad one. Taking the handgun with them, they would dress in their sexiest outfits, drive to Sedona in the big truck, and try to talk their way into the party Abby was working. Then rescue her. Somehow. Brittney, a girl who'd been at Black Canyon for a couple of months, gave them vague directions to an expensive house where she'd once worked a job for some famous rich guy.

It was the sort of ridiculous plan only a child would come up with. But then, these girls *were* children, much as they might pretend otherwise. One of the plan's many tragic flaws was Deja's inability to drive a truck.

They hadn't even made it to the highway when blue lights appeared in the side mirror.

Deja pulled over and the three girls looked at one another, collectively regretting their decision to leave two kids at the house, with one rifle, to guard six men.

***

The Ghost waited a few minutes after he heard the kid nail the door shut again, then sat up quietly in his seat. The pain from the stings was otherworldly, not to mention the pain from the gunshot. But he was able to shut it all out for the moment. Breathing was the biggest challenge, but so far, so good. He wasn't dead yet.

But *someone* would be dead soon. That soft-headed kid. And Dillard. The thought of making them pay for their actions brought a rush of life into his nerves and muscles. He *willed* himself to full alertness.

Sitting up in his chair, he worked out the steps he needed to execute.

First, he stood, slipping his tied wrists up over the chair back. Then he turned and knelt on the floor, his back toward the desk. Hands behind him, he quietly opened the bottom desk drawer, where Paolo kept items he'd confiscated from the kids. He groped about, and his hands found a box cutter. With surprising ease, he opened it, flipped it around, and cut the band off his wrists. He freed his ankles next.

A flash of motion caught his eye. A two-inch scorpion scuttled across the tile floor toward him, lifting its stinger-tail in a telltale arc. The Ghost pressed his thumb down on the creature, crushing it and deliberately absorbing the pain of its sting—the same way he had absorbed the pain of cutting his own ear off years ago. Pain was not his master.

He took a few labored breaths. Tried to work some oxygen into his system. Then he rose and stepped softly to the closet. That was where Paolo kept his "medicine cabinet," a milk crate filled with drugs and other remedies off limits to the kids' access. It was pretty well-stocked against desert mishaps. He saw a snakebite kit but didn't think it would work on scorpion stings. But he did find Benadryl syrup, some Oxy pills, various calamine and steroid lotions, a big bottle of off-brand Tylenol, and a long, stretchy bandage.

He swigged a quarter-cup of Benadryl, then smeared some steroid lotion on his face, neck, and hands. He considered taking Oxy, but that might not be wise on top of the Benadryl. He was pretty sure the pain was too lively for drowsiness to occur, but he opted for Tylenol instead. Just to be on the safe side. Needed to keep his mind sharp

He sat in the chair, thinking, for a few minutes, until he could feel the Benadryl working. His tongue felt thinner, and his breathing came a bit easier. He pressed a wad of tissues onto his abdominal wound and wrapped the bandage over them and around his torso.

He reached down into the rear of his underpants, where he had stashed the e-fob for his car. Then he got up and examined the window. The idiot amateurs had nailed the door shut but had failed to account for the window. People in this part of Arizona never opened their windows. He thought most people forgot they even *could* open.

The window was a sliding type. It was sticky; probably hadn't been opened in years. He took his time, inching it open in short bursts.

The drop to the ground wasn't far, maybe six feet. He landed with an explosion of pain, shook his head to clear his mind, then hobbled away from the house.

The car chirped loudly when he unlocked it, but he didn't care. There was nothing they could do to stop him now. The van had already left. Oddly, so had the moving truck.

He sat behind the wheel of the Audi R8 and focused his pain into an emotion he could *use*. Fury. He fired up the car and sped off toward Sedona.

CHAPTER 46

I t wasn't until the adrenaline wore off a bit that I remembered how hard I'd been hit on the head. My temple thundered with every pulse-beat. But that wasn't the worst of it. Waves of dizziness washed over me every few minutes.

Dizziness and driving don't mix. I struggled to keep the van between the dotted white lines of Route 17 North and to keep my speed constant. I didn't report my mental condition to Tommy. I didn't want it to scare him as much as it was scaring me.

Even worse than the dizziness were the Caroline intrusions. It was as if the blow to my head had shattered whatever thin wall remained between her "realm" and mine. Or between me and madness, as the case might be. Her voice came through continually now, whether imagined or "real." As if she were riding in the van beside me.

Stay calm, Joe. I love you. Prepare yourself; you're going to see things that will enrage you. Don't lose control. Don't set more chains in motion.

Thus went her running commentary. I tried to take in her words, but not to let them distract me. No easy task on top of the driving and dizziness.

Bringing Tommy with me had been a godsend, though. One of the first things he told me as we drove away from Black Canyon City was something he overheard Paolo saying to Abby before she left. "The man you are visiting tonight calls himself God. Be an angel for him, and you'll make us all very happy."

I called my daughter and told her to relay the "God" info to the team. She called me back a short while later, bursting with energy. She told me the traffickers, whom we all now agreed had taken Abby, were known to be "suppliers" to some very high-end clients, including Godfrey "God" Edelberg. World-famous scumbag.

He was hosting a "golf weekend" right now.

In Sedona, Arizona.

Lilly then emailed me some photos from an online real estate magazine. They showed Godfrey Edelberg grinning slickly from various rooms and decks of a gorgeous house in the Sedona mountains. A long shot of the house was included.

Edelberg's house.

I stepped on the gas, despite a rush of dizziness, heading north as fast as I dared go beyond the 75-mph speed limit. I couldn't afford to get pulled over tonight.

"Easy, Joe. Careful," said the voice of Caroline. "Stay in control."

"I will, Darling, I will," I told my dead wife, aloud, then shot a glance at Tommy.

"I understand," he said. "I talk to my brother sometimes too."

***

Same day, 10:07 p.m. Eastern

After meeting with Sarah in her hotel room, Anita White called off her carnival-kidnap plan. The Ghost had been caught. Joe had sent his photo; it was him, no question—the guy White had been tracking. The guy who was in Grace's photo. The one Sarah had seen lurking outside the room. Alec Crandall. With Crandall safely out of the picture, the team didn't want to put Grace at risk. His operatives might still be planning to grab her, but now the risk wasn't worth any potential benefit.

"Can we at least go downstairs to the restaurant, while it's still open, and get a snack?" Sarah asked. "Grace is starving, and so am I. And we need to get out of this room."

Anita said, "Okay, fine." With The Ghost captured, she felt they could let down their guard. Slightly.

Sarah and Grace rode the elevator down to the lobby floor, along with Anita, another TBI agent, and Lilly and Charlie, who had shown up to lend their support to Sarah.

A third agent, a woman dressed like a hotel janitor, met them all in the lobby.

As the group walked together toward the hotel restaurant, Charlie continued to work her phone.

"Come on, Jack, answer," she whispered. "Answer."

***

We made it to Sedona in less than an hour, but still no one had phoned or texted me Edelberg's address. I'd hoped they'd be able to learn it by now, but evidently "God's" property was held by a well-shielded LLC that did a good job hiding its assets from the public.

On the positive side, the pain and dizziness had finally started to ebb.

I spotted a restaurant/bar that looked like a locals' hangout—four pickup trucks in the parking lot—and took a chance. I dashed in and told the bartender I was scouting locations for a movie company. I was looking for a particular home, I said, but didn't have the address. A beer-bellied guy with an A/C company's logo stitched over his shirt pocket wandered over and looked at the photo of the mountaintop house my phone was showing.

"You won't be able to get near that place," he said. "It's up a long, gated private road. Security cameras, the whole nine yards."

I assured him I wasn't planning to enter the property. Just wanted to get some wide-angled night shots of the house's exterior and the surrounding area. He shrugged *no law against that, I guess* and gave me driving directions.

***

After her second refill of lemonade, Grace said she needed to use the bathroom. Anita signaled the janitor-disguised agent to accompany her. The bathroom was down a hall and around a corner. The agent went into the bathroom with Grace, took a quick look to ensure all three stalls were unoccupied, then took up guard duty outside the door, so no one could enter.

Grace chose the last stall and reached for the snap on her jeans.

A nerve-shattering *bang* made her head shoot up. The door to her stall flew open, kicked in by brute force. Before she could process what was going on or find her voice to scream, a man's hand shot forward, clamping her mouth shut.

"Hello, Grace Elizabeth Dillard."

It was him. The man from her photo. The one who had followed her in the woods.

CHAPTER 47

It was too dark to admire the Sedona scenery Caroline had always wanted to see. I didn't have the time or inclination anyway. I spotted the right-hand turn described by the A/C guy, off Route 179, and headed down a narrow road into the mountains. After about three miles, I passed a dirt road on the left with the small "Private" sign I'd been told to watch for. The road inclined steeply upward and hung a right curve. A sturdy gate with a guard shack, set back from the main road, blocked access to the property.

So, Edelberg owned himself a whole mountain. Of course he did. Thoughts of smashing his face to meat-ribbons threatened to overwhelm me. Caroline's voice urged me to breathe.

I drove past the private road without stopping or slowing, in case cameras or a live guard were watching the gate.

I had no idea how to get into a house that sat on a hilltop like a medieval castle and was surrounded by cameras and other security measures. One thing I knew for sure was that I wasn't getting in by vehicle. Not with a manned gate blocking my path. I would need to do this on foot.

I spotted another dirt road up ahead on the right, marked by a tiny wooden sign with an icon of a Jeep—off-road adventures were a major tourist industry in Sedona. There wouldn't be any more tours today, so I pulled onto the red-dirt trail and parked in a patch of shrubbery.

No sooner had I stopped the van and opened the door than another vehicle pulled in behind me, high beams glaring. Looking in the mirror, I saw a man dressed in official-looking khakis and a wide-brimmed hat step out of the car.

"Hands up and step out of the vehicle," he ordered.

***

The smashing of glass dishes caught everyone's attention. Not an unusual sound in a restaurant. But Anita White leapt to her feet and ran in the direction it came from.

"Help!" a young man's voice cried.

Anita dashed down the hall and around a corner.

A teenage food-server in white shirt and black pants stood staring, aghast, at the floor. But not at his dropped tray of broken plates: the TBI agent in janitor clothing lay in a pool of blood. Her neck was slit open in a five-inch gash, and her eyes bulged in panic. An awful gurgling sound issued from her neck.

Anita yelled, "Somebody call an ambulance!" She ran past the fallen agent and shouldered open the bathroom door, gun in hand. Grace was gone, as White knew she would be.

She dashed back into the hall. She quickly knelt in the pooling blood and put her hand on her agent's face.

"Hang on, help is coming," she said. But it looked like help would be too late.

As White ran toward the nearest exit, she phoned her second-in-command and barked, "Go to plan C. Repeat, go to plan C."

***

Tommy and I raised our hands in surrender and stepped out of the van. I turned to look at the cop barking the orders and tried to see his face through the high-beam glare.

"Dang, Brother Dillard, I'm just yankin' your chain. Don't you recognize my voice?"

"Leon?" The man stepped forward. Leon Bates. My jaw dropped. "What the hell are you doing in Arizona? Aren't you a tad outside your jurisdiction? Like, about two thousand miles?"

"Come Monday morning, I won't *have* a jurisdiction, at least not anywhere on this green planet. My resignation letter is already written, and I got nothin' to lose. I flew out here, 'cause I thought my friend Joe might need some help catching some bad guys."

"You got that right," I said and smiled for the first time in recent memory. "How'd you find me?"

"Your daughter gave me this." He held up Caroline's phone. It showed a map with a flashing blue dot on it. "A little app called Family Circle. It's on your own danged phone."

What? So I'd been beaming my location to my family all along? Well done, Joe.

I shook my head in disbelief. "Leon, I'd like you to meet someone who's already been a lot of help to me. This is Tommy. Tommy, Leon." The men shook hands.

Leon told me he would explain his resignation later. For now, there were more important matters. He filled me in on what he'd learned about the sex ring and Edelberg. He explained that Anita White had been trying to get the FBI involved, but that the feds were taking a "wait and see" approach. There was still no hard evidence connecting Edelberg to the girl, and the Bureau was not eager to be sued by him again. The Arizona CID (Criminal Investigations Division), for its part, was taking its cues from the feds.

"Which means it's probably just us," said Leon.

"Won't be the first time," I replied.

We walked to the winding, paved road, reviewing our weapon inventory. Bates had brought a sidearm and a rifle. I had the same. I gave my handgun to Tommy and asked if he knew how to use it.

"Good enough," he replied.

I showed him how to disengage the safety.

We walked down the street toward the private roadway, brainstorming ways to get up to the hilltop home and inside it. We couldn't see the house from where we stood, but the photo on my phone showed it had one road spiraling up to it, which was no doubt well-covered by security cameras. The rock walls looked too sheer and dangerous to climb, especially in the dark, and the cameras would probably spot us there anyway.

In short, there was no way we were getting in.

"Caroline," I said aloud. "If you have any influence over there, we could use a miracle right about now."

And damned if she didn't deliver one. Or maybe it was just dumb luck.

A commercial van came up the road, slowing as it neared the private road. When the driver saw Leon and me with our rifles, he canceled his turn and kept driving. We read the words on the side of the van: *Masterson Catering, Food Service for Discerning Clients.* The driver stopped a little farther down the road, as if trying to decide what to do. Then he commenced a slow three-point turn. As we ran toward the van, I quickly hatched an idea and explained it to Leon. He was already on the same page.

Leon, armed and uniformed, stood in the middle of the road, flagging down the vehicle.

"I'm with the Sheriff's Department," he said, holding up his badge. Not a lie. Technically. He said Tommy and I were plainclothesmen. Also literally correct.

Tommy wisely looked at the ground, hiding his youthful face.

The driver explained that he was delivering food supplies to a private party at the hilltop house and didn't want any trouble. Leon told him a potential crime was in progress and we needed to enter the home undetected. He ordered the driver to allow us to hide in the van and told him to proceed through security protocols as if all was normal. He promised the man he was not in danger.

We piled into the catering van, squeezing in amongst the tubs and coolers.

I couldn't see anything for the next few minutes. I felt the van stop at the gate and heard the driver announce, "Masterson Catering. We have an order for Mr. E." A man's voice replied, "Proceed to the service entrance." Presumably, the gate opened. Up the spiraling road we drove.

I may have breathed once or twice. If so, I don't recall.

The driver made a couple of turns, then backed up, stopped, and shut off the engine.

I heard a roll-up door on the house open quietly.

"I have an extra smock," the driver said. He was cooperating with us. Good. "But it's a woman's size." That ruled out Leon or me. Tommy would have to wear it. "Grab a tub and follow me. I'll show you where the security room is. There's a big monitor in there. And a guy who watches it. All I ask is that you let me get out of here before you do anything."

We made a quick plan. It hinged on Tommy playing a key role. And a risky one. Tommy and the catering guy would make the delivery to the kitchen. On the way back out, Tommy would try to peel away and dash into the security room, fast. He would order the security guy to the floor with his gun. Leon and I would wait till the driver returned to his truck. If Tommy wasn't with him, we would make our move into the house.

The driver and Tommy, wearing their Masterson Catering smocks, each grabbed a plastic tub and headed into the house through a basement area.

Leon and I waited. Game on.

CHAPTER 48

Several cars from the TBI, the state police, and the Johnson City police, working in hasty coordination, moved into position to seal off all streets and arteries around the Vanderbilt Hotel. The hotel was flanked on one side by ETSU—East Tennessee State University—and on the other side by the St. Regis Medical Center, both of which had sprawling campuses.

The front of the hotel and the lobby had been well guarded all evening, and the suspect and victim had not been sighted leaving in that direction, or crossing Route 321, known in that area as West State of Franklin Road.

Anita White had called the Special Operations Commander of the Tennessee Department of Safety and Homeland security to authorize a chopper, with searchlights, to join the hunt. But she hadn't heard back yet.

A dozen officers from various departments fanned out on foot from the Vanderbilt. Their heavy concentration was on the university campus, largely dark at eleven o'clock on a Saturday night and full of potential hiding spots.

Anita White felt confident the suspect and his young hostage were still within the contained area. They'd had, at most, a minute's head start, probably less. But still, her nervous system was jacked up to a 10.

"Anyone you see on foot, regardless of physical description, detain them and question them," she shouted into her walkie-talkie.

***

The tall blond man known variously as The Ghost, The Surgeon, El Espectro, and a half-dozen other names—a man reputed to possess the impossible ability to be in two places at once—ran toward the medical center, dragging Grace Dillard by the wrist. They had exited the Vanderbilt by a rear service door, where he had killed a young cop. He had terrified Grace into submission with threats of unspeakable cruelty toward her and her mother should she disobey him. He'd also told her that he had gotten away with every murder he'd ever committed.

The Ghost reasoned that a hospital would offer multiple means of escape. And though he still planned to get the girl out alive, so that she could suffer a fate worse than death, he would not hesitate to kill her if necessary. And dispose of her body. A hospital offered many creative methods of death and disposal.

He'd been watching the girl and her mother for days. Security around them had been tight. He had come up with several better plans than this one but had received a call from his partner in Arizona that tonight was the night to act. So, he'd been forced to improvise.

He knew the police would seal the area off immediately, and he also knew there would be plenty of cameras in a hospital, but he intended to act fast. He didn't care what the cameras revealed on later examination. He was a ghost. And at this late hour on a Saturday night, he knew the security crew would be minimal.

"Keep your right hand in your pocket," he instructed Grace as he walked briskly into the ER entrance, holding her left hand. "And keep your eyes down. Don't look at anyone's face. I'll see it in their eyes if you do."

***

Grace obeyed the big, scary, blond man. But as she slid her right hand into her pocket, she left her pinkie finger sticking out. He couldn't see it from his angle. She hoped.

She stretched her pinkie out three times. Fast.

She knew what was at stake if he caught her. She'd seen the woman lying in the pool of blood, with her neck cut open, gurgling blood-bubbles. It was a picture she'd never erase.

As she and the man hustled through the ER lobby and down an adjoining hall toward a bank of elevators, she contracted and extended her pinkie. Repeatedly. Three short stretches, three long stretches, three short stretches—the "help" signal her mother had drilled into her. You could do it with anything, that was the beauty of it—hands, feet, eyelashes, objects. Of course, for it to work, someone had to see it. Grace couldn't look up to check if anyone was noticing

All she could do was repeat her finger movements and hope.

Three short, three long, three short. S.O.S. in Morse Code.

Three short, three long, three short.

***

The middle-aged woman leaned into the "girl-party room" and said, "Show time! Let's head upstairs." She looked at Abby as she said it.

The four "party girls" all stood. The two older ones each grabbed a bottle of Veuve Clicquot and bent over to snort another line of powder from the black stone table.

"The men may want you to dance first," the older woman explained. "If they do, act like you're having the time of your life. Big smiles. We don't want to upset our host."

As they filed out of the room, Abby and the other younger girl exchanged silent looks of terror.

***

The catering guy came back to the van without Tommy. He told me and Leon how to get to the security room. We gave him ten seconds to make his getaway, then ran inside.

I liked Tommy and had developed a new respect for him. But still, I didn't have high confidence in his ability to do what we'd asked of him.

He proved me wrong. When Leon and I got to the security room, a uniformed guy with a paunch and a gray mullet was lying on the floor, wincing and holding up his hands. Tommy stood over him with his gun. The arrival of me and Leon, also armed, dissolved any vestige of resistance in the guy.

He told us, upon questioning, that he was a private security employee who worked at the house occasionally, for special events. His job was to watch the massive monitor, which was divided into about thirty camera views. If he spotted unusual activity in any part of the house or grounds, he would notify one of the six other security agents, all of whom were armed.

I was encouraged by what I was hearing. This guard was the only person who had eyes on the whole house, and we had him under our control.

From his supine position, he pointed out, on screen, two of the other security agents. Each was stationed on an outdoor deck on opposite sides of the house. They wore leather jackets and held rifles. Then he showed us two other agents. They were "casually" dressed—polo shirts, jeans— but still reeked of security, even without the sidearms and earpieces they wore. They stood guard outside a room the guy told us was Edelberg's "office."

The final two agents were stationed inside the office, the guard said. It was the only room in the house without cameras.

"The boss man doesn't want anyone knowing, or recording, what happens in that room," he told us. Given the guy's apparent eagerness to rat out his employer, I thought maybe he knew exactly what went on inside that room. "Oh look," he said a moment later, his voice dripping with disdain, "here comes the entertainment."

On screen, a middle-aged woman led a quartet of scantily clad, underage girls toward the guarded door to Edelberg's "office." The two girls in front, carrying champagne bottles, laughed and slapped playfully at each other. The two in back looked sullen. Because of the mature-looking makeup and sequined bikini costume the final girl was wearing, I almost didn't recognize her. But then, at the last second, I did.

Abby Pruitt.

Clashing emotions erupted within me: fear for her safety, eagerness to rush to her aid, hope that I was still in time to save her from the worst, and, of course, my old friend. Anger. Boiling, seething, blistering rage that men of Edelberg's ilk, simply because they had power and privilege, could purchase a young girl's innocence and use her like an object. A disposable commodity to be tossed aside when done with.

"Careful, Joe," spoke Caroline in a voice so clear I looked around to see if the others had heard it. They hadn't. "Keep your cool. Stay in control."

I didn't know if I had the power.

CHAPTER 49

A ngie McCallister was a nurse practitioner doing her residency at St. Regis Medical Center. She planned to specialize in working with victims of trauma. She was on her way to the lobby exit after a long shift. Something about the young girl holding hands with the tall blond man set off her inner alarms. Angie turned to watch them as they headed toward the elevator. That was when she saw the girl's little finger twitching.

Three short, three long, three short. S.O.S. She was sure of it. Yes, there it was again.

The man and girl entered the elevator. It was too late, and probably unwise, for Angie to try to make it onto the elevator car with them. The door closed anyway, eliminating that option.

The "down" arrow lit up over the door.

Angie watched to see which floor the elevator stopped at—B, basement—then ran toward the security station at the end of the hall.

***

House music blared and colored lights flashed as the four young girls paraded into the room known as "the office." Abby had never seen an office this size. It was longer and wider than her whole Tennessee house-trailer.

The girls marched toward an open area where the flashing lights were focused. An impromptu dance stage. Leather armchairs formed a semi-circle in front of it. Sitting in the "audience" seats were seven or eight men, clapping to the music and making whoops and catcalls. They all looked pretty old, at least 40 or 50. Cigar smoke hung blue in the air.

As the girls entered the dance area, the middle-aged woman looked at Abby and made the "smile" gesture with her fingers. Her eyes issued a stern warning. Abby smiled, all teeth, as if posing for a school photo. She had a feeling her life might depend on that smile.

She stepped into the flashing lights and began to dance like the others. The men cheered.

Abby's skin crawled. Her bladder and bowels felt ready to give.

***

Leon had brought nylon cuffs along in his uniform pocket. With apologies to the gray-mulleted security guy, he bound his wrists and ankles but lifted him from the floor and let him sit in his chair.

"Do I need to gag you?" Leon asked.

The guard shook his head no. "Believe it or not, I'm on your side. I can help. I know this place inside out."

I believed him. But still, we told Tommy to guard him.

And then we gave Tommy further instructions. He was to watch the whole house on the monitor and send Leon and me status reports in real time. By text message if possible, by live call if necessary. Bates and I would do the guerilla work, on foot. We had the experience.

Tommy protested, but we convinced him his role was vital. We asked if he knew how to write and send text messages. He said yes.

I gave him Shane's phone. Leon and I each had our own. We exchanged numbers, and Leon quickly set up a three-way texting group.

"How do we get up to the room that has no cameras?" I asked the guard.

"Go up those stairs, take a left, then another left."

Leon and I silenced our ringers and text alerts. We struck off toward the stairs.

***

The security team at St. Regis Medical Center phoned in to report a possible sighting of the suspect and girl. The Amber alert had gone out just two minutes ago, along with special calls to the ETSU and hospital security offices. Agent White had never seen such a quick response.

She raced out of the lobby toward the hospital, calling in backup as she ran. She turned to see Sarah, Lilly, and Charlie running after her, along with a couple of TBI agents.

"Stay out of this!" she shouted at the Dillard women. "That's an order. Remain in the hotel lobby."

The Dillard women ignored her and kept running. Anita White couldn't worry about them right now. She had too much else to focus on.

***

Abby's fear shot into the red zone when the white-haired man with the bright teeth and dark tan stood up, clapping and grinning. He signaled to someone to cut the music and the flashing lights. His wish was immediately granted. She sensed he was used to that.

"Gentlemen," he said. The way the others looked at him, Abby knew he was the man in charge. The host. The one who called himself God. "That certainly was entertaining, was it not?"

The men responded with hoots and applause.

"Ladies, take a bow."

The four teenage—and pre-teenage—girls bowed dutifully, all plastic smiles.

"I can only speak for myself," said the white-haired man, "but my… 'entertainment level' is peaking." He flashed a glance at his crotch, then bobbed his eyebrows up and down. The other men laughed uproariously. "God" looked directly at Abby and held his hand out, his cigar in his other hand. The middle-aged woman shot Abby a warning glance and jerked her head toward the man. Abby approached him and took his hand.

"Miss Abigail, I believe?"

Abby nodded.

"Would you do me the honor of accompanying me to my chambers?"

"God" pulled her by the hand, and they headed toward a side room. At this, the men all stood and clapped. Abby couldn't wrap her mind around this. They were giving him a *standing ovation*. For molesting a kid. What kind of world was this?

A world where money was power, and power was everything. That kind. The kind where no one cared, no one helped, and no one came to your rescue.

Grow up, kid. Get used to it.

Abby felt hope and innocence drain from her like air from a punctured beach ball. She resigned herself to whatever was coming next.

CHAPTER 50

Tommy's eyes gawped in disbelief when the monitor showed the Audi R8 pull up to Edelberg's guarded gate. He recognized the car. But it couldn't be him. The Ghost. He couldn't be alive and moving about. Not after taking a gunshot to the gut and a dozen bark-scorpion stings. And being nailed up in a room.

But the camera showed his face clearly. It was him. Here. Now.

The call buzzer from the gate rang up to the security room. The security guy told Tommy which button to push to answer it, then did the talking himself. "Yeah?"

"Tell Mr. Edelberg that Alec Crandall is here," said the guard from the station below.

"I'll see if I can reach him," said the security guy. He shrugged at Tommy: what do we do now?

"We keep this guy away from here," Tommy replied. "That's what we do."

***

Leon and I crept quickly, but quietly, down the hall, rifles at the ready. At the next left turn, we'd be facing the two security guards standing outside Edelberg's "office."

I looked at my phone for a status report from Tommy at the monitor. A text came in that instant: *Tall blond guy from house is HERE.*

What? Impossible. I should have killed him when I had the chance. I should have known better. I typed *Hold him off* and hit send. I had no idea how Tommy was going to do that, but I had more urgent matters to attend to. *What are guards outside office doing now?* I texted him.

Looking bored came the text reply. Good, maybe we could catch them by surprise.

What should I do about blond guy? read his next text.

Figure something out! I typed. Tommy against The Ghost? Not a chance. But I had the Abby situation to handle now. I'd deal with The Ghost if and when I needed to.

Leon and I reached the turn at the end of the hall. We braced ourselves for action.

***

"Drink?" said "God" to Abby. He held up a bottle of champagne.

The bedroom looked like it was copied and pasted from one of those *Homes of the Rich and Famous*-type shows her mother loved to watch. Low, elegant lighting. Massive bed, soft leather chairs, low tables. All in black and white. The only color in the room was the trail of red rose petals leading to the bed. This guy actually wanted this to be *romantic*?

She was about to reply "no" to the drink offer—and just get the whole thing done with—when a thought inserted itself. *Hawk! Wake up! Come alive!* Coach Jack. Telling her not to give up. The game wasn't over yet. She just needed to find her *stuff*. The will to win.

Despair retreated.

"Yes, please," she said to the white-haired man with a smile. Maybe starting with a drink would buy her time to figure something out.

As he poured the sparkling wine, her eyes darted about the room. On a polished white desk on the far side of the bed sat a black glass vase filled with all-white office tools—pencils, pens, ruler, scissors.

Scissors.

She took the champagne flute and wandered part-way around the bed, playing the part of the sophisticated young woman surveying "her man's" terrain. He looked on in amusement, seeming to enjoy her appreciation of his wealth and taste. But only for a moment.

"Drink up, toots," he said. "Let's get this show on the road."

So much for "romance."

She moved further around the bed, locking her eyes on his, trying to project sensual, womanly confidence. His face fell into a frown. He didn't like that approach.

Of course not, she realized, with insight beyond her years. *If he liked women with power, he wouldn't be paying to have sex with kids.* She dropped her eyes and went back into "shy" mode.

Standing on the opposite side of the bed from him, she turned away to undress. She slowly lowered the sheer robe covering her sparkling bikini, hoping all his attention would remain on her body. *Her* eyes were fixed on the scissors.

This would all come down to speed. She was young and fast. He was old and slow. She hoped her injured leg, still only partially healed, would cooperate.

She reached around her back and fumbled with the clasp to the bikini top, buying time. She heard his belt unbuckle. Her heart galloped.

***

Tommy watched the guard shack at the base of the road. The tall blond man appeared to grow tired of waiting to see Edelberg. He climbed out of his Audi R8 and exchanged words with the guard inside the shack. After a moment, the guard stepped out and approached him. And then, suddenly, the guard was down. Just like that. It happened so fast, Tommy didn't see how. Alec Crandall stepped over the guard's prone body into the guard shack, and then exited by the side door. He began walking up the road. His gait was wobbly but determined.

Tommy, panic rising, explained to the bound security guy how dangerous the blond man was. The security guy had an idea. "We'll call the two exterior guards and alert them to an intruder." That would serve two purposes, he explained. It would pull the guards out of position, which might be helpful to Tommy's friends. It would also keep Crandall occupied for a while, as the armed guards tried to figure out who he was and whether he belonged here.

The guy told Tommy how to initiate the call, on the computer system, to the exterior guards. "Intruder in driveway," said the tied-up guard from his seat. "Respond immediately."

Tommy watched the monitor. The two guards in leather jackets left their posts and ran toward their respective exits.

***

Leon and I sprang around the corner, rifles aimed. "Hands up!" I said, in a voice sharp enough to get the door-guards' attention, but not loud enough to alert anyone in the office. I hoped.

The two guards turned in surprise. They realized we had the drop on them and obeyed my command. Leon gave them the "hush" sign.

We dashed up close to them and ordered them away from the door. Leon took their guns from their holsters as I trained my rifle on them. We marched them into an open sitting room across the hall from the office. Leon bound their hands and ankles with tough nylon bands.

"Make a sound and I'll kill you," Leon said. They didn't. He taped their mouths shut with a small roll of duct tape he'd brought along too. Bates had come prepared.

Now, how to deal with the armed guards in the no-camera "office"? Tommy couldn't help us prepare for them.

***

The tall blond man holding Grace's hand speed-walked toward the garage bay area on the ground floor of the hospital. The place where the ambulances entered and exited. Grace had to half-run to keep up with him. Her little finger was cramping now, and she couldn't flash her S.O.S. anymore. There was no one here to see them anyway.

She wanted to scream. She wanted to cry. She wanted to run.

But the man said he would kill her. And her mother. And she believed him.

***

Tommy's phone rang in the security room. Joe Dillard. Tommy put him on speaker.

Joe spoke in a hurried voice. "Call the two guards inside Edelberg's office. Tell them there's an emergency situation outside the room they need to deal with, immediately."

Tommy pushed the button to call the in-office guards. The tied-up guy relayed the message convincingly. He was all in.

Tommy then switched his attention to the camera view showing the entrance road. The two leather-jacketed guards ran up to Crandall, weapons drawn. From the body language of the three men, Tommy could tell the situation was going sideways fast. The tall blond man was saying something that had the guards' full attention. Whatever it was, the men seemed to believe him. One of them phoned up to the security room. Tommy clicked the button to answer.

"Alert the whole team," said the guard's voice over the speaker. "Security has been breached. Intruders are inside the house. I repeat, intruders are inside the house."

"Roger that," replied the gray-mullet guy. He shrugged at Tommy, his face pale.

The guards moved in to support the weakened Crandall, grabbing him under the arms. The three of them hurried up the hill toward the house, the two guards half-carrying the blond man. Tommy guessed it would take only a minute, two at most, for them to reach the house.

And then, game over.

CHAPTER 51

When Abby heard the old guy's pants hit the floor, she knew that was her moment. His pants were literally around his ankles.

She lunged toward the desk, grabbed the white scissors from the vase, then pivoted on her good leg. She did a lightning-fast one-eighty and jumped up onto the bed. Making a single bounding leap across the mattress, she sprung into the air, the scissors over her head.

"God" looked up in shock as she descended on him. But as the scissors drew near, his racquetball-trained reflexes kicked in. He deflected Abby's weapon with the back of his left hand and punched her, hard, with his right fist. The scissors flew from her hand. Abby fell to the floor, rolling from his forceful blow, and landed on her back.

He jumped on her instantly, pinning her to the floor. He was naked from the waist down.

Abby was utterly overmatched by his size, weight, and strength.

"That was a bad idea, little girl. Now this is going to be fun."

***

Leon and I were waiting, our backs pressed to the wall, when the two guards rushed out of Edelberg's office, guns drawn. They spotted their bound-and-gagged coworkers across the hall and went to their aid. Leon and I came up behind them with our rifles and took them by surprise. We disarmed them easily, bound them, and dashed into the office.

Bates, looking every inch the law enforcement official, stepped toward Edelberg's cronies, sitting in their leather chairs.

"Don't move," he said in a firm, quiet voice, his rifle aimed toward them. The men turned to look at him. Faces paled. Jaws dropped. Hands went up.

"You, hands off the girl," Bates ordered the last of the men. He complied, and the girl scurried away from him to join her two companions, wiping the spot on her waist where the man's hand had rested. "Where's Edelberg?"

A couple of the men pointed.

I stepped toward the closed door they indicated.

"Remember, Joe," said Caroline's voice, sounding like she was right beside me, though I knew she wasn't. "Stay in control. Break the chain. Do it now."

I took a deep breath and turned the doorknob.

***

Anita White ran down the hospital corridor, right behind Sarah Dillard. She wasn't sure when the shift had occurred—when she stopped ordering Sarah to stay back and started following her. All she knew was that, right now, she trusted a mother's instincts more than her own. And Sarah Dillard seemed to be moving on instinct alone. A mother drawn to her daughter by that mysterious homing force a non-mother could never know.

At least that's what Anita hoped.

***

I heard the words—"Stop! You're hurting me!"—before I saw, or understood, what was happening.

When my eyes landed fully on the scene before me, my logical mind dissolved. I lapsed into a state of reality I'd never experienced before. Time slowed to a crawl. I suddenly didn't know where I was. Or when. Or even who.

I couldn't tell what was real and what wasn't.

I'm sure the events that unfolded in that room took less than five seconds, but to me they stretched out over a small eternity. It felt as if I was moving through clear molasses, mentally and physically.

The voice. The girl crying, "Stop! You're hurting me!' It sounded like Sarah. My sister. As a kid.

It *was* her, damn it. It *was* her.

But the man on top of her, pinning her down, was Godfrey Edelberg.

That didn't make sense. But then suddenly the man became my uncle Raymond. Not in an imagined way; in a real way. Flesh and blood. Right in front of me. I knew such a thing wasn't possible. But I couldn't shake the perception.

I was in the past. Not *remembering* the past. *In* it. All the way. My grandmother's room surrounded me, real in every detail. The porcelain washbasin on the dresser, the doily beneath it, that purple-gray floral wallpaper. My uncle Raymond violating my sister, right before my eyes.

My muscles went numb. Paralyzed. I couldn't move.

And then suddenly I was in a room of black and white. A black and white photo? Another image from the past? No. This was black and white *furniture*. And room-décor.

Edelberg's room. Oh. Right. The girl on the floor was Abby Pruitt, not Sarah. Godfrey Edelberg was on top of her. By an act of immense willpower, I refocused my eyes and mind. Abby was wearing the shimmery bikini I'd glimpsed in the security video.

She was still wearing it. Still wearing it! Top and bottom. That meant he hadn't gotten to her yet. I had to act.

My mind plummeted back to my grandmother's room, watching Raymond rape my sister. And then, before I could do anything, I was whisked away to a different place altogether.

The field at my old high school. Football practice. Me ramming my shoulder into the padded tackling sled, designed for three men, and pushing it back eight feet all by myself. The coach's eyes goggling, impressed. Him unaware that every time I rammed that pad, I was ramming my uncle Raymond. Me knowing I had found my chosen sport. A way to vent some of the anger that was already ruling my life.

My brain spun out again. New memories crashed in, dozens of them at once. My time as an Army ranger, all that hand-to-hand combat. All the fights I'd gotten into over the years.

I saw everything with crystal clarity. As I'd grown into a man, Raymond had burrowed down into my unconscious and hidden himself away there. But it was still always him. Always him I was fighting. My whole life.

Suddenly I was back in my grandmother's room again. Raymond was committing his vile act. But now I stood over him as a man, not a child. I felt the paralysis lift.

As it lifted, so did the curtain on the scene around me. Edelberg's secret chamber came back into view. I saw Edelberg straddling the girl. He turned his head, in slow motion, and registered my arrival. His eyes widened. He started to rise, an attempt to escape.

Caroline's voice came through to me. Different this time. Fueled by outrage, not heavenly peace. "Screw control," she said, as if through gritted teeth. "Take this monster out."

I dropped my rifle. It seemed to take forever to hit the floor. I lowered my shoulder, set my feet, and launched myself like a linebacker with a direct shot at the quarterback. That sense of moving through clear syrup remained.

I felt every separate movement of every separate muscle. My feet firing my ankles. My ankles firing my calves. Then my thighs, my hips, my abs, all exploding into action in a perfect chain of unleashed energy.

I took one slow, running step forward. Then another. Faster now. Gathering speed through the clear molasses. Gathering power. Faster.

Closer.

Faster.

Edelberg was only a foot away now. I attained full speed.

My shoulder connected with his chest. The air whooshed out of him with a mechanical-sounding note, like a dropped accordion. I wrapped my arms around him, dug my feet into the carpet, and drove him forward, lifting him off the floor.

And I ran. With everything I had.

Charging. Pounding. Growling like a beast.

The crack of wood snapped me from my daze and called me back to real time.

I looked at what I had done. I'd driven Edelberg straight through the wall-plaster and into the wooden framing beyond it, cracking the frame itself. Edelberg looked at me with stunned eyes, literally embedded in his own wall. Helpless. Immobilized.

But alive.

I knew what I had to do next. Snap his filthy neck.

"No!" shouted Caroline in my head. "That's enough, Joe! End it here. Break the chain."

I paused. Took a breath. Then another. She was right. This was where it had to end. I had Edelberg fully under my control now. There was nothing to be gained by killing him. I needed to stop things here. Let the chips of justice fall where they would. Not play judge and jury. Not anymore. I'd done enough of that in my life. Enough.

Enough.

I felt my rage melt away like frost on a heated windshield. A wave of Caroline's scent moved through me. I lowered my strangling hands.

Edelberg's face suddenly clenched into a knot of agony. The light went out of his eyes. I looked down and saw a white scissor-blade buried in his gut.

And Abby Pruitt holding the handle.

CHAPTER 52

The Pruitt girl stared at her hand as if it belonged to someone else. I could tell by the blank look in her eyes that she had no idea what had just happened.

But *I* did. She had snapped. Gone into a fugue state. Fueled by the trauma that had been piling on her since the night she'd been snatched. Probably since she'd been born. Her body had acted on its own, driven by a program deeper than her conscious mind.

She looked at me with questioning eyes, then at her hand, and I knew she had no clear memory of doing what she'd just done. And I intended to keep it that way. If I could.

"You didn't do that," I said to her, taking her by the shoulders and shaking her lightly. "It was me. Do you hear me?" I hoped that by feeding her an alternate story, right now, while her mind was still a fresh jumble of trauma, she would start to encode my version of events in her memory as her own. "*I* stabbed him, not you."

A decision firmed up inside me, right there on the spot. Whether her mind accepted my story or not, it was the story we were going to tell. To anyone and everyone. Henceforth and forever. Period. There was no way this poor girl was going to pay one more cent of price for what had been done to her.

"*I* stabbed him," I repeated. I put my hand on the scissor handle, as if to emphasize my act. But I was really laying my fingerprints down over hers. "You didn't do anything. You were the victim in all of this. None of this was your fault. Do you hear me? None of it."

"Who are you?" she asked, as if seeing me for the first time.

I realized I hadn't told her yet. "I'm Coach Jack's dad."

The expression on her face melted. This eleven-year-old girl, cursed with early puberty and costumed by terrible people to look like a sexually desirable woman, dissolved into a five-year-old child. She threw her arms around me and burst into tears. And I hugged her like she was one of my own.

Neither of us wanted to be the first to let go.

"Such a touching moment."

I turned to see a tall man with broad shoulders framed by the doorway. If it hadn't been for Tommy's earlier text, I wouldn't have believed it possible. But there he stood. The Ghost.

"Too bad this isn't a Hallmark film," he added.

What happened next went down fast. And in a flurry of confusion, at least for me.

The Ghost reached for his side, presumably to grab a weapon. Probably the post-mortem knife; I never saw what it was. A voice shouted, "Drop it!"

It sounded like Tommy, not Leon. Coming from the office somewhere.

The Ghost turned to look at the issuer of the command. He appeared dumbfounded for a moment. And a moment was all he had.

The outer door from the hall burst open. A stampede of bodies thundered into Edelberg's office as a volley of voices shouted commands. "Drop your weapons!" "Freeze!" "Hands above your head!"

Edelberg's army to his rescue? Or could it be...?

The Ghost hesitated for a moment, then set his jaw with fresh determination and made another move for his weapon.

Five bullets lodged in him at once—four in his back from the armed invaders and one in his head.

From Tommy. Where he stood, off to the side.

The Ghost fell to the floor, dead. I now saw who had stormed the office. Guys in FBI jackets. Six or eight of them. Fronted by a giant of a man wearing a suit and tie. Mike Norcross—a.k.a. Thor. Anita White's old TBI partner, now a special agent for the FBI. Our paths had crossed before. Mike was good people.

I released Abby from my embrace and stepped out of the bedroom into Edelberg's office. Edelberg's pedophile buddies all had their hands raised. As did his two leather-jacketed security guys, who sat atop Leon Bates, having pinned him to the floor earlier, I guessed.

Leon signaled he was fine. Seeing the situation was under control, I said to Mike Norcross, "The FBI: a day late and a dollar short. As usual."

"Joe Dillard," he replied, "sticking his nose where it doesn't belong and gumming things up for law enforcement. As usual." But there was a hint of a smile in his eyes.

"Word on the street was you guys didn't want to get involved," I said.

"We had this, Dillard. All along."

"Sure," I said. "Sure you did."

He rolled his eyes and shook his head. This was a conversation "to be continued later." Over a beer, I hoped. For now, there were more important things to deal with. The FBI men streamed into Edelberg's bedroom, announcing his medical status to Norcross.

Norcross called in ambulances for two, though it was too late for either. Then he knelt beside The Ghost. "Alec Crandall," he confirmed. "It's him."

***

"Crandall! Alec Crandall!" Anita White shouted. She stalked across the concrete floor of the ambulance bays, her gun in both hands. "We know you're in here, and we have the area surrounded."

White and Sarah had ridden the elevator to the bottom floor of the hospital, where the suspect and girl had gotten off. Then White had followed Sarah Dillard to where her mother-instincts had led her. Here, in the ambulance bay. But now the trail seemed to grow cold. Sarah looked uncertain, confused. As did Lilly and Charlie, who had followed Sarah here as well.

White continued to scan the cavernous area, along with three other agents. "Surrender yourself immediately," she shouted. "Don't harm the girl and we will work with you."

***

When White's voice rang out, Grace looked up at the tall blond man called The Ghost. He put his finger to his lips, warning her and his new hostage, EMT Manny Gonzalez, to remain silent. Grace complied, remembering the woman in the puddle of blood.

The three were locked in the bathroom at the rear of the EMTs' lounge, located off the ambulance bays. The Ghost stood before the mirror, wrapping his head and face in the long bandage he'd taken from his waist.

He'd already explained his escape plan to Grace and the EMT:

He, Crandall, would lie in a stretcher, with Grace pressed up against him under a blanket and his face disguised by the bandage. Manny Gonzalez, the driver, would load the stretcher onto his ambulance. He would then call the police, requesting clearance for his vehicle to exit the lockdown area for an emergency patient transfer.

Manny was to talk his way past any police roadblocks, citing the medical urgency of his mission. If he failed in any way to help Crandall escape, Crandall would kill the girl first and Manny second.

"Her life is in your hands," The Ghost said through the mouth-slit he'd left between the bandage strips. "Do you understand?" Manny nodded. "As is your own."

White's voice called out again, closer this time. "Crandall! Surrender yourself!"

And then a second voice: "Grace!"

Grace's Mom!

Grace filled her lungs with air and shouted, "HEEEEEEELP" in the loudest, most high-pitched shriek she'd ever emitted. It echoed off the tile walls, seeming to amplify even more.

Then she dove to the floor, twisting open the door latch on her way down. She scrambled under the sink to escape immediate harm.

When the squadron of agents burst through the door, The Ghost did not attempt to defend himself or escape. He did not panic or surrender. Rather, his eyes went as dead as coal nuggets. He whipped a surgical knife from his belt and plunged toward Grace, raising the blade.

A deafening round of gunfire rang out in the small, tiled room.

The Ghost fell to the floor, dead.

Sarah rushed in behind the agents and threw her arms around her daughter. Lilly and Charlie crowded into the small room after her.

When Anita White had unraveled the bandage from Crandall's head, she studied his face and let out a sigh of relief. She texted Norcross, her old partner: *We've got him! Crandall!*

Norcross texted back, seconds later, *No, WE'VE got him!*

They sent photos of their respective captives to each other. And in that moment, thanks to information Joe Dillard had provided, one of the FBI's thorniest dilemmas was solved.

***

I helped Leon Bates to his feet and asked him if he was okay.

"I've been roughed up worse than that by Erlene Barlowe," he said, brushing his sleeve.

"Yeah, we know," Mike Norcross muttered with a smirk. "So does half the Internet."

Bates laughed humorlessly. We stepped out into the hall, and he explained to me what Norcross was referring to: a viral video of him and Erlene playing naked cowboy games that had suddenly brought his law enforcement career to an end.

I felt terrible for Leon. But I felt *terrified* for Jack. I knew my son would be released from jail shortly, thanks to all the exculpatory evidence that had now come to light, but I'd been counting on Leon to make something happen before tomorrow morning. That was when the attack ordered by The Ghost was slated to occur. And now Leon was powerless to do anything.

"You forget one thing, Brother Dillard," he reminded me. "I'm still Sheriff of Washington County, until I hand in my resignation on Monday."

He stepped off to the side and placed a phone call. After a minute, I heard him say to someone, "This is Bates. I am ordering inmate 249917, Jackson Dillard, placed in protective custody immediately, with a twenty-four-hour guard, until his release, which will likely occur on Monday morning. He is not to leave his cell, and he is not to be left unguarded for one second."

The EMTs came with stretchers for The Ghost and Edelberg, and a pair of agents went off with each of them. Then the remaining three agents filed out of the "office," marching Edelberg's security guys, in handcuffs, before them.

Mike Norcross exited last. He was talking to Tommy as they walked. "It's amazing that you memorized all that information," he said. "That'll be a goldmine for us in prosecuting this case and finding some of those kids. Tell you what. We'll put you up in a hotel tonight, and then we'll bring you into the Phoenix office tomorrow and start taking your statement."

But Tommy had no intention of waiting. He'd bottled up his knowledge for years, and he wasn't keeping it bottled up one minute longer. "List of residents," he said, and then began reciting, in an almost chant-like rhythm, "Year one, June second: Priscilla Ann. Blond hair. Fourteen years old. Red nose ring. Flower tattoo. Born in Boston. Loves Hawaiian pizza. Left August fourth. June twelfth: Rosalita. Curly hair. Big hips. Parents from El Salvador. Brother killed by gang..." Mike and Tommy continued down the hall.

Leon and I followed them, bringing up the rear.

Guess it was on us to turn the lights out.

CHAPTER 53

It was an absurdly beautiful day for a summer wedding in East Tennessee. Pleasantly warm, not hot. Crystal blue sky, low humidity.

I was greeting guests as they arrived outside the Garden Chapel at Millstone Manor, the venue the kids had chosen for their affair. Jack and Charlie, the bride and groom, were inside the manor, getting ready. Abby was inside too. I was feeling lighter and brighter than I had in years and was as proud a papa as had ever hosted a knot-tying. The kids had tried to pay for the wedding themselves, but I wasn't hearing of it. I was so happy to have my son alive and cleared of all charges, I would have sold the clothes off my back to write that check, if I'd needed to. Jack had acquired a permanent facial scar, but things could have been a whole lot worse.

I spotted Anita White a distance away, wearing a yellow floral dress and looking softer than she allowed herself to look on the job. I excused myself from my "post." I wanted to talk to her alone for a few minutes before things got rolling. I hadn't seen her in person since all the troubles had happened, though we'd talked by phone a few times.

We hugged and exchanged some happy small talk, as befit the occasion, and then she caught me up on where things stood. "They've completed their investigation," she said. "There won't be any more inquiries."

I let out a massive sigh of relief. With Mike Norcross's help, the FBI was officially accepting my version of what had happened in Edelberg's bedroom: I had burst in on Edelberg about to rape Abby. He had a pair of scissors in his hands when I tackled him and drove him into the wall. Somehow, he got stabbed in the process, but the stabbing was ruled accidental.

Abby corroborated my version. I honestly didn't think she remembered what really happened. Or maybe that's just what I chose to believe. Or what *she* chose to believe. And that was fine with me. With any luck, the coming years would cement the "official" version of events in her mind, and her psyche would release her from any blame. If anyone on this planet deserved a break, it was Abigail Pruitt.

Tommy caught a break too. The bullet he lodged in Crandall's head was deemed a legal shot under the "defense of others" law.

Anita White and I talked about other things as well. Some of them I knew already, others I was just learning. Mike Norcross had indeed been zeroing in on Edelberg for some time but had been obstructed by his superiors at the FBI. Not because of a potential lawsuit, it seemed, but because the Deputy Director was a crony of Edelberg. When Anita White told Norcross about the Sedona party and Abby's likely presence there, however, Mike pulled the trigger on action.

As for Edelberg himself, the wall of silence he'd preserved for so long crumbled after his death. A dozen young women and female minors came forward with stories of his abuse. More were waiting in the wings. His legacy would be that of a child molester who had skirted prosecution because of his wealth. His estate would undoubtedly be sued for billions. His cronies who had been at the house that terrible night were all being indicted on felony charges. And Edelberg's "little black book," found after his death, had revealed several other prominent names, including that of U.S. Senator Todd McGinty, who was now under criminal investigation.

Crandall's mystery had been fully unraveled too. And what a whopper it was. Alec Crandall—aka The Ghost, The Surgeon, El Espectro, and other names—was actually Terence *and* Martin Lipscomb, the twin cousins of John Lipscomb. Yes, both of them. Two men, one identity.

People who knew John Lipscomb often mused as to how such a dark criminal mind could have emerged from such a privileged background. What they didn't know about was John's twin cousins from his mother's troubled bloodline, who went to prep school with him and were one year older. They introduced young John to violent pornography, the black-market economy, and animal torture, among other "pastimes." They were also believed to have introduced him to his future business partner, a fellow prep-schooler named Andres Pinzon.

John took to his cousins' world like a junkie takes to smack. It wasn't long before he became the master, the cousins mere underlings. By John's freshman year in college, he and Andres Pinzon had built a thriving enterprise, moving kilos of Colombian cocaine every month in the retail market. But John was a man of dark appetites, and one day a young lady died in his bed. He called upon the twins for help, knowing their fondness for "wet work." They disposed of the corpse bit by bit—using garden shears and plastic bags—and, in so doing, cemented their place in the Lipscomb organization. Doing the jobs John had no stomach for.

The brothers rose to legendary status when they discovered one twin could serve as a perfect alibi for the other. They eventually pushed this ploy to the limit by "fusing" into a single legal entity, Alec Crandall, a man who could literally "be in two places at once" to confound enemies and evade prosecution. When Terence was caught and tortured by a rival organization, Martin even cut off half his own ear to mirror the injury his brother had suffered.

"Damnedest thing I ever did see," said Anita. "They had the same driver's license, same medical records, same Social Security number. Legally, they were the same person. And, being identical twins, they even had the same DNA."

So, while Alec Crandall number one had been keeping me prisoner in Arizona, Alec Crandall number two had been stalking Grace, my niece, in Tennessee.

"Pretty brilliant," I had to concede.

"Pretty sick is more like it."

I could have talked to Anita for an hour, but I had a wedding to host. Stepping away from her politely, I spotted Erlene Barlowe arriving, clad in a bright red dress with a plunging neckline and a wide-brimmed hat worthy of the Kentucky Derby. She was on the arm of Leon Bates. They were an item again? Good Lord.

"I must say, I was a little surprised when I got my invitation," said Erlene, breezing herself with a fan that matched her hat.

"Why would that surprise you?" I replied. "You were a big help in getting Jack to the altar in one piece. And besides..." I smiled and opened my arms. "You know I've always found you utterly irresistible, Erlene."

She didn't take my playful bait. Instead, she cast her eyes downward, as if in shyness or shame. "So, you still haven't put the last piece into the jigsaw puzzle, have you? That's not like you, Joe."

I didn't know what she meant. And then it hit me like a blackjack to the head—how the whole chain of awful events had been set in motion. Why didn't I see it before? I had long wondered why the Lipscomb organization had come after *me* for the death of John, not the people who actually killed him. Like, for instance, Ronnie Barlowe—or so I suspected.

Now I saw the obvious truth. Erlene had set them on my trail.

Rage flared up within me, extinguishing my joy. I told Leon I needed to speak to Erlene in private.

"Calm down, Joseph," Erlene said to me behind the chapel, after I leveled my accusation at her. "It ain't fittin' for the father of the groom to be bustin' a blood vessel on his son's wedding day." She then shocked me by validating my charges completely. She admitted she was the one who had set The Ghost on me. I demanded she explain herself.

She did:

When Lipscomb's decomposed body was found by a hiker a year earlier, the Lipscomb organization went on the warpath. Erlene found out about this through a network of underworld "tipsters" she paid for information that could affect her or her business. Crandall was vowing to spare no effort in finding John's killer, Erlene learned. She knew he would sniff his way to her eventually. After all, she *was* the one who had arranged Lipscomb's death.

"I figured I had a choice," she said. "I could live in fear the rest of my days, waiting for the axe to fall or I could make the first move. Set things in motion. Bring the fight to us. Where we could have some control of the results."

"By 'we,' you mean me," I said. "You put out the word to Crandall that it was me who offed his cousin, not you."

Erlene looked at me thoughtfully. "Wasn't it, though, sugar?"

I didn't answer. Because I knew she spoke the truth. And it was time I faced it after all these years. *I* had asked Erlene for the hit on Lipscomb— indirectly, sure, but with full intent—because I knew it was the only way to protect my family. Lipscomb needed to die, there was no other way; Andres Pinzon himself had told me that. If Lipscomb had lived, my family would have perished. His death was the price I had to pay for being able to host this joyous wedding today. And it was a price I would pay again in a heartbeat. So, I supposed it was only fitting that the fight had come to me.

"I had faith," said Erlene, "that you, of all people on God's green Earth, would be able to defeat that animal. Leastwise, that's what I hoped. And it turned out I was right."

"You could have at least warned me," I said, trying to tamp down my outrage. "Why didn't you?"

"That woulda defeated the whole point. I didn't want you going all 'Joe Dillard' on the situation. I wanted to keep things contained, let *them* make the first move. Once they finally did—took 'em long enough—I was in a bind. I knew if I told you your family was in danger, you'd have stuck around to protect them. But going after that girl was what you needed to do. ...If it makes you feel any better, I was getting inside info on what they were up to. And I had men watching your house and your family. If you don't believe me, ask your dog. He knew."

I wanted to be furious at her. I wanted to tear into her for saving her own skin at my expense, for not warning me, for setting events in motion that would cause Caroline to die earlier than necessary. But I couldn't muster the self-righteousness. Because Erlene *was* right. About everything.

And things *had* turned out okay. The risk had been huge, but so had the payoff.

I shook my head as she walked away from me and took Leon's arm. It was hard to imagine what Leon Bates, a career lawman, saw in Ms. Erlene Barlowe. When it comes to matters of the heart, I guess, common sense goes right out the window.

That could have been the official theme of the day, it turned out.

You see, Jack and Charlie's nuptials had a unique angle. Not only were the kids celebrating their own betrothal, but they were also announcing their plans to adopt Abby Pruitt. When I first caught wind of this idea, a few weeks earlier, I'd tried to talk them out of it. I applauded their intentions but told them this was a time in their lives when they should be unfettered by responsibility, free to follow their dreams. Taking on the care of a kid who was almost a teenager when they were not too far out of their teens themselves seemed like biting off way too much. There were other ways to help the Pruitt girl and stay involved in her life, I said.

But Jack had explained that having Abby in their lives was a blessing, not a burden.

Here's how it happened. After the horrible chain of events that culminated in Arizona, Abby had to deal with the news of her young mother's suicide. She'd also learned that her father, Greg Pruitt, was in jail, awaiting trial on meth charges, and was likely to spend several years in prison, thanks to Tennessee's "three strikes" rule. Abby thus became a ward of the state.

Jack and Charlie petitioned to become her foster parents, and, thanks to Abby's enthusiasm for the idea, the process was put on the fast track. And thus far, the arrangement had been a success. Though Abby was going through a difficult period, she had bonded with Charlie as deeply as she had with Jack. Together, they were working through it all. Adoption was the next logical step.

Even Greg Pruitt had given the idea his surprise blessing. He'd asked to see Jack in jail, and the two men sat down together. In the most mature act of his godforsaken life, Pruitt signed the paperwork for voluntary surrender of parental custody, allowing the adoption process to go forward. He hadn't gone so far as to apologize for the scar on Jack's face, but I guess you can't have everything.

Jack had tried to explain to me, in words that sounded suspiciously like his mother's, that "Man plans and God laughs," and that the unpredictable messiness of life was where all the good stuff happened. But in the end, it was Charlie's simple words that convinced me.

"She loves us and needs us," Charlie said. "And we love her."

How do you argue with logic like that?

The ceremony was unforgettable. Poetic. Moving. Funny. Solemn. In perfect balance. And when the bride and groom kissed each other, and their daughter-to-be leapt into their arms with unrestrained joy, all my doubt was erased. The kid was finally catching a break. And that was a good thing, even if heaven and Earth had to be rearranged to make it happen.

There was just one more thing I needed to do to make the day complete.

CHAPTER 54

As the sole living parent of the newlyweds and the author of the feast, it fell on me to make the speech at the reception. I waited till everyone had ample time to visit the open bar and find their tables in the Hampshire Room of the Millstone Manor. I made sure everyone I cared about was present in that room. Lilly and her family. Sarah, Grace. I was glad to see that two of the three guests Abby had invited—Hope and Deja—had accepted my plane tickets and showed up, dressed in bright colors and whispering and giggling like teenagers. Badger Daley was here, too, and already on his third beer. We'd have to keep an eye on him. Jack had managed to finagle him a one-day furlough. Jack was working on a diminished capacity defense for Badger but was really counting on the unspoken "sumbitch had it coming to him" defense to win over a jury in the Eddie Braun case. In the courts of Tennessee, I'd learned, anything was possible.

I grabbed the mic and did the expected clink-the-spoon-on-the-glass thing.

Everyone looked at me, and I took my notes from my pocket.

Lilly surprised me by standing and interrupting me before I could speak. "Actually, Dad, Mom has a few words she'd like to say." She marched toward me holding Caroline's iPad with the flowered case. "She recorded this and asked me to play it today." Dumbfounded, I placed the device near the mic and tapped on the cued-up file.

"Hello, my dears," said Caroline's recorded voice, weak but full of inner strength, through the room's speakers. Faces in the room lit up with surprise. "All the people I love the most on Earth are gathered in this room right now. I can feel it. And I am so grateful. This family has been through hell recently, but somehow, I'm betting we made it through. Like we always do. Why? Because we love each other. We're the Dillards. We're family. And family is everything. So, listen to me, all of you: *stay* a family. For me. Always love each other. Never drift apart. Never let small things turn into big things. I am with you today, I really am, and I love you all so much. Blessings on this wondrous union of my beloved Jack and my amazing new daughter, Charlie. I'll be waiting for you all, out on the luminescent bay. But don't rush to come see me. Take your sweet, sweet time. What we have is a forever thing. It'll wait."

Silence filled the room. Tears welled in every eye. I tore up my stupid little prepared speech and just let the silence stand for a minute.

But I did have one final piece of business.

"And now I have a gift for the bride and groom," I said at last, "and for my soon-to-be granddaughter, Abby." I reached into my pocket and pulled out a key on a tab ring. "Jack and Charlie—and Abby—I want you to have the house. On Boone Lake. The family home. The one you kids grew up in." The looks of surprise and protest on the bride's and groom's faces told me I had some explaining to do. "The place is too big for me now, and I have other plans for my immediate future." Before anyone could press me on that last point, I continued. "If you choose to accept the house, and I hope you do, I have only two rules. The first is that Lilly and her family can stay there whenever they want."

"They'd better!" shouted Jack. Everyone clapped.

"The other is that you keep a room ready for me. So I can visit too."

"Visit?" said Charlie from her seat. "Where are you going?'

I gave her the "wait" gesture; we'd talk about it in private. For now, I wanted to finish my thoughts. "One thing I've always known but I've learned anew over the past few months is what your mother just said. Family is everything. Your mother and I want the Dillards to stay strong. And so, the house needs to stay in the family." I lifted my glass. "To Charlie and Jack. And Abby. May you make as many amazing memories in that house as I have."

And then something happened that will go down in Dillard family lore for all time. As the crowd raised their drinks to toast my final words, an electric buzz rang out from the corner of the room. A neon beer sign hanging over the bar sparked to life and lit up. It took a few seconds for the significance of the two lighted words to hit everyone. And then the room broke into stunned applause, which turned into a standing ovation that went on for minutes on end. Tears and laughter flowed in equal measure.

The two words on that sign? "Bud Light."

***

After dinner, there was dancing and drinking. And toasts to the Bud Light sign. Everyone tried to pin me down as to what my mysterious plans would be after vacating the house on Boone Lake. The truth was, I didn't really know. I just sensed I needed to spend some time alone. Do some figuring out. And for that reason, my plans would start with a solo trip. To the Caymans. Well, not strictly solo. Rio, my aging German Shepherd, would join me. He and I had been needing some "man time" together for a while now.

As the festivities were winding down for the day, I became aware of Sarah, standing against a wall, eyeing me. I knew she wanted to talk. I wanted to talk to her too.

But part of me didn't.

We stepped outside onto the manicured grounds of the Manor and found a spot behind a vine-covered trellis where we could speak in private.

"You've had time to do some reflecting since all that terrible business went down," she said. "So, before you go off on your next grand adventure, I just wanted to ask you: did you find what you were looking for on that road trip?" She looked at me with a meaningful glint in her eye.

I let her question percolate.

"Let me put it another way," she said. "Were you able to put anything to rest?"

I knew what she was getting at, given the nature of my trip and the way it ended. I was reticent to talk about it, but then I realized if anyone deserved my full honesty on this topic, it was my sister Sarah.

I told her about my strange experience in Edelberg's secret bedroom. About how I'd seen our grandmother's bedroom around me.

About how Edelberg had transformed into our young uncle Raymond. About my realization that every punch, every tackle, every act of violence I'd dealt out in my entire angry life had really been aimed at Raymond. Always him. Over and over.

Sarah laughed dryly and shook her head.

"What?" I asked, surprised by her reaction.

"For such an intelligent man, you can be pretty dense when you choose."

I gave her a questioning look.

"It was never Raymond you were lashing out at. Never. It was yourself, Joe. Every time. Our entire lives, you've blamed yourself for what happened in that room."

I couldn't muster a rebuttal. "I may not have committed the act, Sarah, but I should have stopped it. Can you ever forgive me for that? I mean *really* forgive me?"

"I did that forty years ago, Joe. You were my little brother. I never blamed you. And I've told you that. A thousand times. But what *I* say doesn't matter. I'm not the one with the power to forgive you. You are. You need to forgive *yourself*. Can you do that? Finally?"

Could I indeed? The question of a lifetime.

"You've been a good brother to me, Joe. More than a girl could ever hope for. And that's the God's honest truth. That's all I have to say. ...But I think someone else might have a few words to add." She reached into her purse and pulled out Caroline's iPad.

My heart skipped a beat. Sarah pointed to an audio file named "For Joe," cued up and ready to play. "You might want to listen to this one in private," she said.

But I tapped it without hesitation.

"Joe," said my beloved wife's voice from the little speaker. "I want to say goodbye to you in case we miss our chance. I'm recording this on my final night." *Her final night? How could she know that?* "If you're hearing it, then I know you saved the day again. Because that's what you do. You take care of the people you love. Just like you took care of me. Day after day. Year after year. I need to tell you something, Joe. If you're holding anger toward anyone for my passing, let it go. I'm making my exit on my terms." *What?* "I'm hastening the inevitable tonight, and I may not be here by the time you get back."

"Why?" I said to the device, horrified. "Why?"

She answered. "I'm doing it for our son. I'm giving him the only thing I have to give. I'm doing it so you can focus on the task at hand, with all your mind and will. You need to get Jack out of the trouble he's in. You can't be worrying about me. My time is up, and my life has become nothing but pain. But Jack's life is ahead of him. I know you know that. And I know you will save him. Because you have the truest and bravest heart of anyone I've ever met. I loved you before I was born, Joe, and I'll love you long after I'm gone. You're a good man. Remember that. You are a good man, the goodest of them all."

For some reason, those words crashed through to my core. She had said similar words to me before, but I was never able to hear them. This time, though, they made it through. Past all my walls and filters.

And I began to sob. Like a child. Great, loud, chest-racking convulsions. I can't explain why. I didn't just shed a few tears. I bent over and *wept*. I couldn't stop. The chest-quakes just kept coming. In wave after wave.

Sarah wrapped her arms around me. And I let her. For the first time since we were children, I let Sarah be my big sister. And I let her comfort me with her strong, loving arms.

THE END

EPILOGUE

The beach is sunny today on Grand Cayman. As it is most days. I toss a stick of driftwood for Rio. Not as far as I used to throw it back in the day, but far enough to put some spring in his old legs. He trots the stick back to me, as pleased with himself as ever.

We've been here about four weeks, Rio and me. We came down on a one-way ticket. I'm not planning to stay here forever; I just didn't want to commit to a return date. Not yet.

When we first arrived, I had a bit of a fantasy going on. That maybe I'd pull a *Shawshank Redemption* thing. Stay here for good. Buy a little B&B near the beach, take tourists out fishing. But that's not me. I don't like people enough. Who was I kidding?

Retirement? I thought about that too. After all, I started talking about retiring with Caroline ten full years ago. But as I look at it now, I don't even really know what the word "retire" means. What am I going to do? Golf? Collect stamps? Please.

But what *am* I going to do? That's what I need to figure out, I guess.

I'm not in any hurry. I have some work to do first. On myself. Something changed in me that day with Sarah, something fundamental. When I broke down like a child. I felt something lift out of me. Like an evil spirit departing a body in an old movie. I think it was my anger. I think it just up and left.

In the month I've been here, I haven't wanted to punch anyone. Not even once. That's an all-time record for me. When people say and do things that used to tick me off, I just laugh. Or tell myself to get over it. It's strange.

It'll take some time to get to know the new me. Turns out, I don't really know who I am without the anger. It was such a central part of me. I mean, what does Joe Dillard do when he's not secretly trying to orchestrate a face-off with someone or stoking some righteous vendetta? That's what I need to find out before deciding how I'm going to spend my remaining days.

One change I've noticed already, since coming here, is that I've become a bit more philosophical. I've been doing a lot of reading. And thinking. I have the time. And lately I find myself drawn to "spiritual" books and books about the nature of reality. Books that ask the big questions, the ones I never had time for in my busy life.

Maybe it was those strange episodes with Caroline, after her death, that brought it on, that made me question my tidy, materialistic understanding of things. Caroline doesn't talk to me anymore, by the way, not in words—even when I go rowing out on Bioluminescent Bay at night, which I've done several times since arriving.

But I feel her presence in some deeper way. It's as if she hasn't really left, she's just changed form. And if the books I've been reading are right, maybe that's not so farfetched. After all, if time is an illusion, as both the physicists and spiritual masters say it is, then all of eternity is present in every moment. Nobody ever really goes anywhere.

That's how I choose to see it anyway. Whatever keeps Caroline in my life.

I notice I'm starting to feel the tug of home a bit now. But I'm not ready to leave yet. I'm still figuring out who the hell I am. One thing I need to remember, though, is that I *am* a grandfather. Not only to Joseph, but soon to Abby too. And so, whatever I decide to do, it must include regular doses of grandfathering, whatever form that takes.

The truth is, I just don't know what I'm up for anymore. Or what I want from life. Or what life wants from me. Little things like that.

I pick up Rio's stick and decide to try for an old-time Joe-and-Rio throw. I pull my arm back all the way, like a quarterback throwing the long ball, and let it rip. I'm surprised how high and far the stick sails. And how fast Rio races off down the beach to retrieve it. Maybe I've been writing the old boy off prematurely.

Maybe he's still got a few good runs on the beach left in him after all.

Thank you for reading, and I sincerely hope you enjoyed *Last Resort*. As an independently published author, I rely on you, the reader, to spread the word. So if you enjoyed the book, please tell your friends and family, and if it isn't too much trouble, I would appreciate a brief review on Amazon. Thanks again. My best to you and yours.

—Scott

ABOUT THE AUTHOR

Scott Pratt was born in South Haven, Michigan, and moved to Tennessee when he was thirteen years old. He is a veteran of the United States Air Force and holds a Bachelor of Arts degree in English from East Tennessee State University and a Doctor of Jurisprudence from the University of Tennessee College of Law. He lived in Northeast Tennessee with his wife, their dogs, and a parrot named JoJo.

www.scottprattfiction.com

A NOTE FROM SCOTT'S FAMILY

Every man's life ends the same way. It is only the details of how he lived and how he died that distinguish one man from another.

— Ernest Hemingway

This book was a long time coming. We apologize for that. If you are new to Scott Pratt's fiction writing, then you should know that this is actually the tenth installment of Scott's wildly successful Joe Dillard series. The plan was that this would be the last in the series and, although Scott didn't leave behind any written words for this book, it had been cooking in his brain for quite some time. In case you're unaware, Scott passed away suddenly in November of 2018 in a scuba diving accident in Bonaire just five short months after his beloved wife Kristy finally succumbed to the ravages of cancer.

We knew, as a family, that this book must be written for the sake of his fans. However, as you can imagine, making that happen was intertwined with deep sorrow and a complicated maze of emotions. Scott's son, Dylan, however, persisted and here you see the finished product. Our hope is that this book honors his fans, the characters he created and, most of all, he and Kristy's life and legacy.

We'll never not miss you, Scott. We hope this makes you proud.

ALSO BY SCOTT PRATT

Made in the USA
Columbia, SC
29 June 2023

29d03bc8-3ceb-49f1-a28e-9f73c1b42df9R01